Space Living

Also by the author:

Independent Living

Assisted Living

Date Night on Union Station

Alien Night on Union Station

High Priest on Union Station

Spy Night on Union Station

Carnival on Union Station

Wanderers on Union Station

Vacation on Union Station

Guest Night on Union Station

Word Night on Union Station

Party Night on Union Station

Review Night on Union Station

Family Night on Union Station

Book Night on Union Station

LARP Night on Union Station

Career Night on Union Station

Last Night on Union Station

Soup Night on Union Station

Meghan's Dragon

Turing Test

Human Test

Magic Test

Space Living

Book Four of EarthCent Universe

Foner Books

978-1-948691-29-1

Northampton, Massachusetts

One

"If I knew that dancing would be so much work, I never would have let you teach me," Bill groaned as he slumped into the shuttle's seat. "I'm exhausted."

"But Rinka told me that she never saw Julie looking so happy," Jorb said. "And the catering was incredible. Not that there's anything wrong with the food that you and Harry prepare in the cafeteria," he amended himself hastily.

"I still can't believe I didn't get my feet tangled up and fall on my face when the band started playing that modern stuff. What was it?"

The Drazen shrugged and stretched his tentacle. "Some kind of Horten music. The bandleader is Marilla's boyfriend. I introduced you to her."

"You introduced me to more people than I normally meet in a year," Bill said. "I still feel weird about going to the wedding of people I don't even know."

"You met Samuel and Vivian at the Con six months ago when she won the 'Best Drazen' competition," Jorb reminded his friend. "She was still working for Drazen Intelligence back then."

"Vivian is a spy too?"

"Not anymore, unless she's in charge of starting a new intelligence service for the Human Empire," Jorb said. "I'll have to ask her at lunch tomorrow. You and Julie are invited, by the way."

"I still don't understand why Julie and Rinka couldn't come back with us."

"Because they have to escort Vivian to her honeymoon suite on Flower," Jorb explained patiently. "It's a females-only thing."

"Why are Samuel and Vivian following Drazen customs?"

"It's not a Drazen custom. The bridal escort is common courtesy for newlyweds all around the tunnel network, and it made sense for Rinka and Julie to volunteer since they don't have to return to Union Station afterward. Flower is departing as soon as the wedding party is back on board."

"So your friend Samuel is on the shuttle with us?" Bill asked, leaning to the side to look down the aisle.

"He's already on Flower preparing the suite for his bride," Jorb said. "Haven't you ever been to a wedding before?"

"Just once, at the independent living cooperative, when Jack and Nancy got married."

The Drazen gave his friend a look of concern. "You really didn't attend any weddings before you joined Flower?"

"I thought I explained that my mom was in a cult back home and we basically spent all of our time selling grey market stuff out of a pushcart. People like us didn't have weddings, they just moved in together. And then when I got suckered into leaving Earth to work on an unlicensed picking crew, I didn't even see a woman for over a year."

"Well, now that you've been to a fancy wedding, what do you think?"

"That Julie and I will be old before we can afford to get married," Bill said. "Vivian's mother must have spent a thousand creds just on that cake! I captured a bunch of images with my implant to show Harry and my classmates."

"Is that what the hospitality and foodservice students all do at the Open University? Hang around exchanging baking porn?"

"After I finally passed the entrance exam, Flower got me advanced credit for my work with Harry, so I started right in with the cake estimating course. I'm not going to school for credentials—I'm only interested in the practical lessons that I can apply to opening my own business."

"Humans are the only species I've ever heard of who go to school part-time," Jorb said. "You're missing out on the whole student experience."

"You mean the parties and stuff? It's not my thing, and I'm not interested in meeting any more girls. Julie is more than enough for me, and I barely have time to spend alone with her as it is."

"So have the two of you set a date yet?"

"We talk about it, though after seeing what a real wedding is like, I'm worried she's going to start having second thoughts," Bill said.

"That wasn't an ordinary wedding," Jorb said. "Between Samuel's mother being the EarthCent ambassador and Vivian's mother being the cofounder of InstaSitter, they're practically Human royalty. And her father is the Director of EarthCent Intelligence. Do you know what that means?"

Bill hazarded a guess. "They put the whole thing on their expense accounts?"

"It means that most of those guests you saw were invited for political or business reasons. And I'll bet you that the majority of the invitees showed up just to see the other important guests. Maker Dring was there, along with the local ambassadors from all of the tunnel network species, and most of the top business types on the station. My parents even put in an appearance."

"Did you talk to them?"

"I would have tried if I thought they'd listen, but you know they wanted me to marry the daughter of some other major stakeholders in their consortium. They don't approve of me finding Rinka on my own."

"But you and Rinka aren't even officially engaged yet."

"We passed our second compatibility test, so it's just another nine and a half years on your calendar and then we can make it official. Maybe my parents will come around when they see that we're really serious."

There was a high-pitched buzzing from the row behind them which Bill's implant translated into a voice saying, "The two of you sound like a bad Vergallian soap opera."

"Is that you, M793qK?" Jorb asked. "I didn't see you when we boarded."

"That's because I got on before you and I put all the armrests down so I could stretch out and rest my weary chitin," the Farling said. "If the two of you think that dancing is exhausting, try doing it with a carapace."

"You looked better than I did out there and you didn't lack for partners," Bill said over his shoulder. "What do all of those women see in you?"

"Free medical advice. While you were attempting to lose yourself in the rhythm, I was diagnosing everything from an acute iron deficiency to ball-gown-induced anorexia. I don't understand why Human females can't wear dresses with elastic in the waist like normal humanoid species."

"We will be arriving home in one minute," Flower announced over the shuttle's public address system. "If you removed your magnetic cleats to dance and left them behind, there are spares under the seats. And don't forget to return your footrests to the stored position."

"Are the two of you awake enough to work?" M793qK inquired.

"Us?" Bill asked.

"Who else could I possibly be addressing?" the Farling physician demanded irritably. "While dancing with the EarthCent ambassador, I got her final go-ahead for the contract to set up a certification lab for the All Species Cookbook on Flower. This shuttle is loaded with test samples, and I want to get started right away."

"You closed a business deal with the ambassador at her son's wedding?" Jorb asked.

"She brought it up," M793qK said. "Dewey has been on Union Station for a week hashing out the details with the ambassador's special assistant, a charming Vergallian princess who must enjoy slumming with Humans. When Ambassador McAllister mentioned that her only remaining regret in life was taking money to extend the All Species Cookbook seal of approval to anybody willing to pay the license fee, I knew the timing was right. I offered my own services to put the whole thing on a scientific basis."

"Our services," Flower interjected via an overhead speaker.

"Our services," the Farling conceded. "And as the two of you surprised me by remaining reasonably sober at the reception, I shall avail myself of your services as porters."

"Thanks a lot," Jorb muttered as the shuttle set down on the deck of the giant cylindrical hangar in Flower's core.

"So you want us to bring all the stuff to your clinic?" Bill asked.

"Where do you get these insane ideas?" M793qK rubbed out on his speaking legs. "Take it all to our cafeteria, or the kitchen, to be more precise. Flower assures me that you and Harry don't use a third of the storage available."

"You're going to use the aliens who eat in the cafeteria for guinea pigs?"

"Bring it on," Jorb said, releasing his safety restraints and rising. "I enjoy adventure eating."

"Which is what disqualifies you for the role," the giant beetle said, as he maneuvered his bulky body into the aisle. "I'll be setting up a safety lab in the kitchen, after which the samples will be taste-tested by Human volunteers. Their crude digestive systems make them the lowest common denominator on the galactic food chain, which is ideal for All Species Cookbook certification purposes."

"It's nice to find out that we're good for something after all," Bill said to Jorb as he followed the two aliens to the back exit of the shuttle. They shuffled down the ramp on their magnetic cleats, and M793qK led the way to the cargo section where the samples were stored. The access panel dropped down as they approached.

"Take the packages addressed to the All Species Cookbook, care of the EarthCent Embassy on Union Station," the Farling instructed them. "Grab a couple of floating carts and bring everything up through one of the cargo lift tubes. Flower can show you the back way into the kitchen."

"Aren't you going to help?" Bill asked.

"That was originally my plan, but there's been a medical emergency that requires my immediate attention," the giant beetle said, already backing away. "Just leave the samples out and I'll stop by the kitchen later and sort through them. And don't eat any of it."

"I've never seen him move so fast," Jorb observed as M793qK skittered off on his magnetic cleats.

"He did say there was a medical emergency," Bill said. "I don't think he would lie about something like that. Flower?"

"There's always a medical emergency somewhere," the Dollnick AI responded ambiguously. "Be careful when you load those packages. Some of them include large glass jars, and even though they don't weigh much on this deck, their masses are unchanged, and they'll break if you crash them together."

"Let's find a couple of floater carts and get this over with," Jorb said.

Forty minutes later, Flower guided the pair of overdressed cargo handlers through a back entrance and into the kitchen of the cafeteria where Bill helped Harry prepare meals for alien spies traveling alone. Once inside, the young man looked around in puzzlement.

"Where did that door come from?" Bill asked. "I'm pretty sure there was a wall here."

"Give me a little credit for tight seams," Flower replied. "You've just never seen the commercial entrance open before because I have my bots make deliveries during the off hours."

"Why didn't you have your bots deliver this lot?"

"Because you and Jorb were available and I prefer to avoid using automation wherever possible," the Dollnick

AI said. "Are you awake enough to unpack the samples and put the boxes and wrapping in the carts?"

"Will you send bots to pick up the trash?" Jorb countered.

"Recycling," Flower said. "Deal."

"I can't believe we let them talk us into this," Bill grumbled as he tore the wrapping off the closest package. "This is going to take an hour, and I was hoping to see Julie before going to bed."

"She and Rinka will be tied up with getting Vivian settled in for a while yet," Jorb said. "They don't just escort her to the honeymoon suite and abandon her. They have to stay outside the door just in case."

"Just in case of what?" Bill asked, removing a gigantic jar of pickled something from a box.

"In case Vivian changes her mind about being married and wants to back out. It's just a formality. They can't escort her back to her familial home since we left Union Station a few minutes ago." Jorb frowned at a plastic-wrapped brick of small rectangular packages as he puzzled out the English. "What are ramen noodles?"

"Are you being serious? They're one of the main food groups on Earth."

The alien grabbed a kitchen knife, slit open a corner of the plastic, and extracted a package. "I'm going to try one. Do you know how to boil water?"

"Now I know you're not being serious," Bill said. "Put it back or we'll get in trouble with M793qK."

"There are twenty-four identical packages, he doesn't need them all for testing," Jorb said, moving over to where the pots hung over the industrial stovetop. "Two cups of water. Is that like coffee cups or beer cups?"

Bill shook his head in resignation. "You keep unpacking and I'll make the ramen. How much of the flavor package do you want me to use?"

"Do you need the rest of it for something else?"

"No, it's just that it's got enough salt to give you a heart attack. I only use about a quarter of the package myself."

"Give me the whole thing. I live for sodium chloride."

Bill dutifully brought the water to a nearly instant boil on the Dollnick induction stove, dumped in the flavor package, and added the block of ramen noodles. "Do you want anything else in there?"

"What are my options?" Jorb asked, reaching for another box with his tentacle.

"I could nuke some vegetables to throw in, or add an egg. The truth is, you can put almost anything in ramen—it's like a universal base."

"I think I should try it straight the first time to get the full experience." The Drazen looked over as the door leading to the cafeteria swung open. "Hey, Yaem. Did Flower send you to help out?"

"I wasn't expecting anybody to be in here," the Sharf said, and then belatedly attempted to hide the bag he was carrying behind his back.

"Did you miss a meal because we took the day off?" Bill asked. "I saw most of our usual gang at the wedding, I guess some of them knew the bride and groom before joining Flower. And I thought Woojin invited all of you to the wedding to mix with some of the other alien spies. You didn't go?"

"I'm not a fan of dance music," Yaem admitted. "Flower pinged me earlier to say I would be the only one at dinner tonight, so I told her not to bother and that I'd take care of myself." He brought the bag out from behind his back. "I popped over to Union Station to take care of some business and I bought these slug roots to fry up for myself."

"Do you know how to use the stove?" Bill asked, having some experience with aliens like Jorb who never learned how to cook for themselves.

"I was going to ask Flower," the alien admitted.

"My noodles are going to get soggy while the two of you play kitchen," Jorb complained. "Put that bowl back and just give me the pot. And some of those little spears to get the noodles out."

"Chopsticks," Bill said, sticking a pair in the pot and adding a spoon for good measure. "I'll get a pan heated up for you, Yaem. Do you fry the, uh, slug roots in oil?"

"You don't have to cook for me," the Sharf said, but he put the bag on the counter and pushed it in Bill's direction. "A little of that olive oil in the pan would probably be a good idea."

"This is excellent," Jorb said after slurping down a quarter of the noodles on his first go. He grabbed another package of ramen and tossed it to Yaem. "You should try your slug root in ramen."

Bill rolled his eyes and put another small pot on the stove next to the frying pan. The kitchen door opened again and a stunningly beautiful woman dressed in an expensive gown stepped through and came to a sudden halt. "Oh. So the kitchen is in use."

"Join us, Avisia," Jorb welcomed the latest arrival. "Feeling a little peckish after the wedding feast?"

"I only had a sliver of cake and some fruit," the Vergallian intelligence agent who ran a finishing school for girls explained. "Men kept asking me to dance, and by the time I took a break, the vegan food was all gone."

"Ramen noodles might be vegan, though I don't know about the flavoring," Bill told her. He picked up the torn package from the block of noodles he had just dumped into the pot for Yaem and scanned the ingredient list. "This one is vegetarian, but I'm not sure what some of those chemicals are."

"Who cares as long as they're tasty," Jorb said. "You know, I could go for another serving myself." He tossed two more of the small packages to Bill. "What? There's still twenty left for M793qK to destructively test."

"Are those truffles?" Avisia asked, and began peeling open one of the retail boxes that Jorb had unpacked. "This is turning into my lucky day."

"Hey, let me in there," Yaem said. He moved around the counter and started rummaging through the samples.

"Just leave enough for the Farling to test," Jorb cautioned the other two aliens. "He and Flower made a contract with the EarthCent embassy to certify the products that get the All Species Cookbook seal of approval."

"These truffles are already approved so I guess he won't have to test them," Avisia said and held up the package. "See?"

"That only means they paid the fee," Jorb told her. "Just leave a couple in there. Okay?"

"Is somebody making ramen?" a new voice inquired, and everybody turned to see the Grenouthian director had silently padded into the kitchen. "I'll take two packages, and you better make at least four for Brynlan. And he likes them crunchy."

"Didn't any of you guys eat at the wedding?" Bill asked, taking down another pot.

"That was hours ago," the director said. "I have a fast metabolism."

"I thought you'd be taking it easy for a while now that the second season of *Everyday Superheroes* is in post-production," Avisia said from the corner, where she had retreated with her box of chocolate-coated truffles.

"Are you serious? Flower wants to get four new independently produced series up and running for the next season, and our studio has already contracted to do the animation work for a half-dozen others."

"Captain on deck," Flower announced via the overhead speakers. A moment later the kitchen door swung open again and Woojin entered, still resplendent in his uniform that was copied from portraits of George Washington.

"Looks like an intelligence convention in here," Woojin said, and then his eyes lit up. "Are you making ramen?"

Jorb tossed another package to Bill, who snagged it out of the air and added it to the pot he had just put on for the director and Brynlan.

"Ramen is the best thing ever to come out of Japan," the captain continued. "And that's saying something for a Korean." He looked around the kitchen, and then asked, "Where's Razood?"

"I saw him scarf down an entire cheese platter at the reception," Avisia said. "He's probably in his cabin sleeping it off."

An angry buzzing came from the service entrance and M793qK stormed into the kitchen, his wings popping out of his carapace in anger. "Oh, now this is just perfect," he rubbed out on his speaking legs. He snatched the remaining truffles from the Vergallian, glared at her through his multifaceted eyes, and then pulled open a cabinet and placed the box on the top shelf. "From now on, these cabinets are officially reserved for Flower Certification

Labs, and I'm going to have her send a bot to install surveillance cameras. Bill, I'm disappointed in you."

"Go easy, M793qK," Jorb said. "I'm the one who made him start cooking."

"Which is exactly what I'd expect from a Drazen, but I had higher hopes for the young Human, especially since Flower insists he play a role in this new business."

"Another job?" Bill asked in dismay.

"I thought you'd appreciate the chance to earn some extra income to save for your wedding," Flower said.

Two

"Are you sure they want a tour of the ship on the first day of their honeymoon?" Julie asked. "Vivian didn't say anything about it to me."

"I pitched it to them this morning," Flower replied over the girl's implant. "Take down the caution tape and then I'll tell them that you're here. If you wind it up carefully, you can reuse it on your own door one day."

"Stop nagging," Julie replied reflexively. She unstuck the end of the "Just Married" caution tape that she and Rinka had stretched back and forth across the door of the honeymoon suite the previous evening, and began winding it onto her left hand. "How did they get out for breakfast this morning?"

"They didn't. The honeymoon suite has a small kitchen which I stocked with their favorite foods before you sealed the happy couple in, and of course, they had a complimentary basket of fresh fruit."

"So where do you want me to take them on the tour?"

"Let's start with the library and then we'll wing it depending on their reaction," Flower said.

"I meant to ask you yesterday why this caution tape is heavier than it looks," Julie said as she pulled the improvised roll off of her spindle-hand and placed it in her purse. "What do you put in it?"

"Ground-up quality control rejects from a Verlock magnetic monopole manufacturer. They provide just enough attraction to keep the tape in place without interfering with electronics."

"Okay, I'm ready," Julie announced and looked at the door expectantly. "Aren't you going to tell them that I'm here?"

"They're in the shower."

"Together? I mean, of course they can take a shower together if they want to. They're married."

"Hmm, I don't know why I never noticed this about you before," Flower said.

"Noticed what?"

"It's not important. Why don't we take advantage of the time to go over your schedule for the week? Now that your principal animation actor work for the second season of *Everyday Superheroes* is complete, what are you planning to fill in the time?"

"Last year we went back to regular theatre practice. I think I was finally beginning to understand Shakespeare," Julie said.

"The Grenouthian director is going to be too busy for live theatre, so you'll either have to find a replacement for him or choose another activity for your team sport."

"You're asking me to find a replacement director? I'm surprised you don't already have a dozen candidates lined up."

"You and Bill are always telling me that I'm too controlling, so I thought I'd leave it up to you what to do," Flower said.

"What about the aliens in the cast?" Julie asked. "Don't they have a team sport requirement as well?"

"The truth is that they're all active enough without me telling them what to do, so I'm inclined to grant them waivers if you don't keep the troupe together during the offseason."

"I should talk it over with Bill and Harry and see what they think. They're as much a part of theatre practice as I am."

"Didn't you know that M793qK put Harry in a medical stasis pod and shot him off into space?" Flower asked.

"What? Oh, you mean Harry's character on *Everyday Superheroes*. I knew the writers were going to kill Gerryman off at his request, but I didn't ask for the details."

"Stasis was a compromise in case I can convince him to return for a guest appearance. But Harry won't be joining you for live theatre in any case. He and Irene have already signed up for a waltz class in the independent living cooperative that I've certified as a team sport."

"Could I take that with Bill?"

"It's acceptable to me if they'll have you, but you'd be the only ones younger than sixty-five in the class," Flower pointed out.

"Oh. Maybe not. How long do I have to decide about this?"

"Until this evening. You should talk it over with Samuel and Vivian as well."

"Why?" Julie asked. "They're just here on their honeymoon tour."

"That's no excuse to skip their team sport requirement—the rules apply to everybody."

"I know they didn't come out in the corridor to do calisthenics this morning because the tape was still up."

"I gave them a waiver for their first morning after the nuptials," Flower said. "I'm not as heartless as you make me out to be."

"I don't think you're heartless, just oblivious at times. And you change your mind pretty often for a supposedly omniscient AI."

"I never claimed to know everything, or even zero-point-two-six percent of everything."

"That's a pretty specific number," Julie said suspiciously.

"I might have asked my mentor for an estimate of my ultimate intellectual capacity," the ship's AI replied. "And the ability to change one's mind when new facts present themselves is a mark of high intelligence."

"I'll keep that in mind when I see my new business cards. Who am I working for this time?"

"Flower Enterprises. I'm moving you from the entertainment division to the umbrella company that will include all of my major subsidiaries. You start after lunch."

"I'm a twenty-two-year-old former money courier for the drug syndicate who never even went to high school!" Julie exploded. "What am I possibly going to do working in the headquarters of a company that controls Flower Entertainment, Flower Foods, Flower Studios, and the new spaceship construction business you're starting?"

"I trust you," Flower said. "You might not get everything right the first time, but you're smart enough for a Human, and you don't put your hands over your ears and make humming noises when I talk to you."

"Do people really do that? Besides, I granted you access to my implant so it wouldn't help."

"Ah, they're out of the shower and dressed now. I'm telling them that you're here."

The door to the honeymoon suite slid open, and Julie heard a young woman's voice call, "Come in."

"I'm sorry if it's too early, but Flower told me you were ready to take a tour," Julie apologized as she entered the suite. Then she realized that she was talking to an empty room and raised her voice. "Hello?"

"I'll be out in a sec," Vivian's voice came from down the hall.

"Morning, Julie," Samuel said, emerging from the kitchenette. "We've got lots of food if you want anything."

"This suite is huge," Julie said. "I've never been in a cabin that had a hallway like that."

"I think Flower modeled it after the honeymoon suite in the Empire Hotel that's attached to the convention center on Union Station. I've never really traveled, other than a trip to Earth with my folks, but Vivian says that the Empire chain has a convention center and a hotel on most of the Stryx stations," the EarthCent ambassador's son said.

"And you've been in a honeymoon suite at the one on Union Station?"

"The EarthCent embassy rented them out for the alien observers who showed up for the Human Empire launch a couple of cycles ago. I was working for the Vergallian embassy back then, but my ambassador gave me a leave of absence to help my mom, and somehow I ended up swapping jobs."

"So you work for your mom at the EarthCent embassy on Union Station now?" Julie asked, attempting to make sense of the diplomatic musical chairs.

"I got traded to the Human Empire's startup team. Vivian too. In fact, we're sort of the whole thing for now."

Vivian came into the room wearing something like a summer dress, her long hair hanging freely down her back. There was something a little off about her overall appearance, but Julie couldn't quite put her finger on it.

"Thumbs," Samuel said, with a long-suffering sigh. "You promised to stop wearing them after we got married."

"Sorry, I forgot," Vivian said, making no move to remove the Drazen prosthetics. "I promise I'll start weaning myself off them tomorrow. Where are we going?"

"We'll start with the library," Julie told them. "I've worked there part-time ever since I came on board, but lately Flower has been monopolizing my time with her businesses."

"I haven't been to the library in years," Samuel said, as he and Vivian followed their guide out of the suite. "We always pop over to see Jorb when Flower stops at Union Station, but he's more into the food scene."

"I'm going to have to get used to talking to Jorb all over again now that I don't work for Drazen Intelligence anymore," Vivian added. "We used to share secrets."

"How does a human get a job as an alien spy?" Julie asked, forgetting for the moment that Bill now had a part-time gig recruiting agents for the Sharf.

"My father is the director of EarthCent Intelligence and he wanted me to work for him, but the Open University co-op program sent me to the Drazens," the new bride replied. "It's the same way Sam got his job working for the Vergallians. We figure now that it was just the Stryx getting us some practical work experience to prepare for the Human Empire startup, but you can never know for sure."

Julie came to an abrupt halt at the lift tube despite the fact that the door had slid open at their approach. "You mean the Stryx try to manipulate everybody the same way as Flower?"

"Haven't you ever heard of Convergence Theorem?" Samuel asked her.

"No," Julie replied as they entered the lift tube. "Library," she instructed the capsule before asking, "What is it?"

"Supposedly the Stryx manipulate everything to obtain their idea of the best outcome, and they do it by creating an endless series of choices for biological actors until we pick the right one. It's an unproven alien theory, but the idea is that the Stryx influence our decisions just enough that the average result converges to some predestined endpoint."

"Flower's not that subtle," Julie said with a laugh. "She just pushes everybody until we give up and do what she wants."

"That might be a nice change," Vivian said. "Some of us who grew up on Union Station end up second-guessing ourselves all the time about our motivations."

"And some of us don't," Samuel said as the capsule doors slid open. "I'm with the aliens who say that worrying about what the Stryx want is like worrying about the weather on a planet without weather control satellites. My mom thinks that this whole thing with the Human Empire is a Stryx scheme to keep the sovereign human communities from drifting permanently into the diplomatic orbits of the host species on the open worlds. But a thousand years from now, what difference will it make why we got started? The important thing is getting it right."

"Sam's a pragmatist," Vivian said to Julie. "He's actually a good choice to run a start-up empire."

"Aren't you both kind of young to be in charge?" Julie couldn't help asking.

"It's more like a school project," Samuel explained. "We're supposed to start laying the groundwork for building a governmental infrastructure that won't take control for a hundred and fifty years or so. The Stryx had veto power over our faculty advisor."

"Your what?"

"Our mentor, from the Cayl emperor's family," Vivian told her. "She's waiting to hitch a ride back to this section of the galaxy with a Stryx science ship, and we've been putting off doing anything other than gathering information until she gets here. We haven't even rented office space yet."

"Is the Human Empire going to start collecting some sort of tax to pay for everything?" Julie asked.

"We're fully funded by royalties from the All Species Cookbook for as long as we don't spend too much," Samuel told her. "It's another part of my mom's theory about the whole thing being a Stryx setup."

"Shush," Vivian said, putting a forefinger to her husband's lips. "We're in a library now."

"It's not that strict," Julie told them, though she did lower her own voice. "The Dollnicks mastered acoustic suppression technology like a million years ago, and Flower isn't shy about using it to keep the noise down. Is there anything in particular you want to see?"

"Some of my Dad's friends at our wedding said that the Galactic Free Press publishes a *Marriage For Humans* book that I'd better read," Samuel said. "Do you have those?"

"We keep them hidden because the head librarian hates the branding," Julie said. "I don't see her anywhere so it's as good a time as any." She led the honeymooners to a blank section of bulkhead and sent the "Open Sesame" command via her implant. A large panel slid aside, revealing hundreds of identically bound books, the only difference being the title on the spine.

"There," Vivian announced almost immediately, pointing at the book in question. "Between *Mariachi Bands For Humans* and *Mars Colonies For Humans*."

"Wow, you're really good at this," Julie said as she extracted the volume from the tightly packed shelf and handed it to Samuel. "Have you worked in a library?"

"It's just a visualization trick I learned at Drazen Intelligence," Vivian explained. "It takes a little practice, but you can train yourself to only see what you're looking for, assuming that it's there. You have to be careful about applying it to anything other than picking items out of a collection, because if you let it influence your regular data analysis, you'll end up with a wicked case of confirmation bias."

"Making the wedding night a success," Samuel read out loud from the first chapter. "The intimacy of pair bonding is critical to a happy marriage and—" he stopped reading and his ears turned red.

"And what?" Vivian prompted. She reached for the book, but Samuel employed his superior height to hold it out of reach.

"You can look at it when we get back to our suite," he told her, and glancing at Julie, lowered his voice to a whisper. "They have diagrams about—you know."

A man with immersive star looks approached and returned a book titled *Careers For Humans* to a narrow gap on the top shelf.

"Good morning, Dewey," Julie greeted the assistant librarian, a rare human-created AI who had recently purchased an android body to become an artificial person. "It looks like you still haven't made up your mind about continuing at the library."

"I'm going to keep a single eight-hour shift every day and spend the other sixteen working for Flower. You know that I don't require sleep. Are you going to introduce me to your friends?"

"I'm Sam and this is my wife, Vivian," Samuel said, unconsciously staking his claim in the face of the handsome android. "We're on our honeymoon."

"Yes, I knew who you were, but asking for an introduction is a proven sales technique for building relationships," Dewey said. "I met with your mother in her official capacity while I was representing this ship, and Flower suggested that I talk with you about our offerings. Is this a working honeymoon, or are you on vacation?"

"A working honeymoon?" Vivian asked. "I don't think I've ever heard the expression."

"I believe that's how our third officer, Pyun Lynx, described her honeymoon with Captain Pyun back when they were both working for EarthCent Intelligence. They went on a tour of the open worlds and laid the groundwork for the original network of sovereign human communities."

"I guess we sort of planned on working, but I'm not sure we want to jump right into it our first day," Samuel said.

"It's not like I'm a mail-order bride and we met for the first time yesterday," Vivian said. "I've known that Sam was the one for thirteen years."

"How interesting," Dewey said. "I would have estimated your age at approximately twenty."

"Exactly twenty."

"So you chose your mate at the age of seven. Forgive my curiosity, but as an artificial person who until recently occupied a robotic body that most people confused with an industrial appliance, I have limited experience in affairs of the heart. Is it acceptable to ask how long Samuel has reciprocated your feelings?"

"Dewey," Julie scolded the assistant librarian. "That's hardly an appropriate question for a bride on her honeymoon."

"I don't mind," Vivian said. "Sam used to be in love with a Vergallian princess, but I eventually showed him the error of his ways. And we were engaged for two years before we got married."

"And it might have been even longer if her twin brother hadn't eloped with a race floater driver from Chianga," Samuel put in.

"That had nothing to do with it," Vivian objected. "I was waiting for you to quit working for the Vergallians."

"Fascinating," Dewey said. "Well, as long as you're both here in the library, is there anything I can assist you with? We have a fine collection of books about empires that you may find useful."

"We had the Persian, Greek, Roman, Ming, and British empires in a survey course about Earth history at the Open University, but I don't think they would make useful models for the new Human Empire," Samuel said.

"I never would have suggested them," the artificial person said. "I meant recent books about the alien empires. There's an excellent series being produced by an academic community on a Verlock open world that does a good job with the Drazen and Horten empires. They started with the more recent oxygen-breathing tunnel network species and they're working their way backward."

"Why didn't they start with the Verlocks?" Julie asked.

"Because of the amount of work involved. The Verlocks and the Grenouthians have been tunnel network members for nearly seven million years, while the Drazens and Hortens only joined around five hundred thousand years ago. And the series is already up to eighty books without getting to current times, so perhaps it would be heavy going for honeymoon reading." Dewey looked thoughtful for a moment, and then he reached up to the end of the top shelf and brought down a book. "Here's a good primer, *Empires For Humans*."

"Who's the author?" Samuel asked.

Dewey glanced at the title page and reported, "Staff. I've heard a rumor that most of the unattributed books are written by a young Stryx, but the information will be limited to what you could have learned by asking a teacher bot."

"Then why not just ask a teacher bot?" Julie asked. She thought wistfully of the free box-like teacher bot with the kind voice that had provided her with her only formal education while growing up in the slums of Manhattan with a drug-addicted mother.

"With the *For Humans* books, you're mainly paying for the editorial choices," Vivian said. "My aunt Chastity owns the Galactic Free Press, which publishes those books through a subsidiary, so we have a lot of them at home.

The acquisitions editor for the series decides on a general outline of what the average person wants to know about a given subject, and then they contract the work out to an author who can fill in the blanks. I think that Stryx Jeeves used to write a lot of them in his spare time to pick up money, so you have to take it all with a grain of salt."

"Surely you're not suggesting that a Stryx would lie," Dewey said, his face taking on a skeptical expression.

"Not in such a way that we could ever catch them at it."

"I know that Flower trusts the Stryx implicitly," Julie protested.

Vivian sighed, sounding a lot older than her twenty years. "Have you spent much time around children?"

"The library has a program to help children with their reading that I volunteer for when I have time, but that hasn't been often lately."

"How about babies?" Vivian asked.

Julie shook her head in the negative.

"This won't be the best analogy in the world, but start by thinking of the alien species that joined the tunnel network in the last million years as being adults, and humans being children," Vivian said. "Then try thinking of the older tunnel network species like the Verlocks and Grenouthians being the adults, and the Drazens and the Hortens being children, which would make us the babies. Then think of some of the powerful species that never joined the tunnel network like the Cayl and the Farlings being the adults, and the Verlocks and Grenouthians being children, the Drazens and Hortens being the babies. Do you see where I'm going?"

"You're saying that compared to the Stryx, the most powerful aliens are children, so we must be like ants or something," Julie said.

"I don't think ants are sentient, though that's a question for philosophers." Vivian exchanged a look with her husband. "I remember that Sam figured this out before I did when we were little and I cried when he explained it to me. The only reason we understand what our alien friends are talking about is because they are smart enough to assess our capacity and speak accordingly."

"You mean the aliens are always talking down to us?"

"They're just careful not to talk over our heads, like you would be if you were with friends who had different abilities," Samuel reassured her. "And as artificial intelligence, I'll bet Dewey is always restraining himself from bringing up math in his conversations."

"Not always," Dewey said. "Just ninety-eight point two three percent of the time, rounded down to two decimal places."

Three

"What are you doing back for lunch, Harry?" Irene asked her husband as he put his tray down on the table next to hers. "I thought you wouldn't be home until supper, and I already signed up for the afternoon talk."

"Flower told me that none of the single aliens would be coming in for food today," he said. "They had a get-together in the kitchen last night and broke into the samples that M793qK is supposed to be testing for the All Species Cookbook. They left the sink full of bowls and chopsticks."

"So you're taking the whole day off?"

"Flower has been cutting back on my hours since my last birthday. According to some new actuarial tables published by Thark bookies, she's been overestimating my lifespan, and you know she follows Dollnick labor laws on how many hours we're allowed to work on a prorated basis."

"I'm not sure whether that's good news or bad news," Irene said, giving her husband a speculative glance. "You were always busy in our bakery back on Earth, and Flower has kept you employed ever since we joined the ship."

"I wanted to rebuild our nest egg a bit after we lost it in the original independent living scam that brought us here," Harry said. "I don't envision us ever needing the money, but it would be nice to be able to leave the grandkids something."

"The world has changed so much since we were their age that I'm not sure it matters."

"Money always matters. What's the talk you're signed up for? Maybe I'll sit in."

"The two authors who started a writers colony on board are going to talk about their progress," Irene said, and looked over as a couple more people set down trays and took their seats. "You look very nice today, Nancy. Are you and Jack going somewhere after lunch?"

"We're going here," the retired schoolteacher replied. "As the population of Flower's Paradise grows, we're now putting on classes and lectures in the mornings, afternoons, and evenings. Some events work best in different time slots, but I've realized that people only dress up for the after-dinner lectures. I think there's an effect on the professionalism of the presenters, so I thought I'd try dressing for the afternoon lectures and see if it catches on."

"My wife the fashion leader," Jack said, patting Nancy's hand. "The main difference I've noticed between the time slots is that everybody is alert in the morning, irritable in the afternoon, and sleepy in the evening."

"Keep that in mind the next time you catch me snoozing at one of our board meetings," Harry told the retired ag world worker, who served as the president of the independent living cooperative.

Dave, an ex-salesman in his mid-seventies with a bit of a potbelly, set his tray down on the table and gave Harry a friendly nod. "I haven't seen you here for lunch on a weekday in ages. Did you get fired from Flower Foods?"

"Flower can never fire Harry," Irene said. "Her main product is named after him."

"The fruitcake is less than twenty percent of the business at this point, and it's only that much because the Dollnicks can't get enough of them," Harry said. "These days the big sellers are the ready-to-make soup mixes based on the All Species Cookbook, and looking around the cafeteria, I see they're a lot more popular than my pot pies."

"These soups are made from packages?" Nancy asked. "I thought they were from scratch."

"You'd have to ask Flower to be sure," the baker said, carefully removing a section of crust from the top of his pot pie with his fork. He looked up again as Maureen, a retired advertising executive who sat on the cooperative's board, took her seat. She was accompanied by Brenda, who in addition to serving on the board, had been drafted into working full time as Flower's lawyer for dealings with humans. "So all of you went for the soup-and-salad? I thought the pies would be a big hit."

"It's the calorie count," Dave explained. "You know that Flower keeps track of what we eat."

"It's worth being careful at lunch to be able to pick any dessert at dinner," Maureen concurred.

"We all assumed that Flower grants you a waiver since you do research and development for her food business," Brenda added with an envious look at Harry.

"Not that she's told me," Harry said, spearing a chunk of gravy-drenched carrot with his fork. "It's just that after baking for over forty years I've gotten out of the habit of eating desserts."

"You should all eat balanced meals and listen to your bodies," Flower addressed them via an overhead speaker. "I'm troubled by this Human obsession with calories."

"What brought that on?" Irene asked, without even glancing up at the ceiling.

"The deal I made with the All Species Cookbook to certify products for their seal of approval. M793qK has informed me that we will be obligated to confirm all of the nonsense numbers on the packaging."

"Shall I assume that you're referring to nutritional data?" Nancy asked.

"Precisely. Nobody reads it, and even if they did, they wouldn't understand it. I have almost eighteen thousand years experience looking over the shoulders of Dollnick dieticians, and five years of assisting with the eating choices of over a half-million Humans. Do you know what I've learned?"

"I have a feeling you're going to tell us," Harry said in an undertone.

"You have to communicate with people in a vocabulary they understand," the Dollnick AI continued. "Do I tell Dave to watch his calories? No. I give him a list of foods and quantities he can eat throughout the day, and if he goes over that—"

"No ice cream," Dave interjected in a mournful tone.

"—no ice cream," Flower concluded on a note of finality. "And do I tell him three ounces of this or forty grams of that? No, I break it down into pieces of fruit or servings of soup. But those misguided nutritional labels are so ingrained in your collective subconscious that if anybody brings up the topic of diet you all revert to reciting numbers of calories that you can't even measure without lab equipment."

"Isn't that a good reason to put the numbers on the labels?" Harry asked, winking at the others.

"First of all, my infrared sensors picked up that wink when the radiated heat from your left eye blipped," Flower said. "Second of all, if you wanted to be part of the solution rather than part of the problem, you'd volunteer."

"Of course we want to be part of the solution," Irene said. "What do you want us to volunteer for?"

"Taste testing," Flower said, her artificially generated voice overflowing with enthusiasm. "I think you'll find it an enjoyable experience, and it will only take a few minutes of your time to fill out the forms after each sample."

"Forms?" Irene repeated.

"To put your reactions to the products into words while the impression is fresh," Flower said. "After all, the purpose of branding is to create a perception of quality and consistency. The EarthCent ambassador finally realized that allowing anybody to market their products as 'Certified by the All Species Cookbook' in return for an annual licensing fee was cheapening the brand. She's hired us to help relaunch the certification program with a focus on safety and quality. When it comes to food, taste plays an important role in quality considerations."

"I would have thought it plays the only role," Dave said.

"It's that kind of thinking that put you on a restricted diet," the Dollnick AI chided him. "Taste provides an important feedback signal to your brain about what your body needs if the food is unprocessed, but as soon as cooking and additives come into play, your taste buds are easily fooled."

"Just how difficult will these forms be to fill out?" Irene asked.

"Maybe I'll just pay Bill to bring the samples and record your reactions," Flower said. "Now that you've agreed, I'll begin introducing samples to the lunch selections as soon as M793qK finishes his chemical testing."

"For everybody?" Jack asked. "Don't we get to vote?"

"If you recall the review of my food service contract for the cooperative at the last board meeting, informed consent from one regular diner per location is all I require to introduce new menu items," Flower said, and then quickly changed the subject. "Last night's transit took us to a tunnel exit on the Sharf frontier, and tonight I'll be jumping to one of their older industrial worlds for my elective stop. It's quite a distance, so I'll be stretching the jump for twenty-six hours to give your brains time to adjust. The majority of you will be asleep during both transitions, which should ease any symptoms."

"What do you want at an old Sharf world?" Harry asked.

"Mothballed factory tooling for the discontinued model of Sharf two-man traders that have proven so popular with your species. I want to have an assembly line up and running in time to be able to demonstrate the ships and start taking orders when I host the next Rendezvous of your Traders Guild."

"I get that you have plenty of empty decks where you can set up manufacturing, and we all know how good you are at attracting new employees, but where are you going to get the parts?" Jack asked.

"My deal for the intellectual property rights and tooling requires me to purchase the drives and fuel packs from the Sharf, and the ships will be equipped with controllers that the Verlocks produce under license from the Stryx. Our assembly line will fabricate the hulls and mechanical components, and we'll add value with custom interiors for Humans, including the Zero-G exercise equipment, bathrooms, and kitchenettes."

"And you think you can compete on price with pre-owned ships that have been reconditioned?"

"All of the used inventory has already been absorbed by your people—that's the reason I'm getting into the business," the Dollnick AI said. "You asked me to inform you when the guests of honor arrived, Nancy. Geoffrey and Bianca just exited the lift tube."

"Don't jump up," Jack told his wife, putting a restraining arm on her shoulder as he rose. "I'll go greet them."

"You got yourself a real gentleman," Irene said, giving Nancy a wink as Jack went to meet the guests.

"I think he feels guilty about taking a salary as the president of the cooperative while the rest of the board members only get profit-sharing," Nancy replied, after swallowing a bite of lunch. "He works hard at organizing the tours we take at all the stops, and everybody grabs him in the corridor whenever they have a complaint."

Brenda glanced towards the exit to make sure that Jack was out of earshot, and then said, "I think your husband underrates himself because he didn't have much education and worked on an ag world for most of his life. He's the only one of us who shows up for all the board meetings and actually knows everything that goes on with the cooperative, rather than just the parts he's interested in."

"Jack really does make it a full-time job, but he likes to keep busy," Nancy agreed. "Could you grab another chair for the table so that there's room for both of our guest speakers?" she asked Dave, who had already polished off his soup and salad.

"One of them can have my seat," the retired salesman replied. "I'm going to walk up and down the corridor for fifteen minutes. Doc said it might help make my digestion more efficient."

"Immediately after the meal?" Harry asked. "My doctor used to give me grief about eating on my feet and not taking time off after lunch at the bakery."

Dave shrugged. "M793qK has repaired more of my organs than I can remember. If he thinks it's worth trying, I'm game."

Jack returned with an elderly couple, both of whom had been working as authors for over fifty years. "Bianca D'Arc and Geoffrey Harstang," he introduced them to the others. "Some of you already know each other from working on MultiCon, but it can't hurt to refresh everyone's memories at our age."

The occupants of the round table dutifully gave their names, and then Harry said, "Grab a tray and get some lunch. It's free for guests."

"Jack already offered, but we ate before we came," Bianca said. "Your common room seems quite cozy," she added, looking past the grouping of circular tables to the area with overstuffed furniture. "Given the number of people Flower claims live here, I take it most of them must eat in their cabins."

"There's a cafeteria that seats five hundred just down the corridor, and the other independent living cooperatives on this deck have their own dining facilities as well," Nancy explained. "Most of us who eat here are the original cooperative members and we just kept coming out of habit, but the new members prefer the big cafeteria because it employs waitstaff. The people eating there who are coming to your talk will start trickling in any time now."

Over the next fifteen minutes, diners who had completed their meal and weren't interested in the after-lunch talk left the common room to be replaced by cooperative members coming from the large cafeteria. There was a bit of excitement when Geoffrey attempted to smuggle Bianca a cup of coffee, only to be intercepted by one of Flower's maintenance bots. He returned to the table with the glass of milk the bot had given him in exchange.

"Sorry, Bee," he said. "I guess that living in Flower's Paradise has its downsides."

"Are you banned from drinking coffee?" Irene asked Bianca.

"It's my own fault," the author admitted. "I agreed to one a day, and Flower is just helping to keep me on the straight and narrow. The last time I cheated she wouldn't talk to me until I apologized."

"Some people would consider that a bonus," Brenda said with a snort.

"I count on her for too many things," Bianca said. "Back on Earth, I used to hire personal assistants to help with my reader correspondence, especially after I appeared on *Let's Make Friends* and started getting questions from aliens about my children's books. Flower offered to help with all of that here, and she's far more efficient than any of my part-timers ever were, not to mention being able to read all of the alien languages. And she arranges for all of my focus groups."

"You run focus groups to test your children's books?" Maureen asked. "I didn't realize the marketing was that sophisticated."

"I let my publishers worry about marketing, but I like trying my ideas on as many age-appropriate beta-readers as possible."

"It's about time to start," Jack said. "I'll announce the two of you and then sit down and you can do your thing." He walked over to the double lectern that bots had brought in to replace the steam table and tapped on one of the mics. "Alright, it sounds like we're live," he continued, speaking right over all of the conversations still going in the common room. "Our guest speakers today are Bianca D'Arc the Sixth and Geoffrey Harstang, both of whom joined Flower in the last year. They're going to talk about the writers colony they've founded on board, and that's all I know about it. Please give them a warm Flower's Paradise welcome."

The audience responded with a polite round of applause as Jack returned to the table and the two authors moved up to the double lectern.

"Thank you for having us," Geoffrey began. "Our real goal today isn't to tell you about the colony we've founded but to get your feedback on what we've done wrong so far."

"Like starting from scratch rather than accepting Flower's proposal to set up here on the independent living deck," Bianca said.

"And why didn't you?" somebody asked.

"It's something we had planned for a long time, or at least," Geoffrey corrected himself, "talked about a long time ago. Outsourcing all of the work to Flower and simply declaring ourselves open for business would have seemed like a cheat. I had a very specific idea for how I would have gone about this on Earth. My plan was to rehabilitate an old country house for common living and add small cabins to the grounds for people who preferred their privacy. Bianca thought that cooking communal meals together would be important, and we both agreed it would be helpful to have a natural setting."

"In space?" Harry asked.

"Flower was very accommodating and gave us a section of her outermost ag deck, which is mainly fruit trees and pasture," Bianca said. "Then she brought in modular cabins that were either in storage or fabricated by bots, I never got a straight answer from her. We currently have private and semi-private apartments for thirty-six people in the first ring. When we finish filling them, Flower will install a second ring with seventy-two cabins, and then we'll have to see."

"In case you're wondering, the cabins are arranged in a ring around a structural spoke containing a lift tube," Geoffrey added. "And we have a kitchen and dining pavilion with a clear view of a mixed orchard of apple and peach trees."

"But it sounds like Flower did all of the work after all," somebody pointed out.

"So that's the first thing we realized," Geoffrey said. "I'm closer to eighty than seventy-five, and while I like to think that I could still saw a board straight, metal fabrication has never been part of my skill set. Thanks to help from Flower's lawyer," he paused and nodded in Brenda's direction, "I've recovered more of my assets and rights than I dreamed possible after being imprisoned in a locked ward for a decade while my so-called family plundered my estate. So along with Bianca's contribution, we have no issues with financing the work. But Flower is operating so far below capacity that her charges for leasing space and construction ended up being cheaper than I would have expected to pay anywhere else in the galaxy."

"Sounds like you're complaining about having it too good," Dave commented from the entrance where he had remained standing after returning from his walk.

"Except for the one little thing," Bianca said. "We've only convinced nine writers to sign up so far, and all of them were from the group who remained on board after MultiCon."

"Have you advertised?" Maureen asked.

"We both announced the opening of the writers colony in the discussion forums of the professional groups we're members of, and it never occurred to us that there wouldn't be a flood of applications for subsidized housing from authors who have reached retirement age but still want to be productive."

"Advertising would be like spending money to give money away," Geoffrey added.

"How about free publicity?" Nancy asked. "Our cooperative didn't really get off the ground until the local Galactic Free Press reporter ran a series of articles about the financial fraud that led to our banding together. Then Flower stepped in and started making media buys in advance of all of our stops."

"I would be honored to do the same for the writers colony," Flower put in.

Geoffrey and Bianca looked at each other. "We'll think about it," they said at the same time.

Four

Dewey removed his hands from the bookmobile's controls and settled back in his seat to watch the final approach on the main view screen.

"I thought you were flying this thing," Bill said to the artificial person. "Did you hand over control to Flower?"

"It looks like there's some wind shear at the landing field, and I can keep us steadier by linking directly with the controls," Dewey replied complacently. "While my hand-eye coordination is excellent, it's difficult to make precise movements if the whole ship is getting bounced around."

"I haven't felt a thing."

"The bookmobile is quite advanced, even though it's not large. There! That was a bounce."

"I still didn't feel it."

"I keep forgetting that you aren't equipped with my absolute positioning system," Dewey said. "I suppose your brain isn't getting bounced around any more than it usually does just from walking."

"Speaking of brains, I just remembered the dream I had last night. We were about to land at the factory, and suddenly the bookmobile just vanished. It was the two of us falling side by side, but somehow I was sure you could fly and I asked you to hold me up. You answered that flight was an expensive upgrade option and you decided it wasn't worth it when you bought your body."

"Funny, I don't remember telling you about the pushy salesman with the jetpack, but I understand that dreams of falling are very common during jump transitions. Was this around three in the morning?"

"It was," Bill said. "I checked the time on my implant when I woke up because I was hoping it was already morning and I wouldn't have to go back to sleep again."

There was a gentle thump as the bookmobile put down on the ancient tarmac that was surrounded on all sides by an enormous factory.

"That was the roof of a building on the view screen?" Bill asked in disbelief. "I thought we were landing on a pad at the center of a grassy field."

"The Sharf always plant the roofs of their buildings with cereal crops or grazing land," Dewey said. "It's actually a very common practice among the advanced species. In addition to increasing green space, the organic layer provides insulation, protection from radiation, and a healthy habitat for nature."

"But doesn't it cost a lot to put up buildings that can take the additional weight? I remember how the water would pour off of roofs back home, but if it rains here, all that water will get absorbed and add to the load."

"It's less of an issue than you imagine, even without the advanced materials the Sharf produce. I've read some books about commercial architecture on Earth, and people used to build structures in accordance with the depreciation allowances of the tax code, meaning they designed factories for a life of just a few decades. The aliens all take a much longer view, and I wouldn't be surprised if this factory has been here for a hundred thousand years or more."

"Somebody is waving a flag at us," Bill said, pointing at the viewscreen.

"Excellent." Dewey released his safety restraints and motioned for Bill to do the same. "Yaem briefed me before we left, and he said that it's traditional for visitors to Sharf industrial sites to remain in their craft until an escort appears. Otherwise, they might mistake us for industrial spies."

"The aliens sure do a lot of spying on each other." Bill released his own four-point harness and followed the artificial person to the hatch.

Dewey hit the button, and the hatch folded down as a ramp. The two of them went out to meet their escort, who proved to be a youthful Sharf wearing some type of uniform. The alien hurried over and then asked in a loud voice, "CAN YOU UNDERSTAND ME?"

"Yes, you don't have to shout," Bill said. "I have an implant, and he's artificial intelligence."

The Sharf made the logical assumption as to who was in charge and turned to address Dewey. "We packaged all of the tooling and shipped it up to orbit in anticipation of Flower's arrival. Why did she feel that a factory visit was necessary?"

"Flower said she arranged for us to meet with an engineer who had some experience with the discontinued model," Dewey replied. "I'm told he prepared some instructions for getting the line up and running."

"Gaer," the Sharf muttered. "He's an old fogey is what he is, but if you insist…"

Bill and Dewey followed their escort through a sliding door into a dimly lit area of the building that appeared to be operating on emergency lighting.

"Is the whole factory shut down?" Bill asked, peering around the gloomy space. "It's completely empty."

"And why do you think that is, young Human?" the Sharf inquired grouchily.

"Could this be the area where all of the tooling that Flower bought came from? If it is, I guess the equipment is going to take up a lot of deck space."

"Production lines for metal fabrication have a way of spreading out, especially if you have the capacity to build more than a ship or two at a time," Dewey said. "My understanding is that this one factory produced all of the two-man traders of that model that were ever built."

"Millions of them," the Sharf confirmed, pivoting to the left. "Ah, there's Gaer now. Greetings, Engineer Gaer," he said, lowering his eyestalks in respect. "I bring you guests from Flower, an artificial person and a Human."

The new arrival carried a large satchel in one hand and seemed to be bent over from the weight of it. He shuffled forward slowly and then spent a good minute clearing his throat. Finally, he said, "Thank you, Technician Eeeks. You may return to your work and I will take responsibility for our guests."

The young Sharf dipped his eyestalks again, and then hurried off, leaving Bill and Dewey with the ancient engineer. Gaer set the satchel down and tapped a button on a device he wore on his wrist. The light fixture above their heads came on full, almost blinding Bill until his pupils adjusted.

"I'm Dewey and this is Bill," the artificial person introduced the two of them.

"Gaer," the old Sharf said, dropping his professional title, perhaps in an attempt to put his guests at ease. "I've never heard of the intellectual property owners of a ship design licensing it to aliens before, but I have to admit that I'm pleased. Our two-man traders were solid little ships, practically took care of themselves, and the replacement model costs five times as much. I convinced the management to mothball the equipment around five hundred years back when the market dried up completely."

"When did they start manufacturing the old model here?" Dewey asked.

"Long before my time," Gaer said. "I couldn't find any of the manuals for operating the equipment. As near as I could discover, the factory didn't want to pay for them."

"Then how did the original operators learn?" Bill asked.

"Now you're asking me to speculate about something that happened tens of thousands of years ago, but I'll guess they bought a subscription to access holographic materials from the equipment manufacturer and let it expire after the first generation of workers was trained. These days we build our own machinery in-house, and at least we end up owning all of the documentation."

"So up in orbit, as we speak, Flower is loading antique assembly line equipment that comes without any instructions?"

"There's always a wiring diagram and safety warnings on the insides of the access panels," Gaer said, and then his ancient features cracked in the semblance of a smile. "Ha. Had you going, didn't I?"

"You sure did," Dewey said, and to Bill's ears, the artificial person actually sounded relieved. "So the manuals are in the satchel?"

"Just what I was able to draw up from memory since the management informed me of the deal," the old Sharf said. "You have to realize that with a production line this old, most of the equipment had been replaced a hundred times over, with a focus on cutting costs and increasing efficiency. Engineering is the art of creation on a budget. If you have infinite resources to solve a problem, you can just hire scientists instead and they'll get you there eventually."

"But the machines are in working condition?" Bill asked. "We'll be able to build the discontinued model of the two-man trader with them?"

"I'm sure your Dollnick colony ship could have her bots fabricate two-man traders without any of the equipment she just purchased, but it will save you some time and expense compared to doing everything from scratch," Gaer said. "Speaking of which, I wonder what's taking them so long."

"What's taking who so long?" the artificial person asked.

The old Sharf bobbed a single eyestalk, the equivalent of a wink for his species. "Right. Say no more. Why don't you show me the ship you arrived on, Dewey, and then the two of us can go over these operating instructions while we wait."

"What about me?" Bill asked.

"You just remain here a few minutes and I'm sure they'll be along," Gaer said, bobbing his eyestalk again. "You don't imagine you're here just for me to pass over some poorly reconstructed documentation." There was a sharp whistle from somewhere outside of the bright circle of light they were standing in, and the old Sharf nodded. "They're here, then," he said and took Dewey by the elbow. "Three's a crowd."

Dewey resisted being dragged off towards the exit for a moment, but Bill said, "Go ahead. I think I just guessed what this is about."

"We'll be in the bookmobile," Dewey said. "Give me a shout over your implant if anything comes up."

Bill remained alone in the brightly lit area as his friend escorted the elderly Sharf out of the factory. Then the overhead light dimmed again, and another of the aliens approached. This one appeared to be in the prime of life, with more meat on his bones than most Sharf that Bill had met. He stopped about five steps away and said, "Four moons are rising…"

"And a comet approaches," Bill replied, completing the passphrase Yaem had given him in case he ever encountered somebody in Sharf Intelligence. "Do you work for Yaem?"

The Sharf agent barked a laugh. "Work for that dilettante? I'm not even sure whose side he's on anymore. The reports he's been submitting since he transferred on board Flower are so good that I'm sure somebody else must be writing them for him."

"I wouldn't know anything about that," Bill said. "I just help him with recruiting."

"When he's not too busy running conventions or acting like an idiot for that animated series Flower produces." The Sharf paused a second, staring intently at Bill's face. "You're on the show too, aren't you?"

"I was, but I think the writers are going to kill me off as soon as it's convenient," Bill said. "Flower has been holding focus groups for *Everyday Superheroes* and the feedback is that there are too many humans."

"That was certainly my impression," the Sharf said. "So, I understand that you've taken to recruiting agents like a Snook takes to water."

"Is that a good thing?"

The spymaster shrugged. "The Snooks seem to like water, so I suppose it is. And we've already started receiving reports from the Human sources on open worlds that you recruited for Yaem, but our analysts have noticed an interesting pattern. They seem to be avoiding sending us any information about their hosts."

"Is that a bad thing?"

The spymaster paused, uncertain whether Bill was playing dumb or was truly as innocent in the ways of the intelligence world as Yaem had made him out to be.

"It comes down to budgeting," he said finally. "While every station chief in Sharf Intelligence is allowed a certain amount of leeway in developing their own network, we set specific goals by which we can judge their performance. The majority of station chiefs are permanently located on a target world, or at least in a fixed region of space, and they are expected to develop sources of intelligence in that region."

"But Flower is always moving, and some of the people I recruited for you were from worlds we've never even stopped at," Bill said, and then gambled on a little disinformation. "That's why Yaem talked Flower into hosting MultiCon, to bring people from all over the tunnel network to us."

"Thank you for that confirmation," the spymaster said. "Assigning Yaem to Flower was a bit of an experiment for us, and we're paying EarthCent Intelligence a substantial fee for hosting him. When a character so obviously based on Yaem appeared on *Everyday Superheroes*, I was afraid he had sold out to Flower in order to indulge his passion for anime. I recruited him from the entertainment industry, and to be honest, I have my doubts about his dedication to the cause."

"He always puts the Sharf first," Bill said, laying it on thick. "I work in the cafeteria where he eats with the other alien spies, and I've seen them get into terrible arguments over whose culture is superior."

"It's good to hear he's standing up for our interests. Now, what can you tell me about the station chiefs on board? I'm particularly interested in this Lume fellow who seems to be working directly for Flower rather than Dollnick Intelligence, plus anything you can tell me about Captain Pyun on a personal level. All I have is his official EarthCent Intelligence personnel records and they don't say much about who he really is as a man. And you may as well fill me in on whatever you can about the others as long as I have you here."

"EarthCent Intelligence shares their personnel records with you?"

"Not intentionally," the Sharf said with a dry chuckle. He pulled a device from his belt pouch and set it on the floor between them. It began to spin like a top, and then emitted an eerie green glow. "Don't let the holo recording field bother you. It's a secure device that will only play back the recording if one of us is present in the field. The other species would kill for this technology."

"It, uh, sounds very impressive," Bill said, desperately trying to think of a way he could get out of reporting on the alien spies from his cafeteria. "Lume is, well, very tall, and, uh, I know he eliminated an assassin who was on Flower to kill my fiancée, though she wasn't my fiancée yet."

"Yes, yes. I know all about Miss Gold and EarthCent's poor excuse for a witness protection program from our sources on Earth."

"You have spies working on Earth?"

"More than we have any need for," the Sharf said in exasperation. "When we opened an embassy there, your people practically broke down the doors trying to be the first to get on the payroll. And unlike the sources from open worlds you and Yaem have been recruiting for us, the Humans on Earth show no hesitation about providing detailed information about the local governments and power players."

"Well, they grew up there," Bill reasoned. "On open worlds, we're basically guests."

The Sharf's eyestalks shot out like a cartoon character's, expressing surprise. "How could our analysts have failed to make the connection? Of course, that explains why the sources you've recruited are providing excellent information about the Humans and other species visiting the open worlds, but nothing about their hosts. They're simply being good guests. Perhaps we need to look again at the grade we assigned Humans for social graces."

"We didn't do that well?" Bill asked, happy to talk about anything other than the aliens from the cafeteria who he thought of as friends.

"Let's just say that—Hortens," the spymaster cursed, and snatched up his spinning holo-recorder like a kid grabbing his top to run home for dinner. "We're out of time. Write me up profiles of the alien spies on board and have Yaem submit them through our regular channels. It was interesting meeting you, Bill. I'll see about getting you a bonus."

"Thank you," the confused young man called after the rapidly retreating alien's back. Then he looked around the dimly lit factory floor and headed in the direction that Dewey and the old engineer had taken. A minute later, he was outside. Bill took a deep breath of relief and climbed the ramp into the bookmobile.

"So if I can summarize what you've told me, these instructions are mainly for tweaking the controls to get a quality stamping out of worn-out molds, but when it comes to setting up the equipment, we're on our own," Dewey was saying.

"I didn't limit myself to panel production," the old Sharf protested. "You're going to find the order-of-assembly steps invaluable. Imagine welding a bulkhead into place only to find that you haven't installed the wiring harness or the air ducting that runs behind it."

"I didn't mean to minimize your efforts," the artificial person attempted to mollify the engineer. "It's just that we were expecting some basic setup instructions. It's not clear to me that our workers will be able to figure out which parts go with which machines."

"Oh, I almost forgot," the engineer said, and fishing in his pocket, pulled out a data chip. "We took holographic images of all the equipment before breaking it down for shipping."

"That's what I was waiting to hear," Dewey said, and reaching in his own pocket, took out a programmable cred. "A little bonus from Flower."

Gaer flipped the Stryx coin to the side showing the amount and let out a delighted whistle. "If there's anything else Flower needs, feel free to contact me. I don't suppose you'll be coming this way again anytime soon, but I'm officially retired, and the wife has been pestering me about taking a grand tour of the galaxy before we're too old. It's just so cliché. Could I borrow your arm, young Human?"

Bill walked back down the ramp with the old engineer, then he reentered the bookmobile and strapped himself into the co-pilot's seat.

"Did your meeting with Yaem's boss go well?" Dewey asked as he began ticking through the brief prelaunch checklist.

"How did you know? It took me completely by surprise."

"Process of elimination," the artificial person said. "We all know that you work for Yaem, and who else would come all the way here just to meet you?"

"He was a bit intimidating," Bill admitted as the bookmobile slowly rose above the factory. "I'm supposed to send him my impressions of all the other alien spies on board, and he even asked me for information about the captain. I'm not sure what to do."

"Talk to Captain Pyun," Dewey advised. "Your first loyalty has to be EarthCent."

"This being a double agent business is getting confusing," Bill said as the bookmobile began to accelerate. "I'm going to have to start writing things down."

Five

When Julie returned from lunch, the door to her new office in the headquarters of Flower Industries was open. She steeled herself before entering, expecting yet another impromptu meeting with a baffled person who the Dollnick AI was trying to recruit for a job that didn't even exist yet, but it turned out to be a maintenance bot in the act of placing a spaceship next to her desk.

"Is that a large toy or a miniature lifeboat?" Julie asked.

"It's a scale model," Flower replied via the bot's speaker grille. "They're very useful for wind tunnel simulations when engineers are designing craft that can enter planetary atmospheres, though the Sharf worked all of that out for this model over a hundred thousand years ago. I had my shipyard employees completely tear down a two-man trader so they'd learn how it was put together, and then they built a few scale models for practice."

"So you had them turn one big ship that actually flew into a bunch of little ships for office decorations?"

"Laura and Don used the knowledge they gained to build the model, not the actual parts. In fact, they were able to put the original ship back together again, though the technicians are still troubleshooting a few minor problems with the drive and life support."

"So what is it doing in my office?" Julie asked.

"As my executive assistant, it's important that you familiarize yourself with all aspects of Flower Industries. You already have experience with anime production, and I know that Bill is always talking to you about our food business, so I want you to start getting up to speed on the shipyard."

"I don't know the first thing about technology, much less space engineering. I'm not even that good at math when you get beyond counting money."

"Counting is fundamental, and this is why I gave you the scale model," Flower said. "I want you to take it apart and put it together again at least once a day. Think of it as a three-dimensional puzzle."

"And that's supposed to teach me something about shipyard work?"

"The pieces are labeled on the back so you'll learn the names of all of the major components that make up a two-man trader. Gaining an understanding of how they fit together is no small thing. Why don't you go ahead and start?"

"What about my afternoon meetings? I was supposed to see Third Officer Lynx to discuss your long-term plans for this deck, and then you had me scheduled to take Samuel and Vivian around looking at real estate."

"There's been a sudden change of plans," Flower said. "I don't want to steal the captain's thunder because he'll be making a ship-wide announcement in approximately—now."

"This is Captain Pyun speaking," Woojin's voice came over the public address system. "We'll be dropping into regular space in five minutes in response to a distress call forwarded to Flower by the Stryx. Those of you who experience any dizziness with jump transitions may want to take advantage of this notice to lie down. We don't have any details about the nature of the distress call, but I will be updating the ship's calendar as soon as we have more information. I'm requesting that all inhabitants with experience in medical emergencies make their way to the core to be on hand in case your help is required. Don't forget to wear magnetic cleats."

"What was that all about?" Julie asked. "Since when do the Stryx ask people like us for help?"

"The location of the distress call is in interstellar space so it's safe to assume that there's a disabled ship involved. I suspect that we were contacted as the closest vessel capable of providing meaningful help," Flower added, not without a hint of pride. "If their life support has failed, I have the spare capacity to take on board over four million moderate-sized oxygen breathers, more if they're willing to double bunk."

"But you don't know anything about who they are or where they're from?"

"We'll have all of the answers in another three minutes," the Dollnick AI said. "Now why don't you get started on taking apart the model and call me if you get stuck."

"Are there any instructions?"

"You'll miss out on half the fun if I show you the exploded view. Just start from the top and see how far you get. The pieces are held in place by embedded magnetic monopoles so you'll have no trouble pulling them apart."

Julie sighed. "All right. Good luck with your emergency and let me know if you need any help. I picked up some basic first aid while I was working for the drug syndicate as a teenager because the dealers were always fighting over territory."

"Why didn't you say so earlier?" Flower demanded. "The scale model can wait until tomorrow. Hop on a lift tube for the docking bay. And don't forget your magnetic cleats."

"I wore my new walking shoes today in case you wanted me to show Samuel and Vivian the inner decks. The cleats are built-in."

Julie gladly left the intimidating scale model behind and made her way to the lift tube. She clicked her heels to activate the magnetic cleats, and a minute later, emerged in Flower's core. Looking up, she could see hundreds of people milling around over her head on the opposite side of the cylindrical core's inner surface, a reminder that she was living in a giant centrifuge built from concentric decks like a tubular onion. Then a tentacle gripped her shoulder and she jumped.

"Jorb! Are you here to help with the medical emergency?"

"You can't teach in a dojo without picking up the basics of first aid," the Drazen explained. "Did Flower give you any details beyond the captain's announcement? We're all in the dark."

"Apparently she doesn't know any more about what's going on than we do. The Stryx just forwarded her the location."

"I hope we're not showing up for the aftermath of a war or a pirate attack," Jorb said. "Drazen Intelligence made me sit through a holo-course for combat medics and it wasn't pretty."

"Flower assigned you both to me," a mechanical sounding voice spoke from behind them, and Julie turned to see M793qK. The Farling physician was wearing his external translation pendant around what passed for his neck, and he was carrying so many medical bags that he looked like an over-packed tourist heading off on vacation. "Do you both have Dollnick stunners?"

"I brought two," Jorb said. "Just in case."

"Give one to Julie," M793qK instructed.

"Do you think it's a trap and they're going to board us by force?" the girl asked nervously.

The Farling buzzed his speaking legs together, producing his version of a snort. "Can't you see the line of combat bots Flower has waiting just to the inside of the atmosphere retention field? If this is a trap, the bait is going to find that it's bitten off more than it can chew."

"Then what's the stunner for?" Julie asked, accepting Jorb's spare and clipping it to the waistline of her slacks.

"Combat anesthesia," M793qK responded. "And if there are a large number of casualties and I have to set up triage, the two of you will be responsible for making sure nobody jumps the line. I'll be the judge of who to treat first."

For a split second, Julie felt like she was back on the lift tube as Flower dropped into normal space. All of a sudden the view through the transparent atmosphere retention field showed a run-down colony ship with dull red emergency lighting showing through the ports of the outer decks.

"We're right on top of them!" Jorb exclaimed. "How did you do that?"

"The Stryx have been supplying me the location feed via the controller's transponder," Flower replied over their implants. "I came out of the jump as close as physically possible because every second counts in rescue operations."

M793qK had set down all of his bags and was now staring intently at the screen of a Farling device that Julie had never seen before. "That's strange," he said. "I've accessed their internal comms and I'm picking up eleven different languages—make that twelve." His wings flashed out from his carapace and then retreated, as if he had been about to take flight and then fought down the urge. "It can't be."

"Can't be what?" Julie asked.

"Wanderers," the doctor replied grimly. "I just heard some chatter from the Zarent damage-control team—they're telepaths, you know." He paused for a moment before adding, "It sounds like the secondary pile containment field detuned and there was an explosion, but it happened days ago."

The axis of the disabled ship was now perfectly in line with Flower's open end, and the waiting combat bots launched themselves across the shrinking gap in a wave. They passed through the atmosphere retention field, and a moment later, entered the other vessel's core.

"This is Captain Pyun," Woojin's voice echoed through the docking bay. "Flower has identified the damaged ship as a Class One Dollnick Colony Transport, that's the original model that was discontinued over a million years ago. It was decommissioned long before Flower herself was built, but it seems to have found its way into the hands of the Wanderers. I've just spoken to their captain, and life support is failing, so we'll begin taking their people on board as soon as the injured are evacuated. We don't yet have an exact count for the populace, but it sounds like less than twenty thousand oxygen breathers from a dozen species. Captain out."

"That's a relief," Jorb said. "Twenty trips with one of Flower's main shuttles will move all of the survivors. If the number had been much larger we would have had to extend our atmosphere retention field and set up safety lines for spacewalking. It's never a good idea for ships this large to get so close together that they're almost touching."

"Who are the Wanderers?" Julie asked.

"You didn't study the Wanderers in school?"

"I didn't go to school, and my teacher bot never said anything about them. I'd never even heard of them before the awards party where the doctor won the best stand-in award for an anime production. A show about a Wanderer ship was a finalist in one of the categories that *Everyday Superheroes* was nominated for, though I've forgotten which."

"The Wanderers have been around for millions of years, maybe tens of millions," Jorb explained. "They usually move in large fleets called mobs, so I don't know what this ship is doing out here on its own. The original Wanderers were a species that never developed interstellar jump technology, but they excelled at building space habitats. So they set out to colonize space in slow motion, with generation after generation living their whole lives on giant ships. When they reached their destinations, some of them decided that they'd rather continue living in space than returning to planets."

"But the captain and M793qK both said that there are at least a dozen species living on board that ship," Julie said. "Do the original Wanderers encourage alien immigration, like Stryx stations?"

"I doubt there are any original Wanderers on this ship because they keep their vessels in tip-top condition," Jorb said. "Most of the mobs I've heard of lately were comprised mainly of tunnel network species, with a few neighboring aliens thrown in. They've developed a sort of post-employment culture, so they count on their parent species for handouts."

"He means that they're bums," M793qK interjected, then he gestured towards a group of Flower's bots that were returning with something in tow. "All except for the Zarents who do the ship maintenance, and from what I'm hearing, it sounds like they've given up. Those bots are bringing back some stasis pods with Zarents who were badly injured when the secondary pile failed. I'll see to those later, but there are some walking wounded as well, so let's get to work."

The Farling gestured at the numerous medical bags he'd carried, and then shuffled off to meet the returning bots. Jorb sighed and grabbed a bag in each hand, plus one with his tentacle, leaving the remaining two for Julie. She hoisted the bags and followed the giant beetle.

A terrible odor of burned fur greeted them when the lead bot opened the door of the simple transfer pod it had towed over from the Wanderer vessel. A tangled mass of tentacles rolled out, and then it separated into individual Zarents, none of whom stood taller than Julie's waist. With eight tentacles each, she was tempted to classify them as land-dwelling octopi, though their instrument laden harnesses and intelligent eyes marked them as sentient creatures.

"That one first," M793qK ordered, pointing at a Zarent who was having trouble balancing, despite the number of appendages he or she had in contact with the deck. "I told her to stop moving around, so stun her if she tries to insist that I treat one of her co-workers first."

Julie felt incredibly awkward drawing her weapon and couldn't bring herself to point it in the direction of the injured aliens. The Farling's bark turned out to be worse than his bite, and he moved even quicker than when he was warding off attacks as the Evil Mastermind in

Everyday Superheroes. "Jorb, bring the bag in your right hand over here and hold the patient up for me so I can get at her underside."

Jorb dropped the two unneeded bags and used some kind of martial arts to move fluidly into position. While holding the bag open for the doctor, he deployed his tentacle to support the Zarent, who wrapped two of her own undamaged tentacles around his one to hold herself in place.

"Julie," the doctor summoned her as he went to work snipping away burned fur and applying some kind of ointment. "Most of this batch are relatives of the Zarents in stasis, but several of them have crushing injuries. I want you to take the green spray can out of the bag in your left hand and apply it as needed."

"How will I know—"

"I've told the Zarents to present themselves to you," M793qK interrupted

Julie dug around the bag for the can in question, and when she looked up, a ragged line of the little aliens had formed in front of her.

"I'm Fourth Technician Miklat," the first Zarent introduced himself via a speaker pendant attached to his harness. "The doctor said that you have Shurpa."

"If it's the stuff in this green spray can, then I do," Julie said, frowning at the label which consisted of clusters of dots.

"That's the stuff," the Zarent told her. "We used up all of ours on the badly injured." He gingerly extended a tentacle he'd been cradling under his body, and even Julie could see that more than half of it had been flattened right out to the tip. The Zarent used two other tentacles to support it and looked at her expectantly.

"I just spray this stuff on?"

"Shurpa. You have to shake it until the mixing pea stops making noise."

"Right," Julie said, trying her best to look confident in the theory that it would inspire the same in her patients. She shook the can vigorously for about fifteen seconds until the loud rattle became subdued, and after locating the small arrow stamped into the top of the nozzle, pointed it at the damaged tentacle and applied an even coat of the green spray.

The Zarent remained perfectly still during this operation, then a loud buzz came from somewhere below his body, and he scurried to the side, keeping his injured tentacle braced with the healthy ones.

"That's Second Chef Miklat," the treated Zarent informed Julie as the next little octopus limped up. "She burned the tips of four tentacles helping to move the emergency containment panels into place."

Julie obligingly sprayed the tentacle tips green as they were presented. "How are you all getting around without magnetic cleats?" she asked her self-appointed assistant as the next Zarent moved forward for treatment.

"It's a property of our fur," Fourth Technician Miklat explained. "The ends are split into thousands of microfibers, and the molecules they are composed of swap electrons with the molecules of the deck, creating a weak electromagnetic attraction. Does this ship have an active AI?"

"Very active," Julie answered.

"I'm sure it could tell you the name of this physical phenomenon in your language if the translation failed."

"Van der Waals," Flower said over Julie's implant. "I love the Zarents. They're the only good thing about the Wanderers."

"And who is this?" Julie asked as she followed a pointed tentacle to spray a large gash on her current patient's body.

"Third Engineer Miklat," her informant told her. "He was the first one on the scene after the containment failure and he put the survivors in stasis. Check all of his tentacles for burns—he's a stoic."

"Let me see those," Julie demanded, moving to block the engineer as he tried to stagger off on three tentacles.

"Save the Shurpa for those who need it more," the Zarent spoke through his speaker pendant.

"I have plenty of it in my clinic and I can make more as needed," M793qK said angrily without looking over. "Now let Julie treat you or she'll be forced to use the stunner."

The Zarent halted, and then presented five tentacles in states ranging from a little singed to badly burned. Julie sprayed them green, and the creature let out an even louder buzz than the first had before moving off.

"Are you all from the same family?" Julie asked when the fourth technician identified her next patient as Seventh Life Support Specialist Miklat. "And are you sure I should be using this spray on open wounds?" she added, wincing at the depth of the puncture wound that had been hidden by the specialist's fur.

"Why would you assume we're related?" her assistant asked. "And you can spray Shurpa on any wound without worrying. It may not help fast enough to matter if the damage is too extensive, but it will never make the problem worse. It's basically a topical anesthetic loaded with the same cells our bodies use to repair themselves when we're healthy."

"In a spray? That doesn't sound possible."

"We're an artificial biological lifeform, genetically engineered for Zero-G repair work," the Zarent told her bluntly. "The Farlings created us for the original Wanderers, though we've long since forgotten whether we were a gift, or a bribe for the mob to leave Farling space."

Julie looked sharply toward the beetle doctor, who had already completed the surgery and was wrapping a long white bandage around the patient, weaving it between alternating tentacles as he went to create a star pattern.

"So you're all clones?" she asked the technician, even as she sprayed another of the Zarents green.

"No, we simply started on a higher rung of the evolutionary ladder, so to speak, but we reproduce naturally and have moved well beyond our initial design parameters. I'm sure you can imagine our joy at hearing there was a Farling physician on board. What made you think we were clones? Surely you don't think we all look alike."

"Not at all," Julie lied, since she could barely tell the Zarents apart beyond the obvious differences in injuries and variations in fur color. "But you all have the same name."

"Ah, I'd forgotten that those who've never encountered us before can misunderstand our official designations. Miklat is the name of our ship, and the rest gives our job description and rank."

"It's not going to be as bad as I feared," M793qK announced after examining his next patient. "I'm going to take this one back to my clinic to run some diagnostics. Jorb, you come with me and I'll give you the rest of the Shurpa I have in stock. Julie, you stay here, and when you're finished with this group, there's a larger number with more superficial injuries on the way."

"I can use the spray on all of the Wanderers?"

"No, it's specially made for Zarents. All it will do to anybody else is paint them green."

"And what about the Zarents in stasis pods?" Julie asked the Farling as he made his way past, a crumpled looking octopus cradled in his lower appendages.

"They'll keep for now," M793qK said. "Unlike humans, Zarent biology is not trivial, and I need to prepare before dealing with serious cases."

Six

"You're just in time to help with the seaweed," Harry greeted Bill. "Go ahead and make all of it—the Verlock and the Grenouthian will inhale the stuff."

"I thought we were supposed to save all of the certification products for testing on people in your independent living cooperative." Bill groaned on seeing all of the opened packages of dried seaweed. "M793qK is going to kill me."

"He's too busy ginning up replacement parts for those furry little aliens from the Miklat. Flower passed along a message from the EarthCent embassy on Union Station that the seaweed is an experimental product from a Vergallian water world and it gave the ambassador a stomachache. Normally we can eat Vergallian vegan in moderation, so it might have something to do with the mineral content of the alien ocean."

"I've never even eaten seaweed myself. How do I prepare it?"

"Just soften it in warm water from the tap, you don't have to heat it on the stove," Harry said. "Lume stopped in earlier and told me the regulars would all be here for a lunch meeting to discuss the situation with the Wanderers. I've got a bean-based porridge staying warm in the oven that I made especially for Razood, though I think the others will like it as well. And I put two vegetable platters in the fridge for in case they start drinking."

"Are you going somewhere?" Bill asked, dumping package after package of dried seaweed into the large stainless steel bowl he had half-filled with warm water.

"I came in early this morning to work on a peach cobbler recipe for Flower Foods that I haven't made in a decade. I've already burned through my new work-hours quota for the day, so I'm going to meet Irene at the food court in twenty minutes and have lunch out for a change. How were your classes this morning?"

"I'm not sure I'll ever get the hang of estimating," Bill said mournfully as he retrieved a premade vegetable platter from the fridge and removed the transparent film. "Today the instructor asked us to write out a description of how we would go about setting prices if we were opening our own cafés, just as a thought exercise, and then we shared them all on the group discussion board."

"Let me guess," Harry said. "You started with the cost of ingredients, added something for rent and utilities, and figured that anything left over after sales would be your pay."

"I've seen enough of the way Flower does business to have included something for marketing."

"What did the other students do?"

"Pretty much the same thing," Bill said, gathering bowls for serving the bean porridge. "But Renée, a girl Julie used to wait tables with at *The Spoon* is taking the class, and she said that it doesn't work that way and we'd all go broke."

"At the risk of oversimplifying, she's right," Harry said, fishing a strand of softened seaweed from the bowl. "All of those costs are important, but ultimately, there is no simple formula for pricing individual items in a food service establishment. When it comes down to it, you have to make your money on the items that everybody buys. Sure, your highest single ticket in a café may be an over-the-top interpretation of chocolate cake that you can sell for two creds a slice, but what percentage of your customers are going to come in and buy it every day?"

"That's exactly what Renée said. It turns out that the biggest profit maker at *The Spoon* is the coffee, even though it's the least expensive item on the menu."

"That's how it works in bakeries as well. Our highest ticket items were the wedding cakes, though they did take a lot of time and customer hand-holding on Irene's part. But it's the daily bread that kept us in business year-in, year out."

The swinging door that separated the kitchen from the cafeteria pushed open and Razood leaned through the opening. "Do I smell bean porridge?" the Frunge asked.

"I'll bring it out in a minute," Bill told him. "Do you want an extra serving?"

The Frunge held up three fingers and then ducked back into the cafeteria.

"Just give it to him in a salad bowl," Harry suggested. "Everybody knows how much Razood likes beans—they won't be offended." He checked that the seaweed strand he had pulled from the bowl was no longer dripping before lowering it into his mouth, and then spat it out in the sink. "That explains the stomachache."

"What?" Bill asked, pausing at the door with the vegetable platter.

"It's loaded with mineral salts, and I'm guessing it's not just the usual magnesium and potassium ones either.

Maybe it's healthy for us in small quantities, but I wouldn't recommend making it into a meal."

Bill checked the status light above the swinging door to make sure nobody was coming in from the other side and then exited to the cafeteria. Half of the alien spies on board were already sitting around a couple of tables that had been pulled together, and Crute, the Dollnick station chief, was taking drink orders from behind the bar.

"Just in time, I'm famished," the Grenouthian director said, indicating where Bill should place the vegetable platter. "Did I smell seaweed soaking when the door was open?"

"I'll bring it out after the porridge," Bill said. "I just have to drain it first."

"Don't do that!" the director exclaimed, grabbing the young man's wrist with a furry paw. "The water is my favorite part. Just bring out the whole bowl and leave it at this end of the table. I'll save a place for Brynlan. And bring an extra bowl for Avisia, though you know she never eats much, at least not in public."

"And what do you mean by that?" demanded the Vergallian agent, who could easily have been mistaken for a fashion model. "Are you suggesting that I binge and purge in private?"

"Avisia, I didn't see you there. And I meant it in the sense that I've never seen you take the last chocolate from a dish, or the last anything, for that matter. You're too attuned to the needs of others."

"You're certainly welcome to my share of the Wanderers," the Vergallian said as Bill retreated to the kitchen. "Have any of you been down to see them? I've been staying away, but I'm afraid my superiors will expect a report."

"You do know that the Wanderers go everywhere and see everything," the director said, sounding rather satisfied with himself. "I took a stroll around the Con deck where Flower is housing most of them, and I picked up a few worthwhile tidbits about the Gormier Rebellion."

"Are you interested in the Gormier Rebellion?" Lume asked, placing drinks on the table with all four hands and taking his seat. "I stumbled across a fellow Dollnick from the Miklat who had some very detailed information and I made a deal with him for the exclusive rights. That said, I'm always willing to listen to reasonable offers."

"Older fellow with a purple plume and a missing finger on his lower left hand?" Razood asked, shifting his attention to the kitchen door when Bill reemerged with a tray of porridge bowls. "He started me at three hundred creds for the exclusive rights, but I bargained him down to twenty for a data crystal. Want to compare what we got?"

"You too?" rumbled Brynlan as he took his seat. "Good info, I got it for ten."

Lume slammed his lower two fists on the table, almost causing Bill to drop the tray. "He charged me fifty and I had to supply my own blank crystal!"

"The crystal was free with the deal," Razood said, and the Verlock nodded his agreement.

"Did I miss something important?" Yaem asked, taking his accustomed place next to Avisia. "Flower's been running me ragged helping the Wanderers get settled in on the Con deck. She said to treat them as if they were all here for an event. I've got anime and immersives running around the clock in all ten of her theatres."

"How many Wanderers are there in all?" the Vergallian asked.

"A little under twenty thousand at last count," the Sharf replied. "Pretty evenly divided between the tunnel network species, though I didn't see any Grenouthians."

"My people are too industrious to join the Wanderers in any numbers," the director said matter-of-factly. "Was there a Human contingent?"

"Just a few hundred," Yaem said. "I doubt most Wanderer mobs have any Humans at all, they're such a new species."

"Not a mob, one ship," Brynlan pointed out, helping himself to a particularly thick carrot spear that promised to deliver a satisfying crunch. "Are they exiles?"

"Is it even possible to get banished from a Wanderer mob?" Bill asked, offering the Verlock a bowl of bean porridge. "The way Flower explained it to me, they have pretty low standards for, well, everything."

"They have strict rules against working too hard and bringing down everybody's mood," Avisia said speculatively. "Maybe this batch got kicked out for being real go-getters, at least by Wanderer standards."

"It's obvious you haven't visited the Con deck yet," Lume said. "As near as I can tell, they expect to spend their time on board being entertained. They make those con addicts who immigrated to cosplay around the clock look like responsible citizens."

"There's nothing wrong with my ConAnon recruits, and I'd happily take more if I could get them," Flower interjected via an overhead speaker. "Dressing up like aliens hasn't stopped them from participating in the workforce, or from doing the required calisthenics and signing up for a team sport. The Wanderers are already making trouble on that account."

"They won't sign up for a team sport?" Bill asked, placing a leftover bowl of porridge next to the one the Frunge was currently devouring.

"They absolutely refused to come out of their cabins for calisthenics this morning," the Dollnick AI reported angrily. "They're claiming that the tunnel network treaty exempts refugees rescued in space from being forced to abide by a ship's exercise program."

"Is their argument valid?" Lume asked.

"Unfortunately, there's something to it, though I'm sure I would prevail in a Dollnick court," Flower said. "I don't trust these Wanderers and I want you all to pitch in and help me keep an eye on them."

"You want us to spy on your guests?" The Grenouthian did a drum roll on his belly in amusement.

"The Wanderers make trouble wherever they go, and we're stuck with this bunch until their ship is back in working order. The Stryx have agreed to reimburse any direct expenses I incur, but if I could pay a substantial sum and see the Miklat on its way tomorrow, I would do so. There's no telling what effect the Wanderers will have on the morale of my inhabitants. Or their morals, for that matter."

"Does everybody have enough?" Bill asked, returning with the big bowl of seaweed.

"Put it at this end," the Grenouthian directed the young man. "And I could use a ladle to get the liquid out."

"Use a teacup," Yaem suggested, and patted the seat of the chair on his open side. "Sit with us, Bill. You're in the intelligence business now so you should be hearing all of this."

"Reluctantly," Bill said, sitting down where his Sharf handler had indicated. "Can I tell them about the, uh, thing?"

"What thing?" the Sharf asked through a mouthful of beans, and then swallowed. "You mean meeting my boss? Sure, go ahead."

"Is Yaem's superior checking up on him?" Avisia inquired, looking rather amused.

"Our boss is suspicious because the reports you guys helped Yaem with while he's been busy working for Flower are too good," Bill explained. "Then he asked me to write up my impressions of all of you, but I wanted to get your permission first."

"Ooh, a polite spy. What is it that makes Humans so naïve?"

"As long as I get bean porridge once a week, you can write whatever you want about me," Razood offered generously. "I'll even give you my impressions of the others if you run out of things to say."

"Sorry I'm late, everybody," Jorb said, taking the last open chair at the table. "Write whatever you want about me, Bill, but leave Rinka out of it."

"Everybody is here now, so let me bring you up to date while you eat," Flower said. "You probably all know that I've taken the Miklat in tow so I can get back underway before our schedule is irreversibly impacted. I'll have to shave an hour or two from each stop for the rest of our circuit, but I don't anticipate having to make any other changes."

"It seems like a rather large vessel to take under tow," Yaem ventured.

"Fortunately, it's Dollnick-built, and our ships standardized on emergency towing protocols over a million years ago," Flower said. "The energy drain is substantial, but the Stryx will make good my losses since this mission was initiated through their request. The main problem we face is that the Zarents are on strike."

Lume choked on a celery stalk and Brynlan pounded the Dollnick's back, causing the piece to dislodge and shoot across the cafeteria.

"I'll get that," Bill said, grabbing a napkin and going after the projectile.

"The Zarents can't go on strike," Lume said, half rising from his chair. "The Farlings designed them for maintaining vessels in deep space. It's their reason for being."

"And they've been evolving for longer than the Dollnicks have had interstellar travel," the Grenouthian observed. "They aren't slaves, and who can blame them for being fed up with the Wanderers. Is it only the Zarents on the Miklat who walked out, Flower, or did it affect the whole mob?"

"According to what the Zarents have told M793qK, the strike is only on the Miklat, though they informed their brothers of their action before the communications failed. They believe they have been systematically starved of resources needed to maintain the ship in anything approaching good working condition, and when the secondary pile failure led to so many injuries, they decided to call it quits."

"So they laid down their tools and walked off the job," Razood said, pushing aside his empty bowl, the second he had polished off.

"They probably laid down those cute unicycles they ride around on and kept their tools," the Sharf said. "Haven't any of you watched their anime series that gave us a run for the money at the awards, *Wanderer Mob*?"

"The absence of a mob bothers me," the Verlock spy returned to his earlier observation. "What did their captain say?"

"He won't talk to me, and Woojin hasn't been able to get anything out of him on the subject," Flower said. "The Miklat's native AI left the ship when it was originally transferred to the Wanderers, as do all Dollnick AIs facing a similar choice. The Wanderers, in their turn, refuse to talk with us, unless it happens to suit their purposes."

"All of the Wanderers on board are refusing to talk to you?" Bill asked on his return to the table.

"I wish," the Dollnick AI said, sounding almost human. "It's only on an official level they refuse to discuss anything with me—they're perfectly happy to make demands for personal attention around the clock. The Wanderers currently on board represent less than three percent of my population, yet they are monopolizing approximately half of my language processing time."

"Maybe they're just settling in."

"Don't even think it. From this minute forward, our top priority is restoring the Miklat's life support and sending the Wanderers on their way."

"I won't give you any argument there," Avisia said. "I've told my finishing school students to stay away from the Con deck, but young Humans that age are reckless. I've taken the precaution of slipping Gem nanotrackers in their energy drinks so I can make sure they're all still on board before the Wanderers depart."

"Sensible precaution," Brynlan commented, and then addressed Flower without looking up at the ceiling, "Has M793qK asked the Zarents what happened to the mob?"

"He said that it's not an emergency so he refuses to interrogate his patients or their families until they are all out of danger," Flower said. "While I agree that there's a mystery involved, the only way we're going to get rid of the Wanderers is to restore the Miklat to operation, and it's not like the rest of the mob would help with that in any case."

"If the Zarents are on strike, who is going to do the repairs?" Bill asked.

"I have my emergency response bots decontaminating the ship and locking down unstable systems," Flower said. "As soon as the initial damage survey is complete, I'll attempt to match the required tasks with available personnel, but I'm not going to hold back on activating and deploying more of my bots if that makes sense. The Miklat is a Dollnick ship, however obsolete, and I have the complete schematics and manufacturing specifications for spare parts in my archives."

"So what do you want us to do?" Lume asked.

"Spy on the Wanderers," the Dollnick AI replied flatly. "You have the perfect excuse since that's already your job, and it's an excellent opportunity for you to gather information for your employers and recruit new sources. But even Stryx stations put a hard limit on the number of Wanderers they'll allow on board at one time, and we're already way over that on a percentage basis. I want to head off any trouble they brew up before I have to deploy my combat bots for policing duty."

"Keep them entertained," the Grenouthian director advised. "It should be easy to distract such an unmotivated bunch of sentients."

"What's the status of the LARPing studio you were setting up?" Jorb asked. "The last I heard you were investing in hardware upgrades to allow you to handle the real-time holographic aspects."

"I'm in the process of integrating the equipment—it hasn't gone quite as smoothly as I'd hoped," Flower replied.

"But you're always boasting about how the Dollnicks design everything to work together," Bill said.

"I didn't exactly buy Dollnick hardware," Flower admitted. "Some of the hackers from Bits claimed to be experts at systems integration, and I let them talk me into purchasing used Horten hardware a gaming tournament promoter was selling at a steep discount. But they seem to be making rapid progress, and I hope it will be ready for Beta testing in the next few days."

Seven

"At least let us pay for breakfast," Vivian said to Julie. "When Samuel insisted on moving out of the honeymoon suite after the week we reserved was up, I thought we'd just be taking the next available cabin. We didn't realize that Flower would make you play real estate agent."

"You never explained why Samuel insisted on leaving the suite," Julie said, checking the direction of the restroom to see if Vivian's husband was on the way back yet. "Was it the color scheme? I warned Flower about all of the pink."

"It's the idea of accepting anything for free," Vivian explained. "Samuel's mother has been EarthCent's ambassador on Union Station as long as he's been alive, and unlike the other species, EarthCent has rules about diplomats receiving gifts. Now that he's officially the top diplomat of the Human Empire he thinks we should adhere to the same code of conduct."

"And the Human Empire basically consists of the two of you?"

"On paper, we're representing over a billion humans spread across open worlds and space habitats. In practice, they all have their own local governments, and they look to the Conference of Sovereign Human Communities to handle their trade issues. The Human Empire is supposed to eventually replace CoSHC, and ultimately, EarthCent as well. But nobody expects anything to change in the near term."

"But on paper, are you and Samuel really the top two diplomats of a new empire?" Julie persisted.

"It doesn't mean anything to anyone other than the Stryx," Vivian said, handing a ten cred piece to the waitress and indicating for her to keep the change. "Anyway, I'm sorry about Flower making you play nanny for us. I don't know why she didn't just give us the tour herself since we both have high-grade implants. Aren't we cutting into your writing time?"

"Really, it's fine," Julie said. "I put in my two hours at the keyboard before I came out to meet you guys for breakfast, and I save my research for before bed."

"Can you get work done right before you go to sleep? I would end up lying awake all night thinking about unfinished business."

"Did I make it sound like work? My research is reading through the D'Arc backlist. There have been seven different authors in the line since the start of the twenty-first century. If everything works out the way it's planned, I'll eventually take over from Bianca the Seventh, but that's at least ten years away. Bianca the Sixth moved on board after MultiCon, and once a week we sit down for a few hours and she helps me with plotting and characterizations."

"Then you're taking time off from your other jobs to show us around," Vivian said, obviously concerned that she and Samuel were imposing.

"Flower made me her executive assistant and now I work for her full time, if not around the clock," Julie said. "If I wasn't here, I'd be stuck in my office trying to put together a scale model of a Sharf two-man trader."

"Is she going into the toy business?"

"No, she's trying to teach me something about space engineering since she's opening a shipyard, but the whole schedule got put on hold by the Wanderer rescue. Flower used her discretionary stop this circuit to pick up all of the old factory tooling from a Sharf world, but nobody has even had the chance to start setting it up. As soon as it's safe to go across to the Miklat, Flower's going to send over the people she hired for the shipyard to get a little practical experience in jury-rigged repairs."

"Is this really what girls talk about when guys are in the bathroom?" Samuel asked, looking impressed. He remained standing rather than taking his seat, an obvious sign that he was ready to get moving. "I'm beginning to lose faith in the accuracy of Vergallian dramas."

"It can't happen too soon," Vivian said with a vehemence that took Julie by surprise. "Are you ready to look at temporary apartments, Mr. I-can't-accept-free-lodgings-in-a-suite?"

"Come on, you know in your heart that you agree with me," the EarthCent ambassador's son said, ignoring his wife's exasperated look. "Besides, it's good practice for when we get back to Union Station. We already agreed we're not moving in with our parents."

"Would they have enough space?" Julie asked. She rose and took a second to locate the direction of the exit, never having eaten in the expensive dairy restaurant before. "I've heard Flower brag that her residential cabins are larger than the ones humans rent on Union Station."

"That's because all of Flower's cabins were originally sized for Dollnicks, but everything on Union Station is custom-built," Samuel said. "Vivian's parents have a pretty big three-bedroom, though their Cayl hound makes it seem smaller. My folks live in a large hold right on Union

Station's core that was a junkyard when my dad took it over. They actually have plenty of room for free-standing structures."

"My twin brother and his wife are staying with my parents for the time being, because she travels all the time to race floaters, and he isn't in a hurry to live alone," Vivian added, and then noticed Julie's hesitation to lead the way. "You can't be lost, can you?"

"It's just that I've never been in here before and I rarely walk through this area of the food court," Julie said, and then pointed. "But I'm sure the closest lift tube is over there."

Julie set off, with Samuel and Vivian following her single file as they worked their way out of the crowded restaurant. Once they reached the lift tube, she requested the main residential deck, and thirty seconds later they stepped out of the capsule into a familiar scene.

"Isn't that the library?" Vivian asked, looking up the corridor.

"There must have been a glitch," Julie said. She turned back to the lift tube but the doors had already closed. "Flower?" she subvoced. "Is something wrong?"

"The space you're showing is just around the other side of the spoke," the Dollnick AI responded. "I'll open the door when you get there."

"Flower says it's just around the other side, if circles can have sides," Julie told the apartment hunters. "The weird thing is that Jorb's dojo is that direction and I thought it was all commercial space over there."

Samuel shrugged and started around the structural spoke that the lift tube ran through. The two young women followed him, and a set of double doors that Julie had never noticed before slid open when they reached the other side.

"Why are the lights off, Flower?" Julie asked out loud.

"There's a proximity sensor, I'm conserving energy," Flower replied via the nearest speaker. "You have to step inside."

This time Vivian led the way, triggering the night vision implant she'd received while working for Drazen Intelligence. The moment the three of them were inside, the door slid shut, and then a spotlight came up illuminating a gold emblem worked into the marble floor.

"Human Empire?" Samuel read the Gothic script incredulously. "What is this?"

"I only had a week to prepare so I hope you like it," Flower said, bringing up the full lighting. They were standing in front of a semi-circular reception desk, the Human Empire motif repeated on the vertical section, and there were some modernistic looking benches to the side under a sign that read, 'Waiting area."

"Why does it smell so good in here?" Vivian asked. "Is that something baking?"

"Chocolate chip cookies," the Dollnick AI confirmed. "I had a bot pick up the dough from Flower Foods this morning and put it in the kitchen oven. It's supposed to make house-hunters feel at home."

"I don't think you're supposed to tell them that part, Flower," Julie said.

"My legal counsel insists that full disclosure is best in real estate deals."

"Is that an all-species conference room?" Samuel asked, pointing through an open archway at a large conference table with different sizes and types of chairs.

"I modeled it after the one at your mother's embassy," Flower said. "I had Dewey capture images for me the last time he was there."

"You do understand that I wanted to downsize from the honeymoon suite to something we could afford for the next twelve weeks," Samuel said slowly, not wanting to offend the ship's AI, who had obviously gone to great lengths preparing the surprise. "We're just interested in a regular cabin with a bedroom, a bathroom, and a kitchenette. This looks like some sort of luxury complex with a reception desk and shared facilities for professionals. How many residential units are in here?"

"You've got downsizing on the brain," Vivian said. "Flower doesn't expect us to live here—she wants us to establish an embassy for the Human Empire on board."

"What?"

"It's premium space with easy lift tube access, and the library is right down the corridor for all of your research needs," Flower pitched them over the room's public address system. "It comes with an attached suite that's connected to his-and-her offices by hidden passages. If you want an additional cabin for the sake of appearances, I've got a unit coming open right across the corridor from Julie's"

"Bill lives right across the corridor from me," Julie objected.

"He can move into your cabin. The two of you aren't getting any younger."

"We're barely in our twenties!"

"Just hold on a minute," Samuel said, and even as the words came out of his mouth, it struck him that he sounded like his father when the senior McAllister thought an alien was trying to get something past him. "You're going so fast that I can't keep up. We don't even have office space on Union Station and you expect us to set up an embassy here?"

"A headquarters," the Dollnick AI corrected him. "An empire has to start somewhere, anybody can tell you that. I'm a member in good standing, so why not start here? It makes much more sense than basing the Human Empire out of Union Station. I visit fifty sovereign human communities a year, and I'm working on an arrangement with the Traders Guild to become the exclusive supplier of new two-man ships just as soon as I get the Sharf production line up and running."

"She's got a point, Sam," Vivian said, clearly impressed by Flower's pitch. "I know you don't want to rush into any decisions before our Cayl mentor arrives, but creating a little separation between the Human Empire and the Stryx might finally give us some legitimacy in the eyes of the other species."

"We haven't even established a budget for rent yet," Samuel protested.

"It's free," Flower told them.

"We'll take it," Vivian said.

Samuel groaned. "Can we talk in one of the offices for a minute, Viv?"

"I'll open the secret passage and you can inspect the suite at the same time," Flower offered. "Julie? Could you get the cookies out of the oven?"

"I'm not sure that ambushing Samuel with your custom-built headquarters was the right move," Julie subvoced as she followed her nose into the kitchen. "He may only be a year older than me, and Vivian's actually younger, but they both have experience working for the aliens, and they aren't going to appreciate being pushed around."

"I thought that Humans liked surprises. Besides, I've examined all of their options, and establishing the headquarters on board is really in the Human Empire's best interest."

"I'm just saying they might have preferred to work that out for themselves. And I suppose giving them a rent-free headquarters isn't in your best interest?"

"There's such a thing as a mutual benefit, you know, and the advantage goes to the first mover in most of these situations. Carpe diem."

"Why do I think I've heard that before?" Julie asked.

"Because it's one of the few Earth epigrams worth repeating—Seize the day. It's up there with 'Caveat emptor' and 'Primum non nocere.'"

"What's that last one mean?"

"First do no harm. M793qK says that Human doctors take it about as seriously as Captain Kirk did the Prime Directive, whatever that means."

Julie found an oven mitt and removed the tray of cookies. "How do I turn off the oven?"

"I did it already, and I vented the hot air to accentuate the aroma," Flower said. "The cookies should be cooled enough to put on a plate by now. Do you think I should charge a nominal rent to make Samuel comfortable?"

"I doubt this is really about the money," Julie said, locating a spatula and sliding the cookies onto a decorative plate with the distinctive Human Empire branding in gold. "Well, for the apartment maybe, but these offices are on a different scale. It's just that you can be a bit overwhelming at times." She headed back out into the lobby and almost dropped the plate when she saw a group of strangers seated in the waiting area.

"Bring those over here," ordered a man with a white beard who appeared to be the elder of the group. "This is what I call service."

"Who are you?" Julie asked.

"Refugees," a middle-aged woman with platinum-colored hair replied. "Are you in charge here?"

"I was just showing the place to prospective tenants for Flower," Julie said, going around to the old man. Instead of taking one cookie, he relieved her of the entire plate. "What are you all doing here?"

"We came to seek asylum from the Human Empire," a different woman said. "Do you have any literature?"

"There's a library down the corridor."

"I meant promotional literature, a prospectus, full-color brochures showing the life we can expect if we join your empire."

"It's not my empire. I already told you that I'm playing real estate agent this morning. And if any of that stuff you're asking for exists, I've never seen it."

"Who are these people?" Vivian asked, reappearing in the reception area with a reluctant looking Samuel in tow. Judging by his face, she'd won the argument, at least for the time being.

"We're refugees from the Miklat," the old man said, a few cookie crumbs escaping his lips. "Is there anything to drink? I prefer milk with cookies, but I'll take mineral water or soda if that's all you have available."

"We've come to hear what kind of package you can offer," the woman with the platinum hair added. "We don't need to see all of the details right now, but we wanted to be first in line for when you start processing applications."

"I'm afraid there's been some sort of mistake," Samuel said. "The Human Empire is just getting off the ground and we're the only official staff. Besides, we're here on our honeymoon."

"Your empire looks pretty established to me," the old man said, holding up the plate with the Human Empire branding. Julie couldn't help wondering where the cookies had all vanished so quickly, but then she noticed each of the Wanderers was now in possession of a small stack. "Any outfit that can afford an office like this is obviously in the money. You know," he added craftily, "a one-time grant for refugees would get you positive press coverage."

"We aren't accepting asylum claims at this time," Vivian said, stepping up next to Samuel. "It's just the two of us and we haven't even moved into our temporary headquarters yet."

The Wanderers all went silent while they concentrated on stuffing their faces with cookies. Through some mysterious process, this must have led to a consensus, because they all rose and formed up behind the old man.

"I'm Ronald, the senior human storyteller from the Miklat," he introduced himself formally. "I can see at a glance that the two of you are newlyweds and very much in love, so I'll give you a week to get your act together on our asylum application. We'll be back." With that, he turned and led the other Wanderers out to the corridor.

"How did they even know we were here?" Samuel demanded. "Did you tell them, Flower?"

"They asked for you by name," the Dollnick AI said. "My standing policy when anybody inquires after the location of a person living on board is to supply the information unless you've specifically requested privacy. You are listed in the Galactic Free Press directory as the point of contact for the Human Empire. I thought it was better that they find you here than approach you in the corridor. Didn't the waiting area work out well?"

"Has anybody else been looking for us by name?" Vivian asked immediately.

"A number of local businessmen, but when I told them that your headquarters construction was almost completed, they decided it could wait a couple of days."

"This might not be what we planned, but we have to start somewhere, Sam," Vivian said. "We're going to be hearing from all sorts of people."

"I'm not worried about the Wanderers," he said. "Don't forget that my co-op job included dealing with all of the human crazies who came into the Vergallian embassy. I'm just not comfortable with accepting free office space."

"But you agreed already. If our mentor doesn't approve when she arrives we can pay Flower back-rent."

"And then when my mother finds out that I spent her All Species Cookbook royalties on luxury office space I'll never hear the end of it."

"I knew that was it," Vivian said. "You can't base your decisions about what's right for the Human Empire on what your mother will think. Besides, my grandmother is still the embassy manager and your mom put her in charge of our funding."

"We shouldn't be doing this in front of you," Samuel said to Julie. "I don't mean we have any secrets—just that we're talking about people you've never met and leaving you out of the conversation. How about showing us a regular cabin if Flower has one ready?"

"You didn't like the secret passage?" Julie asked.

"It's a bit too much even for me, and I've had spy training," Vivian said. "My mom always taught us that it's important not to bring the office home, and with this arrangement, it would be impossible not to."

"I just finished preparing an alternative option," Flower told Julie over her implant. "Take them to the freight lift tube at the next corridor junction on the way to the dojo."

"Flower says she has a residential cabin for you to look at," Julie reported faithfully. "She wants us to use a different lift tube to get there." The three exited the Human Empire's new temporary headquarters and headed for the designated lift tube. The capsule was waiting with the doors open when they arrived.

"It's smaller than the freight lift tubes on Union Station, but it's still bigger than I expected," Samuel said, as the capsule got underway. "Hey, it feels like we're moving outwards."

"Are you sure?" Julie asked. "The next deck is the reservoir and there's nothing after that but space."

"Ta-da!" Flower proclaimed as the doors opened. Directly across from the lift tube, on the grid of metal catwalks suspended over the lake that rode on the inside of the colony ship's cylindrical hull, was a metal cabin that looked like a two-man trader without the cargo or engineering decks. "Lakefront property."

"But the rent must cost a fortune," Samuel said in dismay.

"It's a concept house. You'll be doing me a favor by living in it and providing feedback."

"We can be your beta testers," Vivian agreed enthusiastically. "Come on, Sam. Don't be a spoilsport. Flower has obviously gone to a lot of work preparing this."

"Welcome to my world," Julie whispered in the young diplomat's ear.

Eight

Woojin self-consciously adjusted his three-cornered hat before exiting the lift tube. A forty-ish man and a nervous-looking woman in her early thirties were waiting to greet him. The two of them were standing so stiffly in their 'Flower Shipyards' lab coats that he reflexively ordered, "At ease."

"I'm Laura," the woman said, hesitating a moment over protocol before offering a handshake. "Flower put me in charge of the shipyard even though my only experience was with building wooden boats back on Earth."

"Don," the man introduced himself in turn. "I used to run framing crews putting up ranch homes, though I would have preferred renovating abandoned housing stock."

"Pleased to meet you both," the captain said. "I understand the two of you came on board for MultiCon a few months back."

"Yes," Laura said. "Flower made me an offer I couldn't refuse to start building two-man traders, though the closest we've come so far is taking one apart and putting it mostly back together."

"And we made two scale models with the help of a three-dimensional scanner and printer," Don added. "Don't sell yourself short, Laura."

"Then what are all of those hull sections you're working on?" Woojin asked, indicating the half-dozen constructions in progress.

"Flower has had us building stand-alone residential cabins for the writers colony to practice our metal fabrication techniques," Laura explained. "They're basically the same as the bridge, which is the living deck of a two-man trader. It's kind of strange, learning fabrication techniques from bots that keep two of their arms behind their backs to demonstrate best practices for humanoids. I don't quite get why Flower doesn't just have the bots build the ships."

"It's like that with all the tunnel network species," Woojin said. "The civilizations that go too far in eliminating jobs end up going into decline and disappearing. If you've never seen the interactive museum at Libbyland, you should visit next time we stop at Union Station."

"Our people aren't due to meet us in the docking bay for another fifteen minutes," Don informed the captain. "We have plenty of time if you wanted to take the tour."

"Early is on time," Woojin parroted a common alien saying. "We're only a minute from the core by lift tube, so I'd like to see what became of all of that equipment we picked up on our jump to Sharf space. My wife told me you ran into some difficulty with the installation."

"I thought Lynx was your daughter," Laura said, and then blushed bright red. "I mean—"

"It's all right," the captain told her. "We have a daughter, Em, and when I pick her up at school, all of the children think I'm her grandfather. Now let's have a quick look at that equipment."

"This way, Captain," Don said, giving Laura time to recover. "We barely had a chance to open the shipping containers before Flower pulled away all of her bots for rescue operations, but it's not clear that the help of every bot on the ship would have made much difference in terms of getting up and running. It turns out the Sharf disassembled the machines for shipping beyond the point where we can put them back together just by looking at holograms of the assembly line when it was still installed in the factory."

"There aren't any instructions?"

"Handwritten, in Sharf. Flower said that the penmanship is so atrocious that she couldn't read half of it, but she got that alien fellow who runs the anime conventions to stop by and give it a look."

"Yaem," Woojin said. "Was he able to help?"

"Yes and no. He could read what the other fellow had written and took it all away to make a transcript when he has time, but the instructions were all for operating the equipment, not for assembling a production line. They sent us the entire factory floor, so we have everything from giant presses for stamping hull parts to machine tools for building the life support systems."

"How about the drives?"

"Flower agreed to buy all of the drives and fuel packs from the Sharf, and the controllers will be built by the Verlocks under a Stryx license," Laura said. "We're going to build the hulls and finish the interiors with all of the plumbing and wiring, life support, everything it takes for humans to survive in Zero-G."

"So what's your plan for all of this now?" the captain asked, surveying the mounds of disassembled equipment and parts in boxes that surrounded the freight lift tube in rings like the detritus around a crater thrown up by an asteroid impact.

"Neither of us has anywhere near the knowledge to even make an educated guess about putting that stuff together," she said. "We're either going to have to find somebody with relevant experience, or Flower will be forced into spending some serious creds buying the information out of the Sharf archives."

Woojin nodded. "If worst comes to worst, we'll be back at Union Station in another five months, and I'm sure somebody there could help out. Just let me stick my head in one of those prefabs you're building for the writers colony, and then we better head down to the core and meet your team."

The captain almost stumbled entering one of the cabins, because he was used to anything resembling a ship providing entry via a hatch that dropped down to form a ramp, not stairs. Once inside, the difference between a small trade ship and a residential cabin became obvious. Instead of exercise equipment mounted upside down on the ceiling for Zero-G workouts, there was a sleeping loft. The main level also included a kitchenette with a full oven and stovetop, not to mention a sink and water taps, all of which would have been useless in a weightless environment.

"Pretty nice," Woojin said after the brief inspection. "It looks like the two of you know what you're doing."

"Interior design for wooden ships and spacecraft isn't really that different, except for the Zero-G part," Laura said.

"And I've roughed in enough kitchens to have a decent idea of plumbing and cabinet layout," Don added. "I'm not sure where Flower got the idea, but building some metal residential cabins loosely based on the two-man trader design was a good way to ease us into spaceship construction. It seems a lot less intimidating now."

When the three of them reached the docking bay, a motley crew of largely untrained shipyard workers was waiting. The group barely filled the seats of the front fifth of one of Flower's large shuttles, which took less than three minutes to make the straight hop directly into the core of the ship under tow. As they filed out the front exit, a young man and an artificial person handed out locator bracelets to everybody who didn't have an implant.

"I see Flower drafted the two of you as well," Woojin said to Bill.

"It's my morning without any classes and I wanted to see the Miklat," the young man explained. "Then Flower said something about catering hot meals for the repair crews, so I guess I might be back and forth a lot."

"We brought the Zarent chief engineer over in the bookmobile twenty minutes ago," Dewey added. "He wanted to recover some personal effects, and even though they're on strike, he agreed to give you a briefing on the condition of the ship. That's him coming now."

The workers from Flower's nascent shipyard gaped at the furry octopus riding a unicycle. The Zarent easily picked out Woojin by his uniform and wheeled right up to the captain, though not even an artificial life form engineered by the Farlings could keep the one-wheeled contrivance upright without a little back-and-forth motion.

"Captain Pyun," the chief engineer addressed Woojin by way of a speaker pendant attached to his tool harness. "It was rude of me not to seek you out to offer my personal thanks after you stopped for us."

"I'm sure that seeing to your injured was your top priority," Woojin said. "Your captain approached me immediately after the evacuation to hand over the access codes to the bridge, and then he told me he was washing his hands of the Miklat. I have to admit I didn't understand."

"You know Hortens," the Zarent said. "They're obsessed with hygiene so they use it in all of their idioms. When he told you he was washing his hands of the ship, he meant he was disavowing any responsibility going forward."

"I understood his meaning, it's the thought behind it that left me baffled," Woojin said. "How can a captain walk away from his duty like that?"

"Don't hold it against the captain, it's the Wanderer way," the chief engineer explained. "They are culturally allergic to hard work, and restoring the Miklat to anything like serviceable condition is too big a task for him to contemplate. If he took the job on and completed it successfully, the other Wanderers would certainly exile him from the ship for behaving in an inappropriately industrious manner."

"Weird," Bill muttered to Dewey, who nodded his head in agreement.

"I encountered a Wanderer mob some years back when they stopped at Union Station, but I had no idea that their post-employment philosophy included the ship's officers," Woojin said. "It's a wonder anything gets done at all."

"We have a saying in Zarent that if you want something done, you have to do it yourself. My only interaction with the ship's officers amounted to begging for resources, which were always promised and never delivered."

"Then I'm surprised they even bothered promising."

"It's easier to agree than to refuse, and you can always count on the Wanderers to take the easiest path," the Zarent said. He pulled something that looked like a flashlight from a holster on his harness. "Although we are officially on strike, I couldn't refuse the request from your ship's AI to bring your repair team up to speed on the

Miklat's most urgent problems. Are all of these people engineers?"

"I'm afraid not," Laura spoke up. "We're in training to manufacture two-man traders using Sharf designs and factory equipment in a new shipyard Flower is establishing on board."

The Zarent's unicycle actually stopped dead for a moment, and the chief engineer had to extend several tentacles to regain his balance. "You mean you're here for on-the-job-training?"

"Flower just wants us to contribute any way we can so all the work isn't done by bots," Don said.

The chief engineer let out a loud buzzing noise, then said, "Is this all a trick to get me to declare an end to the strike? Under any other circumstance, it would be effective, but five of my team are still in stasis due to the unsafe working environment. If they recover and Flower restores the condition of the Miklat to critical, then it will be time to talk about returning to work."

"Isn't critical the lowest possible level?" Woojin asked.

"Observe." The Zarent triggered his flashlight, which turned out to be a hand-held holographic projector of sorts. A schematic view of the ancient Dollnick colony ship appeared, most of it in red. "The green denotes the systems in good working condition," he began. "The blue highlights equipment that is scheduled for maintenance. The yellow shows the infrastructure that is in critical condition, and the red is for the systems that have failed."

"I don't see any green," Laura said, and then frowned. "Oh."

"The Miklat is about ten thousand years overdue for a major overhaul," the chief engineer continued. "The hull, decks, and the spokes are the only components of the ship that aren't either in critical condition or failure mode. We only carried twenty thousand Wanderers on board because that's all that the life support and ag decks could sustain. That's down from the design capacity of five hundred thousand souls if all systems were functioning properly."

"What about the primary pile?" Woojin asked.

"Why do you think the secondary pile failed?" the Zarent countered. "The primary pile hasn't been hot in a millennium, but the Wanderers refuse to comprehend the difference between an emergency backup system and a spare. The only power on board now comes from the fuel pack farm, and that hasn't been fully charged since I was an apprentice."

"What about the ship's bots?" Dewey asked.

"Excellent question," the Zarent said. "Some of the legends say that the ship's AI took the bots with it when it transferred to a new vessel after the Miklat was gifted to a mob as a bribe to leave Dollnick space. Other legends say the ship entered the mob with a full complement of bots but the Wanderers sold them off to pay for goodies. We've been building ag bots from scratch to keep everyone fed, and we used our own funds to purchase some cargo handling bots from the Drazens to use for heavy lifting. We keep those in our living area except for when we need them to move equipment so the Wanderers can't sell them on us. Other than that, all of the work on board is done by tentacle power."

Everyone stared at the little octopus. "It sounds like you should have gone on strike a long time ago," Woojin said.

"Don't encourage him," Flower admonished over the captain's implant. "Inform the chief engineer that our next stop is Chianga, a Dollnick open world, and I've already made a deal with them for several hundred obsolete maintenance bots that can be adapted for the Miklat's systems."

Woojin dutifully passed the message along, and again the chief engineer was so surprised that he almost lost his balance.

"Are we talking about scrap yard bots that will require complete rebuilds?" he demanded. "If we had time for that sort of thing, we would have manufactured our own."

"Tell him that they are all in working condition, currently in use on Chianga's elevator hubs and an orbital that's been undergoing restoration," Flower told Woojin. "I brokered a deal with the Stryx to finance new replacement bots for the current owners so everybody wins."

The captain relayed the new message, and the chief engineer perked up visibly. "If we had even a partial complement of maintenance bots to work with, I could—what am I saying?" the Zarent cut himself off. "We're on strike."

"Flower wants me to pass along that we'll do what we can with our current resources, and by the time we have the replacement bots reconditioned and programmed up, she's sure that M793qK will have your people back on their feet, er, unicycles."

The chief engineer hesitated a moment, rocking back and forth to maintain his balance, and then said, "I suppose I can at least give you a brief tour. Just make sure that your magnetic cleats are all on the highest setting because the Miklat is rotationally locked to Flower for the tow. That means our angular acceleration is lower than normal and you'll find that your weight is less here due to our smaller radial dimensions."

By the time the damage control tour was completed and they returned to the core docking bay, Woojin was beginning to wonder if he was too old to learn how to ride a unicycle. Just as he was taking his leave from the chief engineer who was to return in the bookmobile with Dewey and Bill, a veritable fleet of Flowers bots entered the Miklat's core. They were shepherding an enormous metallic sphere.

"No, it can't be," the Zarent said. "It would be impossible to find a replacement on such short notice."

"What is it?" Bill asked.

"A self-contained Dollnick pile, larger than our primary. We would have to do some cutting to get it in, but it would solve our—" the chief engineer caught himself again. "I'm sorry, Captain," he addressed Woojin. "I can't just call off the strike while some of my injured are still in stasis. It would be like selling them for gold."

"Flower completed her assessment of the Miklat's primary and secondary piles and she reports that they are beyond repair," Woojin relayed what the Dollnick AI was telling him over his implant. "She made a deal with the Stryx to replace her own secondary pile with the latest model in return for donating the current one to your cause. I don't pretend to understand much about technical stuff, but Flower informs me that her secondary pile was only operated for the recommended break-in period, so it's essentially in new condition."

"We would be overpowered!" the Zarent said, unable to hide his enthusiasm. "It's not just that the third generation secondary has more capacity than our primary, it's a complete redesign that operates more efficiently with less maintenance. We could sell the excess power to other ships in the mob."

"Flower informs me that she'll have to remove part of the bulkhead separating the docking area from the Miklat's power plant to install it, so she's going to do the work with bots now while the ship is uninhabited. The work will go much faster if we all leave and she doesn't have to worry about maintaining a breathable atmosphere."

The chief engineer stared longingly after the fleet of bots maneuvering the new pile deeper into the docking bay, and then began furiously pedaling his unicycle toward the bookmobile. The captain, Bill, and Dewey heard the little alien complaining about illegal strike-breaking tactics, but even filtered through the translation device, it was clear that his heart wasn't in it.

"Did Flower really just give up a piece of herself to help the Wanderers?" Bill asked Dewey as they followed the Zarent.

"Nobody expects to get rid of them for free, and if the Stryx offer is what she says it is, Flower will actually come out ahead on this one," the artificial person said. "The fact that the chief engineer didn't call the strike off on the spot tells you how bad the situation must have been working on the Miklat. But I'll bet you twenty creds that Flower has less trouble convincing the Zarents to return than the Wanderers."

"I'm not a gambling man, and even if I was, I would never accept bets related to Flower," Bill said. "She's too good at getting what she wants. Isn't she the one who suggested that you trade in your robot body and become an artificial person?"

"I'd been thinking about that anyway," Dewey said as he headed up the ramp of the bookmobile. "Keep this to yourself, but now she wants me to find another artificial person and set up housekeeping."

Bill stopped dead on the ramp. "Do artificial people do that?"

Dewey shrugged. "Some do. I know a couple who work for EarthCent Intelligence who have been together for years."

"Can they have, uh—"

"Offspring is what artificial intelligence calls the next generation, and yes, though it's not as simple as with biologicals. All you and Julie have to do is to let it happen."

"That's what Flower keeps telling us," Bill said.

Nine

"How long do you plan to stay on the surface?" Julie asked Vivian. "Chianga is one of our regular stops, and there are always thousands of people already waiting at the space elevator hub to zip over when we arrive. They were some of our best customers when I worked in the library, though the guests from the Verlock academy worlds borrowed more books per capita."

"I'd skip the visit altogether if I thought I could get away with it," Vivian said. "I barely know the girl my brother married, so staying with her parents just because they happen to live here isn't at the top of my list. But her father is the mayor of Floaters, and Sam wants to get his input on how we should be proceeding with the Human Empire. The mayor is also on the ad hoc committee that sort of runs the Conference of Sovereign Human Communities and he's pretty influential."

"You really are making this a working honeymoon," Julie said.

"I could have dealt with more of a vacation, but you've seen what Sam is like. Sometimes I feel like I've spent my whole life keeping him busy so he doesn't wander off and find somebody who needs him more. Did I tell you that when we were children we used to practice Vergallian ballroom dancing three hours a day?"

"Three hours?" Julie asked, still trying to process her new friend's unexpected revelation. "You must be really good."

"We placed in the Vergallian Junior Championships on the station a few times, but they were never going to give the top prize to a human couple," Vivian said, and then backtracked. "No, I'm not being fair. Maybe they would have given us first place if we had been the best couple there, but there are upper-caste Vergallians who start their dance training before they can walk. I honestly thought we had a shot towards the end, but then they disqualified Sam from the Juniors based on his age after they prorated for our lifespans."

"Ouch," Julie said and took another sip from her gourmet coffee. "You know, it's kind of fun just sitting in an upscale café like this and talking. I've been on board for almost two years and I've never come in here."

"Don't you have a crowd you hang out with?"

"Flower has been enough of a crowd for me, though since Jorb and Rinka started dating, they bring Bill and me out with them everywhere. And I guess I sort of think of all the aliens on *Everyday Superheroes* as friends. There's something about fighting evil as principal animation actors that brings people together. Oh, and I should be getting to work."

"Want to show me your office?"

"Sure, but won't Samuel miss you? Where is he, anyway?"

"Flower heard from Jorb that Sam has a lot of experience LARPing, so she asked him to take a look at the studio she's setting up," Vivian said. "As soon as we arrive at Chianga, I'll contact my in-laws, and then we'll figure out the best way to get to the surface. If there aren't shuttles running back and forth, we'll have to rent an atmosphere capable ship or find a trader willing to bring us, because the space elevator takes around twenty hours each way. No, let me get that."

"You always want to pay," Julie protested. "This is my chance to pick up a tab that I can actually afford." She gave the waitress the only ten cred piece in her purse and was visibly surprised at only receiving four creds in change, but she left two of them as a tip.

Vivian blushed slightly as she rose to follow her new friend out of the café. "Sorry, sometimes I forget that everybody doesn't have a rich mother. I mean, we never went around buying jewels or vacation homes on luxury worlds, but when it comes to eating out, I always went wherever looked interesting. Sam complains about my spending habits sometimes because he wants us to live on our own income."

"Doesn't the Human Empire pay well?"

"We don't even have official job titles yet," Vivian said. "The sovereign human communities chose the Thousand Cycle Option to become an empire, but it's short on details and long on timeline—like a hundred and fifty years. That's why we're waiting for our mentor to show up before really digging in. The Cayl run one of the more successful empires in the galaxy, and Sam's mother hosted the emperor in their home when he visited Union Station around fifteen years ago."

"I thought the Cayl were some scary military power from the other side of the galaxy," Julie said as they entered the lift tube. "What was the emperor doing on Union Station?"

"Trying to abdicate, if I remember the story correctly. I was just a little girl at the time, but the Stryx held a sort of open house to attract new members to the tunnel network. The Cayl emperor showed up with representatives from the principal species in their empire to see if some sort of merger was possible. I wasn't old enough to understand what was going on, but in the end, the emperor decided to stay on his throne, which was probably what the Stryx intended from the beginning."

They exited the capsule across from the impressive doors embossed with the new Flower Industries logo, and Julie led the way through the labyrinth of halls to her office.

"Wow, are you sure you aren't earning a big salary?" Vivian asked. "An office with a door is an upper-management perk on Union Station. Everybody else works in cubicles or open-floor schemes."

"I thought this was normal," Julie replied honestly. "I guess that Flower doesn't like people seeing all her unused capacity, so she spreads things out as much as possible to fill the space better."

"And this must be the famous scale model," Vivian said, examining the two-man trader that stood higher than she was tall. "It looks like you got it all back together right."

"I haven't exactly had a chance to take it apart yet. I was going to try again today."

"Whoa!" Vivian wavered on her feet and grabbed the corner of the display desk to steady herself. "I think we just arrived at Chianga."

"Have we?" Julie asked. "I didn't even feel it. I guess after a couple hundred tunnel transitions and jumps I've gotten used to the little ones."

"The women in my family are famous for being sensitive to space travel. My mom used to date a guy who invented a sort of system that deployed a counterweight on a cable so the ship and the mass could spin around a common center of gravity and create weight."

"What happened?"

"He dumped my mom and married Aisha, who became the host of *Let's Make Friends*."

"I meant, what happened to the counterweight system?"

"Oh, it worked, that's just physics, but it turns out that there isn't any demand," Vivian said. "Zero-G doesn't bother any of the advanced species, and the humans who live on small ships are a self-selected bunch, so it didn't make sense to try to commercialize it. I think my mom said he was planning to design ships that could split into two sections rather than hauling the extra mass around. But for big ships, the simple solution has always been to build cylinders like Flower and spin them so that everybody is living in a centrifuge."

"This is your captain speaking," Woojin's voice came over the public address system. "I regret to inform you that Chianga traffic control is refusing to grant us a low orbit, and we've been instructed to keep our shuttles in our docking bay. They will send officials on board to inspect any commercial shipments scheduled for drop off and will provide their own transportation. Any merchandise on order from Chianga will be delivered as promised, but we've been placed in quarantine. Under the circumstances, our departure will be moved forward to as soon as our business here is completed. I will provide an update when we have more information."

"Looks like I just missed out on three fun-filled days with the in-laws," Vivian said happily.

"What's going on?" Julie asked out loud.

"It's the Wanderers," Flower replied via the overhead speaker grille. "I attempted to suppress the information, but unfortunately, word got out. Nobody wants to find themselves stuck with guests who refuse to go home, and the Dollnicks running Chianga have decided to play it safe. It's a bit insulting that they won't allow me to launch any shuttles for fear that I'd try to sneak Wanderers off the ship."

"Would you?" Vivian asked.

"Maybe a few," the Dollnick AI admitted. "It appears that the Chiangans choreographed our visit in advance because one of the planetary patrol craft requested permission to dock as soon as we came out of the tunnel. And I was asked to relay a request to Mrs. McAllister that she be present."

"Who?" Julie asked.

"That's me," Vivian said. "I took Samuel's family name since my mom took my dad's name when they got married. This must have something to do with my in-laws."

"Maybe I should go with you," Julie said, casting a glance at the imposing scale model of the two-man trader. "Flower?"

"It seems that the Chiangans are in such a hurry to see my departure that the shipment of obsolete bots I negotiated for is already waiting for us in high orbit. I want you there to help with receiving."

"I live to serve," Julie said, flashing a grin at Vivian. "Let's go."

When the two young women exited the lift tube on the docking deck in the core, the Dollnick patrol craft had just landed. The hatch popped down and a team of four-armed marines wearing space-armor trooped out and formed an honor guard. Next came a particularly tall Dollnick, who had a long silvery feather stuck in a holder at the back of his environmental suit's helmet, marking him as the highest official in the group.

"Do they have trouble breathing the atmosphere on board?" Julie subvoced.

"No," Flower responded, as the rest of the similarly garbed inspection team exited the shuttle. "Those suits are totally unnecessary. They're acting as if the Wanderers were a communicable disease rather than a social aberration. Now I know what a plague ship feels like."

The last Dollnick to exit the patrol craft was wearing an ill-fitting environmental suit that bagged up below the knees and above the waist. Then Julie realized that the lower arms were empty because the suit was occupied by a human.

"That must be my brother's father-in-law," Vivian said, waving to the suited figure. "I better go meet him before he trips. Come on, I'll introduce you."

Julie and Vivian shuffled over to the mayor, their magnetic cleats preventing any embarrassing high-steps. Bob waited for them at the foot of the ramp. He began to speak, and they could see his lips moving behind the transparent faceplate, but no sound came out.

"The mayor has requested that I relay a message for him," Flower announced. "The biological hazard suit he's wearing was designed for a Dollnick, and the external vocalization system is activated by high-frequency whistling, so the mayor's speech won't even trigger the transponder. First of all, he expresses his regrets to Vivian that he won't be able to host her and Samuel during our stop."

"Tell him that we were looking forward to meeting the rest of the family and we'll have to return another time," Vivian said diplomatically.

Bob nodded and produced a package with fancy wrapping paper from one of the oversized pockets. "A small gift to express our regrets that we couldn't attend your wedding on Union Station," Flower relayed for the mayor. "I spent almost a month away from Chianga with the ad hoc committee work leading up to the decision on the Human Empire and I couldn't get away again."

"Your daughter told us how sorry you were you couldn't make it," Vivian said, accepting the package. "She made my brother dance all night to make up for it."

Bob chuckled behind the faceplate, and then Flower said for him, "She's a firecracker, that one. But apologies aside, I asked to meet you to pass on a bit of information from a holo-conference I attended yesterday morning. The leaders of most of the big sovereign human communities attended, along with Associate Ambassador Daniel Cohan. I stayed on for a few minutes after it ended to chat with Daniel and a few of the more forward-thinking committee members. All of us were struck by the fact that in a three-hour holo-conference, the topic of the Human Empire never came up."

"Not even as a joke?" Vivian asked.

"Zero mentions," Flower confirmed for the mayor, whose lips continued to move soundlessly. "The consensus among us was that the thousand cycle timeline allows everybody to put the entire subject out of mind. We're all very busy and none of us will be alive long enough to see how it turns out in any case."

"I'm not sure whether that's good news or bad news, but I'll discuss it with Sam," Vivian said. "Thank you for coming all the way up here just to deliver a gift and pass the information along."

"I would have come even if you weren't here," Bob admitted. "Earth is far and away our biggest customer for floaters and we look forward to these semi-annual stops to take advantage of the low freight rates Flower offers. Given how dependent our city is on the shipment, I always come up to oversee the loading in person."

"That's a relief," Vivian said. "I was worried that I was dragging you out of the way."

"My wife handles publicity for our factory, and she suggested that you and Samuel might want to prioritize raising the profile of the Human Empire before everybody forgets that you exist. She says that it's easier to keep a flame burning than to kindle a fire from scratch. Ah, there's the first barge with our floaters coming in so I have to run. Very nice meeting you both."

Bob began shuffling off in his baggy environmental suit, and Flower returned to speaking for herself, "The first shipment of bots is here and I'm putting it down close to a freight lift tube at the next spoke ring. Do you mind walking?"

"I'm just glad I don't have to wear one of those Dollnick environmental suits," Julie said.

"Nobody has to wear them," Flower said in frustration. "You don't catch laziness from a handshake or a sneeze."

"Can I come along?" Vivian asked. "All of a sudden I have nothing on my schedule, and Sam is really into helping set up that LARPing studio. He said we can discuss the mayor's message at lunch."

"Did you just talk to him? You're really good at subvocing."

"Yes, we have a private channel. We actually tried linking our implants as an experiment one time but it turned out to be a disaster. There's no way to selectively block out what the other person is hearing, so if you're both with people, it's incredibly confusing."

"You know, if you're interested in publicity, we have a Galactic Free Press reporter on board who's very nice. Dianne interviewed me about my history with the drug syndicate and I actually felt better after talking to her. The paper didn't add any stock images to make the story more lurid or anything like that." Then Julie remembered something and had to restrain herself from slapping her forehead with her palm. "I forgot that your aunt owns the Galactic Free Press. Never mind my babble."

"No, it's a good idea, and if you could introduce us to the reporter, Sam won't feel like we're taking advantage of my family relations," Vivian said. "I don't want to dump a lot of teenage angst on you, but the reason I kept working for Drazen Intelligence after completing the Open University co-op assignment was that I wanted to prove to everybody that I could accomplish something on my own. When your mother is the co-owner of InstaSitter, everybody just assumes you're being handed life on a silver platter. My brother was always a lot more involved with the family business than I was, even though with his new cooking show, I think he's stepping away from it."

"I'll ask Flower to ping Dianne for me as soon as we take care of this shipment of bots," Julie said, and then hesitated before adding, "You might not believe this, but I know exactly how you feel about people thinking you're being handed everything on a platter. When I first came on board in the witness protection program, I had a pretty normal job in the library that covered my basic expenses, and I worked half-time as a waitress for spending money. But since I started working directly for Flower, she gives me jobs I'm not qualified for and then micromanages me so I can't fail. It's sort of how I figure it must be for rich kids whose parents want the best for them."

"Then I'm glad I didn't grow up with any rich friends," Vivian said with a laugh.

"Take this shipment of bots," Julie continued, finding relief in being able to talk about her fear of being promoted beyond her level of competence. "What do I know about bots, or shipyards for that matter? I never even went to school."

"Do you know how the Stryx pick the EarthCent ambassadors?" Vivian asked.

"Excuse me?" Julie said, knocked off-kilter by the seeming non sequitur. "Actually, I thought there was a civil service exam."

"There is now, and we plan to use it for the Human Empire as well. But the test is a new thing, and the Stryx still have approval for all of the high-ranking positions in EarthCent since Earth is officially a protectorate. You're not going to be able to guess so I'll just tell you. The Stryx pick humans who can empathize with artificial intelligence and aliens."

"Can't everybody?"

"Are you serious?" Vivian laughed again. "Not even close. Don't take this the wrong way, but there's something about you that reminds me of Samuel's mom, the EarthCent ambassador. I must have seen her a hundred times at parties putting all of the alien diplomats at ease, and she's the only one of them who can come right out in the middle of a conversation and start asking the Stryx station librarian questions like they're old school friends. You're like that with Flower."

"I've noticed that people look at me weird sometimes when I start talking to her, but I thought that was just because I forget to subvoc," Julie said.

"No, Flower needs you as a go-between, and Bill is the same way," Vivian said. "I've seen him and Jorb together a few times now, and you can tell that Bill doesn't see Jorb as an alien, even with extra thumbs and the tentacle."

"I've seen *you* with extra thumbs and a tentacle," Julie reminded Vivian, who had mastered prosthetics while working for Drazen Intelligence. "And I don't notice them anymore myself when I'm taking my singing lessons from Rinka."

"That's exactly my point. You might think that everybody is comfortable around aliens and AI, but if you start paying attention, you'll notice that most people aren't. Tell me, what do you think of the Zarents?"

"The furry octopus aliens that the Farlings created? The little ones are so cute I wish I could take them home. I saw them make a puppy pile in Zero-G and it looked like a giant fuzzball with hundreds of tentacles."

"For most people, that would be a nightmare," Vivian said. "You and Bill are actually pretty rare, so don't sell yourselves short."

"But you and Samuel are at home with AI and aliens," Julie pointed out.

"We went to the Union Station librarian's experimental school, and Sam's mother always had aliens visiting. I grew up around my aunt's friend, Tinka, a Drazen who manages InstaSitter, not to mention that over ninety-five percent of our sitters are aliens. We learned how to be comfortable with all forms of sentient life, but you're a natural."

"Flower?" Julie subvoced, as they approached the barge transporting the obsolete Dollnick bots. "Were you listening to all of that?"

"Vivian is largely correct, but I wouldn't have made you my executive assistant just because I like you," the ship's AI replied. "There should be two hundred and four bots in this load. You're good at counting, and somebody has to sign off on the delivery."

Ten

"You want me to burn these potato chips?" Bill asked the Farling. "What's that going to prove?"

"Whether or not the caloric information on the label is correct," M793qK said. "I agree with Flower that the nutrition labeling Humans put on food packaging is misguided, but part of our deal with the All Species Cookbook is confirming that the data presented is accurate."

"And the only way to do that is to start a fire?"

"Earth's calorie unit is defined as the energy required to raise the temperature of a specified mass of water by a specified number of degrees. Didn't you learn about this in the Open University?"

"I've only been going for a couple of months and I'm not taking the Food Science track," Bill said. "I guess I can see it working for a potato chip because of the oil, but what about wet food, like fruit?"

"That's what the dehydrator is for," M793qK said, pointing a limb at an appliance suspended under the cabinets. "I already set up the burner, and you'll use the infrared temperature reader on this scientific tab rather than a contact thermometer which would alter the outcome when using a small mass of water. The most important things are to make sure the food samples are completely burned and to top off the water to the line on the beaker after each test run."

"How about all of the other numbers on the label?" Bill asked.

"I've got an atomic spectroscopy setup in my clinic that I can use to fill in the rest of the data," the Farling said. "I'm working on outsourcing all of this busywork to a Horten who joined up at MultiCon—they like making finicky measurements. In fact, forget about burning the potato chips." The giant beetle pushed the lab equipment to the back of the counter with one appendage while grabbing the bag of chips with another. "A more important part of our contract with the All Species Cookbook is to supply the sort of enhanced labeling that the other species expect to see."

"Jorb told me that Drazen snack foods have to list the cyanide content."

"The Drazens are a strange species," M793qK said. "We'll be focusing on the three main figures of merit that most sentient species require on their food labeling, and it all starts with the crunch factor."

"You mean, like, whether or not the food is crunchy?"

"Exactly, but we put it on a scientific basis. The crunch factor is determined on a scale from one to six hundred and thirteen, where one is water, and six hundred and thirteen is quartz."

"Who eats quartz?" Bill asked.

"Verlocks. Not all the time, but they claim it's a good way to encourage new tooth growth," the Farling said as he opened the bag of potato chips. "Go ahead, take one. Then again, better take a few."

Bill did as he was told and stood ready.

"Now we chew them," M793qK said, and holding the bag above his head, poured the rest of the contents into his maw and began masticating. "Not quite as good as those pretzel things Humans enjoy with their beer, but not bad either," he rubbed out on his speaking legs.

"They're pretty crunchy," Bill said after swallowing, feeling a momentary pang of jealousy that the Farling could talk with his mouth full since he didn't use it for speech. "But I think I would need to try some foods that already have an assigned value on the scale to come up with a number."

"Three sixty-one, or maybe three sixty-two," M793qK said after a moment's contemplation. "How good is your sense memory?"

"I'm not sure I understand the question."

"Could you tell me the temperature of this room on any scale of your choice without consulting a thermometer?"

"I'd just be guessing," Bill admitted.

"Then I'm not going to try to train you up on crunch factor because it requires the chewing equivalent of a sommelier's nose and sense memory," the giant beetle said, crumpling up the potato chip bag and tossing it in the recycling bin. "Let's move on to something that will be easy for you to measure. Open up that jar of white stuff."

"The mayonnaise?"

"I thought it was marshmallow fluff, but it will do. Now enable the stopwatch function on your implant."

"I didn't know it had one," Bill said. He accessed the heads-up display that Julie was coaching him on when they had time. "Oh, there it is. Huh, it's kind of annoying," he added, as a zero with a decimal place followed by a long string of zeros appeared in the corner of his vision.

"Two significant digits will be sufficient," M793qK informed his assistant, and produced a ruler of sorts from his utility pouch. "Now, take this ruler, hold it upright on the counter, and crouch down so your eyes are level with the first major gradation. I'm going to place a large dollop of mayonnaise right in front of the ruler. As soon as the mayonnaise is free from the spoon, I want you to start your stopwatch and note the color of the ruler gradation that most closely marks its height. When your stopwatch reaches sixty-four seconds, call out the color at the final height."

"Is this a real thing?" Bill asked suspiciously as he crouched to eyeball the ruler.

"Slump. It's a universal measure for foods that ooze. Ready?" Without waiting for his assistant's response, the Farling took a big spoonful of mayonnaise and plopped it down in front of the ruler. "Go!"

Bill noted the blue line on the ruler and triggered the stopwatch with a movement of his pupil. A long minute passed, and when the counter reached sixty-four, he noted that the mayonnaise was now closer to the red line.

"It went from blue to red," he reported.

"Ten percent," M793qK said. "We'll do it twice more and see if we get the same result. It's also temperature-dependent, of course, but I've noted that on the tab."

"Doesn't the shape of the mayonnaise when it comes off the spoon make a difference?"

"That's why I'm the one dropping the dollops, but you're correct that you wouldn't be able to do this test yourself." The giant beetle tossed the spoon in the sink while drumming a few of his middle appendages on the counter in thought. "I've got it. You can do the splat test."

"Is he making these up?" Bill subvoced to Flower.

"I can see your lips moving, and no, I'm not making it up," M793qK replied before the Dollnick AI could answer. "The splat test produces a binary outcome so it should be easy for you to perform, but you can always check with me if you run into any borderline questions. Let's start with the potato chips."

"You ate them all."

"I think we can fudge the results without worry in this case. If you dropped a potato chip on the floor, do you think it would make a splat?"

"No, it's too light, and it's hard, so even if it weighed more it would just crumble or break."

"Precisely. How about an orange?"

"I guess it would depend on how hard it hit the floor," Bill said.

"It's just a regular drop at average gravity, not a sporting contest," M793qK said. "An orange would have to be rotten soft to go splat. And mayonnaise?"

"A real mess."

"So just note it down on your tab when you bring the test products to Harry's independent living cooperative tonight. I had planned to be there myself for the first tasting, but my Zarent patients require more attention and I should really be getting back."

"So no burning, no measuring, just note the splat," Bill said.

"And any other reactions the taste testers have," the Farling physician said. "They're supposed to self-report any issues with the food beyond taste, but if I've learned one thing treating Humans, it's that they can't be trusted to describe their own physical responses. Just yesterday I had a patient stop in complaining about a headache. I had to analyze all of his bodily fluids to diagnose that he was suffering from caffeine withdrawal after quitting coffee because he lacked the sense to tell me what was wrong."

"I'll try to watch for everybody's reactions, but I can't make them eat in front of me one by one."

"Do your best, and clean up this mess," M793qK said on his way towards the door. "When I have some free time again, I'll teach you how to determine alcohol content with Frunge strips. That's an easy one because all you have to do is soak the strip and read off the number."

"I don't know any Frunge," Bill said.

"It's just numerals, you'll learn."

Bill cleaned up the mayonnaise and the potato chip crumbs after M793qK left, and then he double-checked the list the Farling had drawn up to make sure all of the products scheduled for testing were on the catering cart. He disengaged the parking brake on the cart so it floated free and set out for Flower's Paradise. The common room was full of diners when he arrived.

"Over here," Harry called, waving at Bill. "I've had my eye on those olives in brine ever since they showed up on the kitchen shelves. M793qK finally released the products for testing?"

"Some of them," Bill said. "It depends on how many samples we have and how much further testing needs to be done. Have you ever heard people talking about the splat or crunch factor for food?"

"When you and Julie have a baby you'll become splat-factor experts," Irene said. "We used to talk about the schmear factor too."

"Mainly for bagel spreads," Harry added. "Schmear factor might have been a regional thing, but everybody cares about splat and crunch."

"On a scale from one to six-hundred and thirteen?" Bill asked.

"You know how some aliens like quantifying things. Now let me have those olives."

"I didn't know there were such things as purple olives."

"They're actually black, but the brining process lightens them," Harry said, then grimaced after trying and failing to unscrew the lid. "Here. You have the young wrists."

Bill took the jar of olives and twisted off the lid, taking care to make it look more difficult than it really was. "Who else wants something from the cart?"

"Is that salt water taffy?" Dave asked, pointing at a package of pink candy.

"Oh, that's actually for me," Bill said, grabbing the pack and sticking it in his pocket. "M793qK specifically prohibited it for your group. He said it could pull your dental work out."

"Those digestive crackers look interesting," Irene said. "Why don't you open the pack, Dave, and I'll share them with you."

The retired salesman grumbled, but he tore open the package at the small notch, took one, and passed it around the table. The only other person to take one was Irene.

"They aren't that bad," she said. "Nice and crunchy."

"How crunchy?" Bill asked, pulling out his tab. "I mean, on a scale from one to six hundred and thirteen."

"That's rather specific. Perhaps around two hundred? What do you think, Dave?"

"I think I'd have to eat some of those potato chips for comparison," he said, eyeing a bag that was the twin of the one that M793qK had recently subjected to destructive testing.

"Does anybody want to try almond butter on their digestive cracker?" Bill asked hopefully.

"I will," Irene volunteered immediately and nudged her husband.

"I suppose we all agreed to be guinea pigs," Harry said reluctantly. "Why don't you just assign us each a product to try, Bill. That's the way they would do it in a real testing lab. If you only get reactions from people who are predisposed to like something, it won't be very useful."

"Great," Bill said and began sliding packages of ready-to-eat foods around the table like he was dealing playing cards. "I'll just take these around to the rest of the room and then I'll be back for your reactions."

But when he tried to move the cart to the next table, he found the way blocked by a trio of elderly women dressed in garish robes.

"Stop right there, young man," the woman in the middle told him. "Bertha, get the nuts."

"These are test samples for certification," Bill objected as one of the women outflanked him and grabbed a double handful of individual serving size packages of pistachios and cashews. "You have to give me your reactions and I need to note the crunch factor."

Behind him, the president of the cooperative rose from the table and stepped forward to greet the women. "I'm Jack. Welcome to Flower's Paradise. I don't recognize any of you so I'm guessing you're here to explore our independent living cooperative."

"That's right," the woman said. "We saw the advertisements and it sounds like you'll provide for all of our needs."

"Well, we like to think we have a pretty good system in place," Jack said. "The rent is competitive with living in a regular cabin, but we also have a flexible meal plan, meaning Flower only charges if you eat in one of our cafeterias. We have classes and workshops on a daily basis, and we're developing new activities that will meet our team sport requirement."

"Excuse me, I don't think I heard you right," the woman said. "Did you say you pay to live here?"

"Of course," Jack said, somewhat taken aback by the question. "Nothing is free on board Flower, but we—"

"It's free for us," the woman interrupted. "We're Wanderers. We don't pay for anything."

"I don't really have any experience with that, but this cooperative is owned by the membership. We may reduce the fees for hardship cases, but the rent is required to reimburse Flower for—"

"There you go with rent again," the woman interrupted irritably. "And who would choose to attend classes or workshops at our age? Are you all loonies?"

Nancy jumped up from the table, looking remarkably spry for her eighties, and stepped in front of Jack.

"Learning doesn't stop with retirement," she told the Wanderer who towered over the former school teacher by a head. "Independent living isn't about sitting around watching each other atrophy. We're an active community."

"We're an active community too," the woman declared, tearing open the package of salt water taffy she had fished out of Bill's pocket while he was maneuvering the cart through the trio of Wanderers to escape. "We all work full time as unpaid entertainment critics. Ask me something about Vergallian dramas."

"I wouldn't know the first thing about them," Nancy said.

"And you put on airs like you're educated." The Wanderer tore off a bit of taffy with her teeth, and then a strange look came over her face and she stopped talking.

"These nuts aren't salty enough," Bertha called after Bill. "The pistachios are about a sixty-three on the crunch scale without the shells and five hundred and twenty with."

The third Wanderer, who hadn't spoken yet, leaned towards Irene and whispered something. Harry's wife blanched and then handed over her butter knife. The woman brought it to the leader of the trio, who accepted it with a nod and immediately started trying to work it in between her jaws.

"Wouldn't you like to sit down to do that?" Jack asked, offering his chair.

The Wanderer just shook her head and continued probing and twisting with the flat knife.

"Better go easy on that almond butter, Dave," Harry advised his friend. "It's healthy, but it's high in calories, and I know you don't want to lose your ice cream privilege."

Dave dropped his third digestive cracker like it was radioactive. "Are you sure? Flower told me I'm already on a short leash today because I had a water roll with lunch."

Bertha burst out laughing. "You let a Dollnick AI tell you what you can and can't eat?" Even the head of the Wanderer trio whose teeth were still stuck together took the time off from prying to manage a sort of chortle.

"Flower's dietary suggestions are a valuable contribution to our independent living cooperative," Nancy said indignantly. "She coordinates with the Farling physician, who holds a regular wellness clinic on this deck tailored for our age group. Nobody is forced to follow the diets they prescribe, but—"

"If they don't, no ice cream," Bertha interrupted derisively, and then stopped to demand, "What?" as the third Wanderer tugged at her sleeve. The two put their heads together and began exchanging whispers.

"You know I try to keep an open mind about people," Irene said to Harry in a low voice, "but I don't think the Wanderers would be a good match for our cooperative."

"Hey, you," Bertha yelled in Bill's direction. "Adel says that the granola bars you're pushing are a four-eighty-six on the crunch scale, and they have excellent tongue feel."

"Thank you," Bill called back, taking a moment to note it on his tab.

"Blech," the leader of the trio exclaimed, having finally pried her mouth open wide enough to speak. "I'd score the taffy thirty-seven out of a possible forty on the Horten stickiness scale, but there's something off about the sweetness. Is it even possible to substitute for sugar in taffy?"

"Do Wanderers know about all these alien scales?" Bill asked, returning to the table.

"Of course," the woman said. "Why would we use Earth's archaic nutritional labeling for anything? It's hard enough to keep the other species from laughing at us as it is."

"I've got some jerky in the bottom section of the cart that M793qK didn't want me to test on any cooperative members, but if you—"

"Real jerky?" Bertha interrupted. "Bring it on. I'll cut my expert consultation fee in half."

"You charge for eating?"

"No," the woman said, grabbing the proffered snacks. "I charge for telling you what I think. If you just want me to take this stuff home and eat it, you don't have to pay me a single cred."

"Oh," Bill said. He realized that possession was nine-tenths of the law and he wasn't going to get the jerky back. "I don't really have a budget, but I guess I could pay a couple creds out of my own pocket."

"Each," the leader of the trio said, and hooking the young man's arm, began moving him towards the exit. "Bertha, bring the cart. Good food is wasted on these old fogies, they probably prefer raw vegetable sticks." She tossed the butter knife to the third woman, who shot Irene an apologetic look and then dropped it in the dishpan on her way out.

Eleven

"How did it go?" Julie asked Dewey when the latter emerged from the bookmobile. "I'm sorry again about bailing out at the last minute, but Flower told me to wait here."

"And it's a good thing that she did," the artificial person said. "When I approached the Vergallian orbital, they told me if they detected any biological life on board larger than a bread box they would open fire."

"I don't get what the aliens are so afraid of," Julie said as she helped Dewey begin removing packages from the bookmobile's cargo compartment. "Sure, the Wanderers are obnoxious and they don't like to work, but—"

"No buts," Dewey said. "Once you let them in the door you can't get them to leave. I'm surprised at how calm Flower has remained about it to this point. The Stryx may be subsidizing repairs to the Wanderer's ship, but who knows how much business we're losing through being turned away at stop after stop. Some of the vendors in the bazaar and the amusement park have basically shut down for the duration."

"The Zarents are nice," Julie protested, placing another box on the cargo floater.

"They aren't Wanderers, they just live in the ships and take care of the maintenance and repairs."

"And these are the vector-whatsits that Flower was waiting on?"

"Vector processors, specifically built for accelerating holographic computations," Dewey said, retrieving the final box and triggering the hatch to close. "Flower tried to save money on the LARPing studio by using cheaper parts, but the quality of the holograms just wasn't up to snuff and she had to work too hard herself just to get to that point. These weren't cheap, but if they operate the way they're supposed to, Flower will be able to serve as the game master without having to do so many calculations."

"I thought all AI loved doing math," Julie said, shuffling alongside the artificial person as he guided the small cargo floater towards the nearest lift tube.

"There's fun math and there's boring math. Keeping an illusion wrapped around a bot for the sake of letting a role player think they're battling an ogre is boring math. And maintaining a virtual reality environment for hundreds of players at the same time in a large space takes an insane amount of calculating power," Dewey explained. "It's no big deal for the Stryx, of course, but the only LARPing studios on planets run on huge banks of vector processors."

"Will these be enough then?"

"They're the latest generation from the Fleet Vergallians, and Flower ordered twice as many as she thought would be required just to play it safe." Dewey shoved the floater into the back of the lift tube and instructed the capsule, "Con deck."

"So was that your first time on the Vergallian orbital?"

"I was there once before in my robot body and everybody ignored me," the artificial person said. "Now I could probably pass as Vergallian if I wore the right clothes and touched up my cheekbones a little." The lift tube door opened and he pushed the floater out onto the Con deck. "Has Flower begun training you in building LARPing studios along with all of your other jobs?"

"She just wanted me there since it's officially part of her entertainment division. Other than my one experience on Union Station during MultiCon, I've never LARPed. I think Flower is putting so much effort into this because she wants to get the studio certified for the professional LARPing league. That would allow us to start staging those events on board, and maybe even do a live broadcast over the Stryxnet. Have you ever LARPed, Dewey?"

"Holographic illusions won't work on me unless I go out of my way to match my frame rate to the projection, but I'm curious to try." The artificial person scowled at a mixed group of Wanderers who were wearing the equivalent of T-shirts for their respective species, all of which were printed in English with misleading identifications.

"Was that Horten wearing a T-shirt that says he's a Verlock?" Julie asked Dewey. "That doesn't make any sense at all."

"They're mocking the cosplayers who try to stay in character around the clock. You know, the way Grynlan and the Grenouthian stole the best-in-species awards at MultiCon without dressing up by pretending to be each other."

"You were there?"

"The Grenouthians kept rerunning it on their network before the late show for a whole cycle," Dewey said. He came to a halt at doors in a partition wall that stretched from the deck all the way to the ceiling. "Try waving your hand over that scanner. It looks like somebody added security to keep the Wanderers out."

"I've got it," Flower said over Julie's implant, and the doors slid open. "Bring the vector processors over to where Bill and Zick are working with Jorb and Razood."

"Why isn't Bill in class?" Julie asked.

"I had to cancel Open University classes this morning. Around a thousand Wanderers showed up and staged a sit-in."

"Why?"

"They must have heard somewhere that student protests are a good way to make the administration crazy," Flower said, and Julie would have sworn she could hear restraint stretched to the limits in the Dollnick AI's artificial voice. "First, they asked for life experience credit for having visited so many places, and when I tried to humor them by granting it, they immediately followed up with a whole laundry list of demands for new clothes and other personal items. They're claiming that under the tunnel network treaty, students living in temporary quarters due to disasters, including life-support failure on residential spacecraft, qualify for special aid."

"What are you going to do?"

"Today is a loss, but I plan to tempt them out of the campus facilities with a banquet later, and tomorrow I'll ask the captain to deploy his security team to limit entry to properly registered students."

"I still think you should throw them all in the brig," Dewey said. They reached the group working on a section of deck where all of the plates had been removed, and the artificial person announced, "One shipment of Vergallian vector processors with K-type edge connectors in retail packaging."

"K-type?" Jorb's tentacle drooped in disappointment. "We just finished installing a full array of J-type sockets."

"The K-type supersedes the J-type," Zick said confidently. "They don't need as many signal leads, but the new processors work with the old slots."

Julie and Dewey opened the cartons and began handing out individually packaged processors. Razood puzzled over the molded plastic protection for a moment, failed to tear it open on the dotted line, and then tried with his teeth. "I think we're going to need scissors."

"There's a trick to it," Jorb said, and then failed to open his own package. "And that trick is scissors."

"I can't believe we're traveling in interstellar space and we still can't get the stuff out of blister packs," Bill said. "Back on Earth when I sold toys from a pushcart with my mom, we used to keep three pairs of scissors chained to the display just so people could open the packages they were buying."

"Earth!" Dewey exclaimed. "Good call, Bill. I'm carrying a Swiss army knife my EarthCent Intelligence friends gave me. I think it has a scissors attachment."

"If it has a knife, that would work even better," Zick said.

"You open the packages, Dewey," Flower joined in the conversation. "Humans are apt to slice into their fingers when they try opening those molded plastic packages with knives. I've seen the blood dripping on my thermal imaging."

"Bucket brigade," the artificial person declared cheerfully, unfolding the knife's largest blade. "I'll slice down the dotted line, and you pull apart the packaging, Julie. Let's get to work."

It took over an hour to populate the array of vector processors, and then Flower sent a pair of maintenance bots to replace the heavy deck plates.

"Don't we want to turn it on to see if everything works before sealing it all in?" Julie asked.

"Safety first," Jorb told her. "This type of computational hardware sucks a lot of power, and we've mixed and matched parts from several different species. If there are interoperability issues, it might express itself energetically."

"He means it might catch on fire," Zick said, "but I've never seen it actually happen with any of this alien hardware. There are too many fail-safes built in."

"How will we know if it's working properly?" Bill asked.

"I think there's your answer," Razood told his former apprentice, pointing off toward the right. An improbable wave of vegetation seemed to be rolling towards them, and suddenly they found themselves standing in a dense jungle, complete with a cacophony of bird song.

"This is incredible," Julie exclaimed. "I thought LARPing was all about running around with medieval weapons and bashing stuff. Will we get to see the tropical birds that are making all this noise if we explore?"

"Noise?" Flower said indignantly. "I'm playing Dollnick opera for the intro, and the closest thing to birds in this jungle are the Horten vampire bats. Now don't be surprised, I'm going to try something."

"Try what?" Julie asked, and then her eyes went wide when she saw that Bill's clothes had been replaced by a medieval outfit, complete with accessories like a large pouch slung over his shoulder and a short sword at his belt. She looked down at her own body and saw that her belly button was exposed because she was wearing a sort of halter top and a short skirt that would have been more appropriate on an anime schoolgirl. "Hey, timeout," she called, making the universal hand signal. "How come the guys are all dressed like warriors and I look like a cartoon bimbo?"

"I thought you'd like it," Flower said. "It was the hot outfit for young women at MultiCon."

"You've got a cool sword hilt sticking up over your right shoulder," Bill told her. "Like that Vergallian anime from the award show, *Class Assassins*."

"You would remember that," Julie said, but she turned her head enough to see the sword hilt, and then reached for it with her right hand, which passed right through. "Hey, that's not how it worked on Union Station."

"It's a hologram," Flower told her. "It's the same sort of illusion I'll wrap around bots so that your weapons will have something to hit when you're fighting monsters. I'm sure it works the same way on Union Station."

"You're thinking about that experimental setup that Stryx Jeeves was working on where everything was real," Jorb told Julie. "You never actually got to try the regular LARPing studio."

A bearded dwarf who was as wide as he was tall stepped out of the jungle and dumped an armful of weapons on the path. "Compliments of Flower," he grunted in a thick brogue. "I'll be drinking in yon pub if ye need anything else."

"I'll go with you," Dewey said. "I'm more of a pub type than a traipsing around the jungle with a sword type."

Jorb and Razood leapt forward as the dwarf and the artificial person headed off. The Drazen seized a double-headed battle axe and the Frunge grabbed a war hammer and a small round shield with a spike protruding from the center. Bill and Zick took their turn next, each going for classic claymores. Everyone looked at Julie expectantly.

"I don't want to be a party pooper, but killing monsters really isn't my sort of thing," she said. "And what if I mess up and hurt somebody?"

"You can't," Jorb said, and his axe flashed out at Razood, who deflected the blow with his small shield. "No, let me hit you so she can see how noodle weapons work," the Drazen said.

"Hit Bill," the Frunge suggested. "That's the sort of sacrifice a man should make for his betrothed."

"Go ahead," Bill said. "But you don't have to put your back into it like that."

Jorb shifted the axe to his tentacle for longer reach and then brought the blade down on Bill's shoulder. It deformed into a silver goop on impact, though it remained in one clump, and reformed the axe head when the Drazen pulled the handle back.

"Did it hurt?" Julie asked Bill.

"It felt about the same as when I throw a laundry sack over my shoulder," he said.

"Well, I'll take that dagger for self-protection, but don't count on me to kill anything I don't have to."

"What's the quest?" Zick asked.

The Dollnick opera playing in the background suddenly halted, and a baritone voice echoed through the jungle.

"An ancient civilization destroyed by dark magic, their temple complex overgrown by vegetation and lost in the mists of time. Legend has it that a necromancer lives on in the pyramid of the Death God, building an unholy army in preparation for an all-out war with the forces of light. Find the temple complex, kill the necromancer, and the loot of an entire civilization will be yours."

"Was that you, Flower?" Julie asked.

"Stop asking questions," Zick told her. "You're ruining the suspension of disbelief."

Jorb tilted his head back and sniffed the air. Then he struck a heroic pose and pointed dramatically with his axe. "It's that way."

"How can you tell?" Bill asked as they all fell in behind the Drazen.

"It stinks of death," he proclaimed in an accent that sounded suspiciously like the vanished dwarf's.

"Shouldn't we be going the other direction then?" Julie whispered to Bill.

"I think the whole point of these LARPs is to find action," Bill said. "Besides, it beats sitting in estimating class and getting all of the cake prices wrong."

After a few minutes on the overgrown path, Jorb turned off into the jungle, clearing away vines with broad sweeps of his axe. Before they had proceeded far, the weapon clanged off something with a shower of sparks.

"This must be it," the Drazen said, using his tentacle to pull some vines away from a large block of stone. "I'll bet it's a step pyramid."

"Do we climb it?" Bill asked.

"Not unless you want to see the top," Zick said. "The entrance is usually hidden at ground-level somewhere on these. Look for carvings of faces and try pushing on the eyes. That's super popular with lost pyramids of Death Gods."

"Why don't you and Jorb go right and I'll take the newbies around the left?" Razood suggested.

"You want to split the party already? What's your hurry?"

"Some of us have jobs," Razood said. "Those apprentices from Bits I took on are nice guys, but if I leave them alone in the blacksmith shop for too long I know they'll try to forge something."

"I'm with Zick on this," Jorb said. "Splitting the party is always a last resort and we aren't there yet. I bet that Flower can just save our place if you have to leave."

"You guys are totally ruining the vibe," Zick complained. "Can we not talk about the game engine for five minutes?"

"Over here," Bill called from just a few steps away, where he pulled back a mat of vines from a stone block to reveal a high-relief carving. "It looks like an ugly guy, but his eyes are completely missing."

"Maybe they were jewels that have been stolen. That happens a lot in jungle quests."

"Stick your fingers in and see what happens," Razood advised.

"I like my fingers," Bill said, regarding the holes nervously. "I don't want to spoil the suspension of whatever, but does anybody ever lose body parts in these things?"

"I'll do it," the Frunge offered striding forward. He held his war hammer cocked behind his head for a blow, and reaching forward with his free hand, thrust his index and middle fingers into the eye sockets. There was a metallic screech, and the whole stone began to pull inwards with a low rumbling noise. In just a few seconds, a stairway leading under the pyramid was revealed.

"Wait," Julie said as the warriors all pushed forward. "If this is an ancient temple complex that's been lost in the mists of time, who lit all of those torches in the wall sconces?"

"Somebody always lights the torches," Zick said, gripping his sword tighter. "Hey, I hear fighting somewhere."

The torches suddenly dimmed, and a willowy Dollnick female materialized in a shimmering haze, her four hands held palms out in a calming gesture. "We have a bit of a problem," she announced.

"Flower?" Julie asked.

"In here I'm a goddess, or I will be as soon as I come up with a decent back story," the Dollnick AI said. "Keep in mind we're just testing the basic game engine today."

"Did you let more people in here?" Jorb asked as the sounds of fighting grew louder.

"Somebody spilled the beans to the Wanderers about this walled-off section being a LARPing studio, and they made such a fuss that I agreed to allow a group of them into the sandbox area so I could gather more data. It turns out that a couple dozen of them had noodle weapons from somewhere, and I thought it would be a good way to accelerate testing of the non-player characters I'm supplying as bots dressed in holograms."

"So what's the problem?" Julie asked.

"You know that the bots have to fight back or the whole exercise would be pointless, but I don't have any experience with this so I'm being extra careful not to cause injuries," Flower said. "The Wanderers have no such compunctions. They've slain half of my orc defenders and are ganging up on the rest in a very unsporting manner. I'm afraid they'll be able to break through, and their Verlock mage has already performed a ritual that allowed her to speak with the undead and learn about the pyramid."

"But the undead aren't real, you're supplying them," Julie objected. "Why didn't you just refuse to answer?"

"She's a real Verlock mage and she performed the ritual correctly. Not answering would have been cheating."

"Jorb, get the door," Razood said. "We'll have to defeat the dungeon boss before the Wanderers find their way in."

The Drazen set down his axe and then jumped upwards, stretching with his tentacle, which just reached the top of the stone block that had withdrawn into the pyramid. He pushed in the eyes on the face that operated the door and then dropped back to the stairs. The block began moving outward with a loud grinding sound.

"Flower, I mean, Goddess. Can you turn the lights back up?" Razood asked.

The torches flared and the ghostly hologram of the Dollnick female disappeared.

"Why aren't we moving forward?" Bill asked as the Frunge headed back up the stairs. "Isn't it a race now?"

"Some dungeons gloss everything over with magic, but I think that Flower is more likely to—there," Razood said, pointing at a complicated arrangement of gears and rods. "Everybody stand back and give me room." He went to work with his heavy war hammer, bashing the mechanism at its weakest points. "That should do it."

"But how will we get out now?" Julie asked in dismay.

"By beating the dungeon boss," Zick told her. "There's usually a teleport scroll in the loot."

The next twenty minutes went by in a blur of combat, with Jorb and Razood tanking for the party and defeating most of the undead before they could get to the second rank, composed of Zick and Bill. Each time one of the zombies or skeleton warriors nearly broke through, Julie felt like her hands were burning, and she was about to call upon the goddess for help when they found themselves in a giant throne room.

"Who dares enter my pyramid without an invitation?" the corpse-like figure on the throne demanded. He rose with surprising grace for one who looked like his better days were centuries behind him, and then stalked forward towards the group of adventurers. "Those who slay the undead are destined to replace them," he continued, raising a scepter and letting out an evil laugh.

"Rush him?" Jorb asked Razood under his breath.

"It can't be that easy," the Frunge replied. "Zick?"

"I saw a scenario just like this last season on the professional LARPing league channel with the same throne room and everything," the former game designer from Bits said. "As soon as the adventurers attacked the necromancer, he smashed his scepter and teleported back onto the throne. Then those other three doors opened, and the whole room filled with undead. The party wiped."

Julie looked around and saw that the passage they had arrived through was indeed one of four possible entrances to the throne room, though the doors to the other three were closed and covered with cobwebs.

"No guts, no glory," Jorb muttered. "Plus I'm teaching a class at the dojo in an hour so I can't stay down here forever."

"Agreed," the Frunge said, and then stared at Julie strangely. "You're a spellcaster?"

"A what?" Julie asked.

"Your hands are glowing," he told her. "That means you have some kind of magical ability. Try something."

"Point at the dead guy," Bill suggested.

Julie felt silly, but she pointed at the necromancer, and on a sudden impulse, trying her best to sound scary, declared, "Abracadabra."

Flames shot from her fingertips and engulfed the undead sorcerer, whose clothing went up like a torch, and then the spot where he was standing was empty.

"Well, that was easy," she said.

An evil laugh chilled her to the bones, and the necromancer reappeared on his throne, now garbed in black cloth that made him near invisible. Without even bothering to rise, he smashed the crystal on the end of his scepter against the stone arm of the throne.

All three sets of the doors to the throne room burst open, and a seemingly endless supply of reanimated dead in various forms streamed through two of them. But the third passageway only yielded a few limping skeletons and a shuffling zombie with a spear protruding from his back, followed by a horde of hard-charging adventurers from every alien species on the tunnel network.

"Kill the mobs and keep Flower's group from the throne," a glowing Verlock female boomed, her words coming slowly despite the excitement of the situation. "The necromancer is all mine."

Jorb and Razood fell back in defensive positions as a dozen heavily armed warriors got between the party and the throne. Bill and Zick closed up around Julie, and the rest of the Wanderers charged gleefully into the undead hordes, slicing and dicing like they were engaged in a kitchen showdown.

"Let's get out of here," Jorb said, backing towards the passage the Wanderers had emerged from. "Those guys are wearing magical armor, and some of them have enchanted weapons. Who would have expected a Verlock mage on a Wanderer ship?"

"You guys go," Zick said, slipping his sword back into its scabbard and folding his hands behind his neck in a sign of submission. "I want to stick around to see the end."

The ghostly Dollnick female reappeared to lead the way up the passage as the remaining members of the original party exited. "I think it was a success from a technical perspective," Flower said, though she sounded a bit apologetic. "Sorry about letting the Wanderers ruin your fun."

Twelve

"I'm Dianne from the Galactic Free Press," the reporter introduced herself. "Thank you for agreeing to meet with me."

"Samuel McAllister, I don't have an official job title yet. Vivian was here a minute ago, but she just realized that the coffee Flower stocked in our kitchen is all decaffeinated, so she ran out to get some real beans for us."

"That works for me," the reporter said. "It's going to be exciting with the headquarters for the Human Empire on board. I haven't submitted a story worthy of the front page in two years."

"We haven't made any decisions about that yet," Samuel said, though he realized how odd that must sound given the luxurious office suite with the Human Empire emblem literally carved in stone. "All of this is just an example of aggressive salesmanship on the part of our hostess."

"Flower does try to be proactive," Dianne said. "So do you mind if I take a few images over my implant? Your office is very impressive."

"You mean the book collection." Samuel reddened. "Flower had them all brought in overnight and we haven't decided what to do about it yet. I can't even read any of those languages, other than Vergallian. It reminds me of when my mom's embassy sponsored a charity book sale on Union Station. Some of the aliens were buying books by weight to use for interior decorating. On the bright side, most of the academic monographs would have ended up in recycling otherwise."

"I won't use the images if the collection is just random nonsense," the reporter said. "I'll ask somebody at the paper to check."

"The Vergallian titles are all legal books and treatises on governing, mainly written for queens. The only English titles Flower thought worth stocking are from the *For Humans* collection."

"That's even better then," Dianne said, spotting the distinctive spines of the trademarked series. "They're published by a division of the Galactic Free Press so it's good publicity for us. Did Flower pick out the furniture as well?"

"Initially she did, but Vivian made her take most of it back, and then insisted I go shopping with her," Samuel said, looking even more embarrassed. "This desk cost more than I saved working for the Vergallian embassy last year."

"Well, I did hear that the Human Empire is backed by the All Species Cookbook, so I don't imagine a little splurge on office furnishings is going to hurt."

"Vivian paid for the new furniture herself. She says if we get fired, we can take it with us and start a new business."

"That's right," Vivian announced her presence from the door. "If the Human Empire gets into financial trouble, we'll move out the furniture we own and replace it with rentals from Flower. I'm going to put the coffee on but I'll be back in a minute. Do you take anything in yours, Dianne?"

"One sugar," the reporter replied, and Vivian disappeared again. "She seems to know a lot about business. I guess the apple doesn't fall far from the tree."

"Her brother and my sister are pretty sharp too," Samuel said. "I seem to take after my mother when it comes to business sense."

"So what did the future first administrator of the Human Empire want to be when he grew up?" the reporter asked, settling into the chair next to the expansive desk.

"First Administrator," Samuel repeated as if it was a formal job title. "I like that. It doesn't make it sound like we're putting ourselves on the path to royalty, and it could work as a permanent job title for whatever my position here turns out to be. Like the first officer of a ship, or First Consul on a Vergallian Fleet world."

"Feel free to use it," Dianne said. "In fact, we can roll it out in my article if you want. But seriously, readers like to see a little background in an interview with somebody important who they've never heard of. What did you want to be when you were growing up?"

"A space engineer," Samuel replied, figuring it would sound better than admitting his early aspiration to become a Vergallian gentleman and a consort to a queen. "But a year at the Open University convinced me that I was wasting my time. The math was just too much, even with my background from the station librarian's experimental school. And I guess I had an aptitude for statecraft after growing up with an EarthCent ambassador for a mother. When I started taking the diplomacy courses, I knew it was the right decision."

"Some people would call your mother THE EarthCent ambassador," Dianne prompted.

"She'd be the first one to tell you that's not the case," Samuel said. "Mom doesn't know herself how she ends up in the middle of so many historic events, but all of the EarthCent ambassadors have pretty impressive track records. It may be as simple as the fact that the Grenouthian news network is headquartered on Union Station so it's a logical place to stage diplomatic summits."

"The Galactic Free Press is also based out of Union Station," Dianne pointed out.

"Humans are the only ones who read that," Samuel said, and then corrected himself. "Humans and some Open University students, because it's free and it has a great local classified section that lists all of the bands playing in off-campus bars, plus coverage of the LARPing leagues."

"I understand that you chaired the Open University committee responsible for vetting student business proposals for Flower while she was being refitted at Union Station for her current mission. I interviewed the Grenouthian director of *Everyday Superheroes* last season, and he said that if you hadn't selected his proposal to start an immersive training studio on Flower, he would probably be eking out a living on the regional theatre circuit."

"He made a very strong proposal, though from what I've heard, Flower immediately roped him into starting multiple theatre groups as team sports. Then they went into the anime business together so his original concept never really got a chance. Do you know Razood, the Frunge blacksmith?"

"Everybody knows Razood," Dianne said. "When you visit Colonial Jeevesburg, you can usually hear him hammering away at the forge."

"Our student committee actually passed on his business proposal but Jeeves decided to sponsor him directly. In the end, we only approved around a dozen businesses, so it's not like we had a major impact."

"I think you're too modest," the reporter told him. "I interviewed Flower about the new Open University campus she launched during our last circuit, and it turns out she began planning for it after your committee visited her. It took a deal of convincing and years of good behavior on Flower's part to persuade the Stryx to expand the franchise."

"They take the Open University seriously," Samuel said. "I suppose they wanted to make Flower work for it enough that she would do the same."

Vivian entered with a tray and handed Dianne a coffee. Then she set the tray on Samuel's desk, took her own mug, and sat in the remaining open chair. "What have I missed?"

"We were just talking about the student committee for outfitting Flower at the Open University," Samuel told her. "How did you make the coffee so fast?"

"I don't really know myself," she admitted. "It's the first time I've used the new machine, and as soon as I poured the beans in the top, coffee started coming out the bottom. I didn't even hear the grinder."

"Oh, this is good," Dianne said after taking a tiny sip. "It's hot, but not too hot." Without setting the mug down, she used her other hand to navigate through a couple of menus on the reporter's tab on her lap. "Do the two of you mind if I record this?"

"Doesn't bother me," Samuel said, and looked at Vivian.

"I can always ping Aunt Chastity and beg her not to run the story if we say anything stupid," Vivian said.

"Don't worry, I'm not the gotcha type of investigative journalist," Dianne said. "I'm mainly interested in what your plans are for getting the Human Empire off the ground. I understand that you're waiting for your mentor to show up before making any big decisions, but you must have some idea of where you'd like to start."

"I think for the next few years it will basically be an exercise in learning," Samuel said. "We've been studying the other empires on the tunnel network, and EarthCent Intelligence has tasked an analyst to help us identify best practices. Some of the administrative departments are about the same across everybody's empires, some are more species-specific, like the Horten Bureau of Hygiene, or the Verlock Ministry of Volcanoes. The two of us aren't going to change the galaxy on our own, so the first goal is to hire the right people to head up an exploratory team for each department."

"And I believe I heard you're looking for young people, rather than experienced diplomats."

"It probably sounds funny, but we think that's the best way to avoid accidentally falling into the same old ruts that humans have been carving out since the Bronze Age," Samuel said. "And then there's the whole longevity thing."

The reporter motioned for him to elaborate.

"One of the things that we've learned working with aliens is that they place a high value on building relationships with individuals, both in diplomacy and intelligence," Vivian answered for her husband. "With the exception of the Vergallians, who are always rotating queens through their ambassadorial postings, the aliens consider a few hundred years on the job to be the minimum for a serious career diplomat."

"So by hiring young diplomats and administrators, you hope they'll stay in place long enough for the aliens to take them seriously," Dianne said.

"That, and we're so young ourselves that it might be hard for professionals with more extensive experience to work under us," Samuel admitted. "And we really expect that the next few years will be spent re-educating ourselves to see things from the perspective of an empire. It will almost be like going back to school again."

"I could offer a course in empire building through the Open University," Flower announced via an overhead speaker. "I have extensive experience working in an imperial structure myself, and it will be easy to bring in guest faculty. I've read up on how Earth trained people for careers in public service and there were several schools of government associated with famous universities."

"That's not a terrible idea," Vivian said, either not noticing the expression on her husband's face or choosing to ignore it. "Leveraging the Open University's infrastructure makes more sense than our setting up a parallel effort with the classrooms, administration, and all of that."

"We aren't talking about making hundreds of hires right off, or even dozens," Samuel protested. "If we could just find a few good people—"

"And here we are," a voice announced from the door.

"How did you get in?" Vivian demanded. She jumped up from her chair to confront the woman who walked right into Samuel's office. "I'm afraid I have to ask you to leave."

"Sit-ins don't work that way," the woman said, slipping around Vivian and dropping into the just-vacated chair. Then she grabbed the still-warm mug of coffee from Samuel's desk and downed the remains in one gulp.

"That's an excellent brew. And to answer your question, we walked right in when the doors opened."

"Flower?" Samuel inquired.

"I told you I could provide twenty-four-hour security but you turned me down," the Dollnick AI responded. "The Wanderers began entering Human Empire headquarters just forty seconds ago when the doors opened to allow in the delivery man with the lamps Vivian ordered from the Frunge distributor."

"Why didn't you close the doors after the delivery man came through?"

"Because the first Wanderer lay down in the opening and I didn't think that chopping him in half would be an auspicious start for the Human Empire."

"What do you want?" Samuel demanded, turning to the woman.

"I'm just here to hold the seat for Ronald, he's a bit old to rush around," she said. "And here he is now."

The senior storyteller from the group of human Wanderers shuffled into the office and exchanged positions with his assistant while that worthy prevented Samuel's wife from recapturing her seat. Ronald crossed his legs and began stroking his white beard, obviously in no hurry to speak. Vivian was visibly fighting to restrain herself from inflicting bodily harm on one or the other of the unwanted guests, but then a crash from the reception area sent her running out of the office.

"What do you want this time?" Samuel asked wearily.

"When a week went by without you processing our refugee application, I wrote it off to the newness of your administration and the demands of young love," the old man said. "But it's been almost three weeks now, and we don't even know what sort of UBI you'll be providing."

"I don't have a clue what that is."

"UBI. Universal Basic Income. How else will you support the non-working citizens in your empire?"

"I've already told you a hundred times that we don't have any citizens in our empire yet, other than my wife and myself. We're just in the planning phase."

"And I refuse to accept that," Ronald said. "Just look at me, will you? What species do you think I am?"

Samuel took a moment to reply, looking for a trick. "Human."

"And what's the name of your empire?" the old storyteller demanded triumphantly.

"You're missing the point. I'm not saying you won't be welcome to join someday, I'm just saying we're not in a position to do anything for you right now. Flower is taking care of all of your needs and I just don't understand what you hope to get from me."

"More than Flower is giving us," Ronald replied bluntly. "Sure, we get free food, a place to sleep, and there are plenty of people wandering around in outlandish costumes to make fun of, but man does not live by bread, blanket, and free entertainment alone. We need cash."

"I'm not in a position to give you any cash. Why don't you get jobs?"

"I offer them work every day, but they won't even take well-paid positions restoring their own ship," Flower interjected.

"You stay out of this," the Wanderer said irritably, glancing up at the ceiling. "There's nothing worse than a bossy Dollnick AI that won't let us sleep in the morning."

"We all have to do the calisthenics," Dianne put in. "They're mandatory for everyone on board, including the aliens."

"Well we don't do them, but she plays loud music in all of our cabins every morning in an attempt to force us out into the corridors to stretch. It's inhuman, and I want to file a complaint."

"With who?" Samuel asked.

"With you," Ronald declared in exasperation. "You're our official government, aren't you?"

"I have no power to accept or process your complaint, and I do not acknowledge being your official government. My job function as, uh, First Administrator, is to get the ball rolling for the sovereign human communities which were tendered empire status by the Stryx under the rules of the tunnel network treaty. You are not a part of a sovereign human community, nor have I seen any evidence beyond your own claims that you represent the humans from the Miklat. Please leave my office and stop wasting my time."

"Not very diplomatic of you." The old man sniffed and produced a roll of parchment. He handed it to his assistant, who spread it out on the desk.

"What is this?" Samuel asked.

"A list of demands. We refuse to leave the Human Empire headquarters until they're met."

"They knocked over one of the new lamps," Vivian announced angrily as she stormed back into the office. "I'm going to contact Captain Pyun and ask him to send security to clean them all out of here."

"What an interesting idea," Ronald said, stroking his beard. He turned to Dianne. "I see from that I.D. hanging around your neck that you work for the Galactic Free Press. How much would you pay for an exclusive interview?"

"With you?" the reporter asked.

"Of course with me. I'm eighty-three years old, the legitimate leader of a sovereign human community whether or not we ever applied to EarthCent's little club, and I'm about to be forcefully evicted from a peaceful sit-in protesting the inaction of the Human Empire on the behalf of refugees. How could you ignore a story like that?"

"Her aunt owns the paper," Dianne said, pointing at Vivian.

Ronald smiled, then began to laugh, and it took him a full minute to regain his composure. "I'm glad to hear that. I was beginning to think that you were a couple of lost kids playing empire, but now I see that you're as well connected as they come. How about we start over?"

"The lobby is full of Wanderers," Vivian reported. "There must be over a hundred of them in there. It's a good thing that you agreed to let Flower operate all of the individual office doors on voice identification or we'd never get them out."

Samuel pulled the scroll closer and began to puzzle over the script. "It's English, right? What are all of the little curlicues and connecting lines? I can barely make out the words."

"Calligraphy is a valued art among the Wanderers," Ronald said. "My own daughter invests at least three hours a month in practice."

"Three hours a month!" Vivian practically exploded. "Samuel and I spent that long every day practicing our ballroom dancing for nearly ten years."

"To each his own," the old storyteller said. "Perhaps if you had spent more time reading and less time dancing you wouldn't be having so much trouble with a perfectly good scroll."

"Number one," Samuel said, having finally deciphered the odd hand. "I cannot give you control of this ship because I'm a guest here myself. Number two. I cannot stop Flower from playing loud music in your cabins every morning unless you agree to go out in the corridors and do your stretching exercises like everybody else. Number three. I cannot agree to represent your group to Flower because you have no standing as members of the Human Empire. Number Four—"

"Now that's where we disagree," the old man interrupted. "You keep saying that we aren't part of the Human Empire and I keep saying that we are. Is there a test we need to take? Do you need blood samples, family trees? What will it cost you to just listen to our problems and offer your help? I'm beginning to think that you just aren't cut out for a career in government."

"You aren't our constituency," Vivian said coldly.

"We aren't leaving either," Ronald said. "How's the take-out on the ship? Will they charge it to the room?"

"I didn't want to do this, but desperate times lead to desperate measures," Flower said. She triggered the office door to open again so they could hear her making a public address announcement in the lobby. "Attention all Wanderers. Flower Entertainment has opened a second LARPing studio on the Con deck. The first five hundred players will receive a starting bonus of—"

The rest of the announcement was drowned out by the Wanderers shouting at each other and trying to squeeze out the doors of the Human Empire headquarters at the same time. Ronald's middle-aged assistant shot him a pleading look, and he gave a sigh and waved his hand for her to go.

"This isn't over," Ronald said, rising slowly from his seat. "Dirty trick that, breaking up a sit-in with a new entertainment attraction. Still, I can probably work it into a story one day. Just so you aren't surprised when you hear it, I'll be the hero and you'll be the villains."

Thirteen

"I can't believe I let Flower talk me into this," Julie complained to her voice teacher. "I thought I'd seen the last of my Refill costume until next season."

"You look really cute as a superhero waitress," Rinka said, and then checked her own outfit in the corridor display panel that Flower had helpfully set to mirror mode. "Do you think the green ribbon suits my tentacle?"

"It's lovely," Julie said, wishing for a moment that she had a tentacle of her own to accessorize. "Aren't you nervous about singing in front of a bunch of aliens? At least all I have to do is pretend to throw a tray and autograph my action figures."

"Drazens don't suffer from stage shyness, at least not when we're singing. And you should consider doing a number yourself. You're quite good for a Human with less than a year's training."

"Not a chance," Julie said, leading the way to the lift tube. "Do you have your magnetic cleats on?"

"They're built into this pair," Rinka said. "Will the boys be coming to watch us?"

"Bill and Jorb? I hope they don't even know we're performing. Flower didn't finalize her scheme until after lunch. Did you mention it to Jorb?"

The lift tube capsule set off before Julie could tell it where they were going, which was only fair as the whole outing was Flower's idea.

"I hate to bother him while he's at the dojo because I know he'll drop everything and rush over," the Drazen girl said. "Who knew he would turn out to be such a gallant."

"Is that a word in English? If the meaning matches the sound, I could probably use it in a book. It's weird how you have a bigger vocabulary in my language than I do."

"I studied up so I can beat Jorb at Scrabble," Rinka admitted. "Gallant is a seven-letter word, and it fits him well."

"Can you come up with a seven-letter word that describes Bill?" Julie asked. "I see so little of him these days that I could use something to remind me that we're really engaged."

"Loverly."

"Is that even a word?"

"It is in an old Earth musical I found," Rinka replied. "I'm hoping to have the travel chorus perform it. You know, you'd make the perfect Eliza…"

"Did you feel that?" Julie asked. "The capsule has shifted to one of the radial tubes and we're moving pretty fast."

"Flower told me that the show will be in her engine room, or rather, the space between her jump engines and the bulkhead of her docking bay. I can hold the high notes better at a lower weight so I'm looking forward to it."

"I guess I never really thought about how far her docking bay on the axis reaches into her hull since I haven't had the time to explore. Flower?"

"The docking bay extends for exactly one-quarter of my length," the Dollnick AI replied immediately. "The rest of the core, or hollow keel if you prefer, is occupied by my physical plant."

"And why are we doing the show there rather than in a theatre?" Julie asked.

"Your audience prefers Zero G. And don't let the little ones climb all over you or you'll never be able to pose properly."

The capsule slowed, changed directions again, and then the lift tube doors opened on a scene that somehow reminded Julie of the rigging of a pirate ship from an old movie. There were giant nets stretched every which way, with plenty of solo ropes as well, all swarming with furry little Zarents.

"It looks like they have thousands of sleeping bags strung along the axis where they're completely weightless," Rinka observed. She stretched her own tentacle as if she yearned to grab hold of one of the ropes and swing herself up. "I'm not sure I can tell which part of their anatomy is which, other than the eyes, but they sure seem a lot happier than when they first came on board."

"That doesn't look like Dollnick text on the banner," Julie said, pointing at a giant printed sheet stretched across the bulkhead. "I wonder what it says."

"Club Flower," the Dollnick AI informed Julie by way of her implant. "Don't forget the plan. Now I've told the Zarents that you're here, so get ready for—"

"Puppy Pile," Rinka squealed as dozens of young Zarents piled onto the two girls. Without their magnetic cleats to help hold them in place, the swarm of little aliens might have carried the girls away onto the nets just like real pirates, but an older Zarent arrived on his unicycle, and the little ones fled back into the rigging.

"Allow me to introduce myself," the new arrival said through his external speaker device. "I am Chief Engineer Miklat, which makes me the official representative of our community. Flower informed me that the two of you asked to perform for us while we rest and recuperate."

"That's right," Rinka said, not contradicting Flower's characterization of the volunteering process on board. "I understand that Zarents were designed to communicate telepathically and have limited vocalization abilities, but I've also been told that you have excellent hearing. I'm a certified Drazen choral mistress, and I'd like to try singing a few pieces to see if they suit you."

The chief engineer performed a sort of a bow by tilting his unicycle forward. "We enjoy the music of other species, the Drazens foremost among them. Do you require a special platform?"

"Anywhere is fine," Rinka said. "Flower assured me she could correct for the performance space with acoustic reflection and suppression fields, but it would be good if anybody who wants to listen gathered in front of me."

"Ah yes, acoustics are a Dollnick specialty." The chief engineer waved his tentacles around for a moment, and Zarents from all over the core began making their way through the nets and ropes towards where the girls were standing near the lift tube.

"Do you have a name other than Chief Engineer?" Julie asked.

"Snap," the Zarent replied. "It's a nickname that attached to me after an unfortunate incident in my youth when I was attempting to prove that a flawless crystal rod I had grown couldn't be broken by tentacle strength alone. I know from the anime that Flower showed us that your name is The Waitress, but do you have a nickname you would prefer we use?"

"Uh, Julie," she said. "I hope I don't look too funny dressed in my costume, but Flower assured me that the short skirt wouldn't offend anybody's sensibilities."

"You all look funny to us, and if you're talking about the propensity some bipeds have for covering their skin, keep in mind that all of us are naked," Snap said.

"Could you tell me something about the frequency range of your hearing so I can calibrate my performance?" Rinka asked.

"Our auditory organs were optimized for troubleshooting, and while we hear perfectly over the entire range that's typical for tunnel network species, we're especially well adapted to sounds above seven hundred and fifty cycles per second, where the frequencies associated with containment field tuning begin to manifest."

"So basically, soprano," Rinka said. She nodded and passed two little plugs attached by a cord to Julie. "You might want to put these in your ears."

"Earplugs?"

"I don't think you've ever heard me hit the high range on the Drazen scale, but I know that some Humans find it to be hard on their nerves," she said apologetically. "Oh, look how many Zarents are coming!"

"Our group includes some three thousand individuals, though a third are apprentices," the chief engineer said.

"Plus the children?" Julie asked.

"Our children are apprentices from birth," Snap explained. "See how they arrange themselves with perfect symmetry."

It looked like all three thousand Zarents had decided to attend Rinka's concert, most of them hanging from nets that had been pulled down near the deck level. The furry octopus-like creatures had ranked themselves by size, with the littlest front and center. Between the stretching of the nets and the distribution of weight, within minutes they had formed their own natural amphitheatre. The chief engineer whipped out a device that let him check the curvature in three dimensions and he expressed his approval with a loud buzz.

"We're ready when you are," he said and pedaled off on his unicycle to take his place near the back.

"Do you want to hold my music tab for me, just to have something to do?" Rinka asked Julie. "It's only a prop as I'll be sticking with old classics that I've known since I was a child."

"I'd probably get nervous and drop it," Julie said. "I think I'll stand near the lift tube and make sure nobody interrupts."

The Drazen cleared her throat, stretched her tentacle, and announced, "I'm going to start with a little folk song for a warm-up and then we'll get to the good stuff. If anybody has heard this one before, feel free to join in telepathically."

She began to sing a song about a Drazen farmer who had a whole collection of animals, and even though Julie had no telepathic sensitivity, she somehow knew that the little Zarent children were all joining in for the chorus with their interpretations of the noises made by the farm's inhabitants. When Rinka finally wound down with the Brizat, an elephant-like creature that made a "Zratt, zratt here, and a zratt, zratt there," all of the aliens, young and old, were practically radiating happiness.

"Next I'd like to sing the first aria from *Hard Rock Asteroid Mining,* a classic of early Drazen space exploration that

I'm sure you've all heard," Rinka said. She glanced over at Julie, gestured at her own ears, and delayed a moment while her friend reluctantly installed the earplugs. Then she let out a high, clear note and Julie winced.

The Zarents hung enthralled from their nets, occasionally poking one another with a tentacle to express their admiration of the Drazen soloist. The performance continued for just over an hour, and not a single one of the aliens, down to the littlest furry octopus, moved from their spots. When Rinka brought the performance to an end, looking both exhilarated and exhausted, the Zarents all linked their tentacles and performed a sort of a group bow in her direction.

Snap rode forward again on his unicycle as the aliens began to disperse. One of his tentacles was kept suspiciously behind him, and then he brought it around and presented Rinka with a bouquet of fresh-cut flowers.

"That was truly lovely, the best vocal performance most of us have ever had the pleasure of attending," he enthused. "Please accept these flowers as a token of our appreciation, along with membership in the honorary guild of Zarent friends. Chief Purser Miklat will bring you the medallion as soon as she can manufacture one. And you," he continued, turning his unicycle toward Julie, "Some of the anime fans in our group bought a whole case of The Waitress action figures and we understand you are willing to sign them and pose for souvenir images."

"Of course," Julie said. "I never would have guessed that Zarents would have an interest in *Everyday Superheroes.*"

"But then again," Snap said, tilting closer on his unicycle before having to lean back to maintain his balance, "we both know that's not the only reason you're here."

"It's not?"

"Club Flower?" the Zarent asked by way of a reply. "Not many sentients can even decipher our written language, yet Flower went to the trouble of producing an expensive banner. While I'd like to believe that she means it as a sign that we are permanently welcome, I suspect that the reality of the situation is that she's desperate to rid herself of the Wanderers and sees no way of doing it unless we agree to return to the Miklat."

"There's some truth to what you're saying," Julie allowed, "but that's not the whole story. Flower feels that the Zarents have been treated as outcasts by the galactic community, and as an outcast herself, she empathizes with your cause, even though you may have different goals." A little alien landed on Julie's shoulders and wrapped several of its tentacles around her neck, and the girl paused to stroke the soft fur. "The Farling doctor has told Flower that the Zarents he revived from stasis are undergoing treatment and will all live, but he prescribes a long period of recuperation in Zero-G, away from the temptations of endless work. So returning them to the Miklat is out of the question."

"We agree on something," the chief engineer said. "But Zarents cannot survive without a community of at least several hundred members. It's an acquired form of co-dependency that we have no desire to outgrow."

"Exactly," Julie said. "That's why Flower really does want you to stay on board. She told me that this whole section of her core is underutilized because the bipedal species all prefer to weigh something more substantial and they aren't comfortable around operating power plants the way the Zarents are."

The unicycle stopped its constant motion, and Snap would have fallen over sideways if he hadn't reached out with a pair of tentacles at the last second, steadying himself between the two girls. "The Dollnick A.I. is offering us a home?"

"As much as she would love to have you all on board permanently, she's afraid that your work ethic would eventually lead to clashes with the way she does things," Julie said, reciting the memorized lines as if she was thinking them up herself. "Flower's idea is to create a resort for Zarents, a place where any of you living in the Wanderer Mobs can come for a few cycles of vacation and then return to your large communities refreshed. Of course, as the seed group, we'd need at least several hundred of you to stay on with the injured, whether the others decide to sign up with another ship or end your strike and return to the Miklat."

"That was smooth," Flower murmured over Julie's implant. "Get him thinking about it as an option again."

"My people have no experience with resorts, but I understand them to be expensive," the chief engineer said slowly. "Since the Zarent way is to retire within our working communities when we can no longer function, we've never seen the need to build up substantial savings. On the Miklat, we were compelled to spend whatever money came our way for repair parts."

"Flower was hoping to come to a barter arrangement," Julie said. "She's undertaken the startup of a small shipyard for producing Sharf two-man traders and has acquired the original factory tooling, but we've run into a snag trying to set it up. I realize that it may not be your thing, but—"

"Sharf two-man traders?" The chief engineer lifted his body from the seat of the unicycle and let out a buzz of laughter. "Why, the little Twelfth Apprentice Life Support clinging to your neck can already trace the schematics for one. Many Zarent communities keep a Sharf two-man trader in the preschool playground, something the youngsters can take apart and put together without adult supervision."

"So you think you'd be able to help set up the assembly line?"

"Certainly, and if there's any difficulty with the existing equipment, we could manage something from scratch. They really are some of the simplest ships of any practical value in the galaxy."

"Then I think that your help getting the factory started would be a fair trade to cover the expenses for the share of your community who want to remain behind with the recuperating patients," Julie said. "Flower apologizes that she doesn't have the sort of social connections that could help the rest of you find a place where your work would be appreciated…" She let the sentence hang.

"No, I don't expect that Flower would," Snap said. "We have feelers out on the Stryxnet to the other Wanderer mobs. To be perfectly honest, labor actions such as ours are rare, and they carry with them a stigma of laziness."

"That's so unfair," Rinka said. "Even Drazen consortiums recognize the validity of strikes for forcing resolutions to problems that resist amicable solutions."

"But there's nothing as disheartening to a Zarent as the order to down tools. We aren't even in negotiations because the captain of the Miklat resigned his commission as soon as Flower took us all on board. In the Wanderer legal system, the Miklat no longer exists as a mob ship. I heard a rumor that the entire ship's company has requested refugee status on Flower, with the exception of the Humans, who are holding out for the Human Empire."

Julie hesitated for a moment while stroking the twelfth apprentice's fur before springing the last part of Flower's stratagem on the chief engineer. "As of four hours ago, we have a legal ruling from the Stryx declaring the Miklat abandoned and granting us the salvage rights. I'm authorized to offer the ship to you."

All motion in the giant open space came to an abrupt halt, and even the little alien wrapped around Julie's neck froze as the telepathic connection the Zarents shared spread the news instantaneously.

"Flower is gifting us the Miklat?" Snap asked, his electronically synthesized voice emerging like a whisper.

"I'm sure you've noticed that Flower is operating at less than twenty percent of capacity herself, even with all of the refugees on board," Julie explained. "If she was full up, we could repurpose your ship as a tender or warehouse space, but there's just no need. If the Miklat had been built by any other species, Flower might have sold it for scrap, but since it served honorably as a Dollnick colony ship, she won't consider that option. Yet the Miklat's condition means that selling it on the open market would create an enormous liability. You'll be doing her a favor by accepting."

"It's too big of a decision to make without discussion," the chief engineer said. "In the history of the Zarents, we've always served on the ships of other species. It's why the Farlings created us."

"If it's a philosophical issue, perhaps you could talk it over with M793qK," Julie suggested. "I'm just Flower's executive assistant and I can't pretend to understand the inner workings of her mind."

"This could change everything. If we returned to the mob as the owners of the Miklat, we could set the rules for any Wanderers who want to join us."

"I don't think you'd convince them to work," Rinka cautioned him.

"We aren't asking for miracles," Snap said, finally letting go of his two humanoid supports and resuming a tilting back-and-forth motion on his unicycle. "Just that they report when things start to break rather than waiting until the damage is beyond repair, and contribute to a replacement parts fund like most of the other Wanderers. Please ask Flower to give us until the next meal period to think about this."

"I'm sure she'll welcome any decision you reach," Julie said. "It was very nice meeting you. We'll see ourselves out."

"Aren't you forgetting something?"

Julie looked to Rinka, hoping that if the Zarents had an official parting ceremony, the Drazen would know about it. Rinka gestured at her own neck.

"Oh," Julie said, and began gently removing Twelfth Apprentice Life Support's tentacles. The task proved beyond her ability, due to the little Zarent's numerical advantage in appendages. She gave Snap an apologetic smile. "I'm afraid I'll have to impose on you for help."

"Certainly, but I wasn't worried about your absconding with our apprentice," the chief engineer said and pointed towards a table where a line of Zarents was forming. "You have a box full of action figures to sign."

Fourteen

"Who wants something that's not from the All Species Cookbook testing samples?" Bill asked. "Harry made vegetable tempura. Everybody except for Razood likes that, right?"

"Stop holding out on us," Jorb said. "I know that Dewey brought back a new shipment of junk food in the bookmobile, and my information says it includes a case of barbeque chips, the kind with the flames on the package."

"You're spying on the EarthCent embassy's shipments to Flower?"

"It's part of my job," the Drazen said. "It's part of your job too."

"No, Bill's a double agent working for EarthCent," Yaem said, taking his seat at the table. "You know they wouldn't let him work for me long-term without supervision."

A giant beetle entered the cafeteria and seemed to be looking everywhere at once through his multifaceted eyes. "I better not see any packaging from our new shipment of test products lying around," he rubbed out on his speaking legs. "Sometimes I think that you lot are as bad as the Wanderers."

"Wait until they start paying you with this," Razood said. He flipped a five-cred coin to M793qK, who snatched it out of the air with one of his appendages.

The Farling didn't need two seconds to examine the coin. "Counterfeit. How much have they passed?"

"I don't know," Flower joined in via an overhead speaker. "I've put Lynx in charge of assessing the damage since she's the point of contact for bazaar vendors, but it looks bad."

"This is why the Stryx limit the number of Wanderers they'll allow to visit a station at one time, even when a whole mob is parked right alongside," Lume said. "There's always a rash of bad coinage, and the five cred pieces seem to be the most common target."

"Valuable enough to pay for a meal, small enough not to draw undue attention," Razood agreed. "I've started running every coin through my miniregister, but the problem is that they're already in widespread circulation, so the people bringing them in probably aren't aware they're passing counterfeits. Fortunately, most of my business is for high-end weapons that are paid for with programmable creds, but I took that coin for sharpening a set of chef's knives."

"The Stryx make good the counterfeits for the local merchants after a Wanderer mob comes through," M793qK said. "Of course, the Stryx also begin scanning visitors from the mob for counterfeits after the first wave appears, so the damage isn't that great."

"Why do the Stryx wait if they know that it's going to be a problem?" Bill asked,

"Just sit, already," Yaem said, pushing an empty chair at the young man. "And while not a tunnel network member myself, from what I know of the Stryx, they are probably applying an excess of caution in not prejudging the Wanderers based on the conduct of the last mob."

"But Lume just said that the Stryx limit the number of Wanderers they'll allow aboard a station at one time."

"That's because the Stryx aren't stupid."

"I don't like the implication of your statement," Flower said.

"Nobody is accusing you of anything," the Sharf amended himself hastily. "And I've finished translating all of those instructions for operating your assembly line should you ever get it assembled."

"I believe I have that under control now. The reason I asked you all here today is to come up with a plan for dealing with the Wanderers. We haven't been able to conduct business as usual at our last four stops, and several species have added me to their quarantine list."

"I actually haven't seen as many Wanderers hanging around the food court the last few days," Lume said.

"That's because at any given time, there are hundreds of them Live Action Role Playing, and thousands gathered outside the studios waiting in line for their turn," Flower said. "It's the first time I've ever heard of Wanderers waiting patiently for anything, and some of the Con deck food vendors are doing a good business selling them snacks."

"But are they getting paid with real money or counterfeit?" Razood asked.

"A mix of both," Flower said. "I think the Wanderers have already run through most of the counterfeit supply they brought with them, and I'm hardly going to allow them to set up shop on the ship. During my inspection of the Miklat, my bots discovered a number of small counterfeiting setups which I've put into storage to deliver to the Stryx for their collection."

"I thought that Stryx creds couldn't be counterfeited," Bill said. "Somebody told me they have quantum things in them and every coin is unique."

"If you put a coin in a Stryx register, or even a miniregister like the one I have, it will immediately identify them as counterfeits," Razood told his former apprentice. "But most people don't bother with one-cred and five-cred denominations, so then it's just a question of the look and the feel."

"Can I request dipping sauce with that tempura?" Jorb asked. "Something with a little heat to it?"

"Sorry, I forgot all about the food," Bill said, jumping up. "I'll be back in a second."

"I believe the rule is that he who makes one of us get up should fetch the drinks for the rest," the Grenouthian director drawled. "And if this is an all-hands-on-deck meeting, where are Brynlan and Battle Royale?"

"Avisia refuses to leave her students during school hours while there are young Wanderers on the loose," Flower reported. "I told her that most of the Human males would be too busy LARPing to cause problems, but she said it's the ones who don't play games that worry her the most. As for Brynlan, he undertook a mission to the Verlock contingent of Wanderers for me, but he's on his way here now."

Jorb installed himself behind the bar and began taking drink orders. By the time he brought them out, Bill was back with an enormous platter of vegetable tempura and several bowls of dipping sauce. Bill set down the bowl covered with tin foil at Jorb's place and explained, "The foil keeps my eyes from watering while I carry it out."

"If you've all seen to your creature comforts, we have a serious problem here," Flower said as the spies began crunching away. "The Zarents have accepted my gift of the Miklat, and tomorrow I'll present them with the maintenance bots I purchased and reprogrammed. I've been employing my own bots more than I'd like in effecting the Miklat's repairs, but I estimate that the Zarents will now be able to finish putting her back into operating condition in less than two weeks. The problem will be getting the Wanderers to go."

"You're confident that the Zarents will have them?" Razood asked.

"Eighty-four point two percent," the Dollnick A.I. said. "It's a risk, but I'm hoping that the bots will tip the balance in my favor. The Zarents themselves may not realize it yet, but as the owners of the Miklat, for the first time they'll be able to prevent the Wanderers from selling off the ship's equipment. In fact, I specifically programmed the bots to require approval from one of the Zarent engineering staff for any mission that takes them outside of the ship's hull."

"A wise precaution," M793qK said. "I've spent more time with Zarents this last cycle than in the previous ten thousand years, and it strikes me how independent-minded they've become. While this group may be outliers due to their untenable conditions of employment, I'd like to believe that the whole species is undergoing a growth spurt, in the sense of social evolution. I think the idea of working for themselves and tolerating the Wanderers as supercargo will be a very attractive proposition for them, at least until they develop the desire to live wholly on their own."

"But won't their newfound confidence make it less likely that the Wanderers will want to return to the Miklat, even if invited?" Yaem asked.

"In my experience, the Wanderers crave authority," the Farling said. "One of the mistakes the Zarents have made in the past is constantly seeking authorization and approval for their maintenance activities. Since the Wanderers owned the ship, this was an unavoidable ritual for both sides, but now the Zarents will be able to remain in the background."

"Excuse me," Bill said to M793qK. "Did you say something about associating with the Zarents for over ten thousand years?"

"Only on the rare and unavoidable occasions that I crossed paths with a mob," the giant beetle replied.

Yaem elbowed Bill and whispered, "Don't ask him about his age. It's considered a challenge of sorts in the Farling hierarchy."

"As long as the Zarents are willing to accept them, we could just chase the Wanderers back onto the Miklat," Jorb said energetically. "I know you have a full complement of combat bots for repelling boarders, Flower. It's clear to me that the Wanderers turned our rescue into a sort of stealth boarding, and now that we know they don't have any intention of leaving, you have every right to give them a push."

"You forget that I'm representing EarthCent here," the Dollnick AI responded. "As much as I'd like to employ my bots to deport the Wanderers, eventually the Humans will bear the brunt of it. You know what's happened to species that got on the wrong side of the Wanderers in the past."

"What?" Bill asked.

"Word gets around the mobs, and more and more of them start showing up at your homeworld," Razood said. "Can you imagine billions of needy sentients on hundreds of thousands of vessels clogging up your space and making all kinds of mischief?"

"Why don't you just, you know. You all have war fleets."

"Shoot them?" Razood took a sip from the wine Jorb had brought him and asked, "Who wants to explain it to him?"

"Wanderer mobs include large numbers of members from all of the tunnel network species except for the Grenouthians, and they avoid Grenouthian space," Lume told Bill. "They don't present a threat in the military sense, they're just a terrible nuisance. But you never know when a mob might include that uncle or cousin that nobody in the family ever talks about. When it comes down to it, we're all willing to pay to keep them away as long as they don't come around looking for hand-outs too often."

"And the Stryx seem to think they serve a purpose in the greater scheme of things," Jorb added. "There are even rumors that the mobs have to clear their visits with the Stryx beforehand. It's extremely rare for a solo Wanderer vessel to put out a distress call like this, and we just got unlucky."

"But if it's not the first time, there must be some sort of history," Bill persisted. "What happened after the last rescue?"

"According to my records, the Koffern took a similar number of Wanderers on board some four thousand years ago after responding to an emergency distress call," Flower said.

"Koffern," Jorb repeated. "Why does that name sound so familiar?"

"It's the featured ship in that *Wanderer Mob* anime that was up for one of our prizes at the awards," the Grenouthian director said.

"It also stopped with the mob that came to Union Station a few years back," Razood added.

"In other words, once the Wanderers got on board, they never left," Flower said grimly. "The crew either joined up or abandoned the ship to their guests."

"You should definitely evict them by force," Bill said.

"Unless this is a test," Lume said thoughtfully.

"You think the Wanderers are testing us?"

"I think the Stryx may be testing Flower."

"My mentor did mention something about wanting to show the other Stryx how much I'd progressed," Flower said. "If this whole experience was intended as a compliment to my growth, I would have preferred an insult. But it does give us another reason to keep forcible eviction as the last option. Any other ideas?"

"Trick them," the Grenouthian said. "When the Zarents have finished their work on the Miklat, lay a trail of take-out food to the docking bay and onto your shuttles."

"I meant serious ideas. I'm beginning to think that your immersion in the anime market is leading to a distorted sense of reality."

"Maybe not take-out food, but trickery could be our best option," Yaem said. "Is there any way you could extend the LARPing environment so that while the Wanderers think they are acting out quests in virtual reality, they're actually boarding shuttles and returning to the Miklat?"

"That's a brilliant idea, but no," Flower replied. "The Stryx could do it, but it's far beyond my capacity. I can only maintain high-quality interactive holograms inside the

LARPing studios where the hardware we installed is doing most of the work."

"How about the old emergency evacuation trick?" Jorb suggested. "I know that the Fleet Vergallians have used it successfully to clear the undesirables off of their orbitals. You fake some technical problem with your radiation shielding or an impending catastrophic pile failure and announce that everybody has to move to the Miklat for safety. We know that the Wanderers are going to push to the front of the line, and you could seed in a couple of thousand Humans for show who would return on the last shuttles."

"Would the Wanderers fall for that?" Bill asked.

"It's hard to think straight when the klaxons go off and the emergency lighting comes on," Lume said. "And if Flower simulates the right disaster, one that gives us a little time for evacuation, it would only be natural that the long-time occupants would lag behind as they have more belongings to gather. The Wanderers would be motivated to leave early to claim the best cabin space on the Miklat for themselves."

"The Miklat doesn't have the capacity to take on board all of my current residents," Flower pointed out.

"But the Wanderers won't care about that. They'll say that if being rescued by strangers was good enough for them, it's good enough for the rest of us."

"Brynlan," the Grenouthian director greeted the slow-footed Verlock who had just made his way into the cafeteria. "You're missing an amusing discussion of whether we should chase the Wanderers off Flower with warbots or trick them into leaving by announcing an emergency evacuation."

"You're forgetting something," the Verlock pronounced slowly. "They are the true experts in this area."

"Evacuations?" Bill asked.

"Attempts to force them to leave," Brynlan said. "I have just returned from negotiations with the Verlock contingent, and providing we can find them a place to go, they are willing to move along for the standard proportional bribe."

"Works for me," Yaem said immediately.

"I'm sure my budget would stretch to it," Razood concurred.

"Hold on a minute," Lume said, looking worried. "You're the only Sharf living on board, Yaem. We only have a dozen or so Verlocks and at most a hundred Frunge. But there are several hundred Dollnicks working in the distribution business alone, and a head tax would run into serious coin."

"I'm sorry to keep interrupting, but what are you guys talking about?" Bill asked.

"Standard operating procedure for mobs is to outstay their welcome and only leave when they've been bought off," Flower explained. "When the Wanderers visit a Stryx station, they typically host a banquet for the ambassadors of all the species that are represented in the mob. The ambassadors are expected to make cash pledges backed by their governments, in addition to providing repair parts for ships built by their species."

"Isn't that extortion?"

"Of course," Yaem said. "Extortion is the entire Wanderer business model in a nutshell. And as the only Sharf resident on Flower, my payment to the Wanderers will just be a symbolic amount to save face for the members of my species. I could probably get away with twenty creds."

like there was a college on every other block, though none of them had many students."

"What else do Humans respect?" Brynlan asked him.

"I didn't really have any experience with high society on Earth," Bill said. "I was just a street vendor with my mom. I guess that people cared a lot about clothes. You could sort of tell what class people came from by what they were wearing."

"Maybe a bespoke suit then," Jorb suggested. "What else?"

Bill didn't want to say that he'd thankfully forgotten most of his life on Earth, so he rooted around in his memory. "People like to be seen with celebrities," he said. "I remember that all the restaurants had a display panel in the window showing images of the owner with famous people who had come in to eat."

"Did the celebrities eat for free in return for getting their picture taken?" the Grenouthian director asked.

"I don't know. But I remember now that important people also had fancy floaters, with somebody who sat in the front and opened the door for them, even though the floaters drive themselves."

"That's a good pitch for getting the Wanderers to board now that Flower has transferred ownership of the Miklat," Razood said. "Samuel just has to convince them that the Zarents are chauffeurs."

Fifteen

"You only have ten minutes before the Zarents arrive at my shipyard," Flower told Julie. "The scale model will still be here when you get back."

"But I almost have it this time. It's just the nose that doesn't want to fit right."

"Given the quality of the scale model and its lack of sentience, I suspect the problem lies elsewhere."

"There," Julie said triumphantly as the nose suddenly settled into place. "Under two hours and I didn't have to ask anybody for help. I'll just grab my purse and—Noooooo!"

"Did you hurt your back?" Flower asked. "My infrared imaging shows you frozen in an awkward position."

"I just spotted a piece on my desk that got left out," Julie reported mournfully. "It's the secondary cooling module. I remember now that I set it aside while I was putting together the primary cooling components so I wouldn't get the two subassemblies confused. Then I got caught up in replacing all of the cargo hold deck plates over the technical deck crawl space and I completely forgot about the secondary system."

"If you were repairing a ship underway and you had to shift cargo around, it would be standard procedure to remove the minimum number of deck plates required to gain access. But when you're assembling ships in a factory, you should delay installing any deck plates until you've done the final inspection and checked the cooling system for leaks."

"But it's a model, it doesn't actually function," Julie protested as she headed for the exit.

"The principle still stands," Flower said. "You've come a long way, from not being able to tell a fuel pack from a microwave oven, to easily identifying all of the primary components of a two-man trader. The final stage is mastering the order of assembly rather than trying to piece the model together like a jigsaw puzzle."

"But nobody ever taught me the order."

"That's because I wanted you to see how far you could get on your own," the Dollnick AI said. "If I had given you the manual at the beginning, you would have followed the instructions without paying close attention to the relationships between the parts and the logic of ship construction."

Julie entered the lift tube capsule and it immediately began moving without waiting for her to give a destination. "You're telling me there's a manual?"

"Of course there's a manual. I just sent it to your tab."

"Is this how Dollnicks teach engineering? Just give the students a model and tell them to take it apart and put it together again until they get it right?" Julie scowled when Flower didn't answer immediately. "I know when you hesitate like that it's because you're trying to decide whether or not to tell me something. Were you just checking with your Stryx mentor?"

"I wanted to give it a little thought, and my gamemaster duties for the LARPing studios are cutting into my spare capacity. I should have postponed building the second one until after the Wanderers left, but it seemed like the easiest way to keep them out of trouble."

"Bill told me that he and Jorb tried getting in to LARP at least three times last week but the lines were always too long," Julie said. "I don't understand how the Wanderers can spend so much time just playing in virtual reality. Don't they get tired of killing things?"

"Apparently not, but the real mystery is the enthusiasm with which they've taken to crafting."

"That means making things in the game, right?"

"Basically light manufacturing, but also gathering materials, farming, and construction," Flower said. "All of the work-related activities they refuse to engage with in real life they've embraced in virtual reality for the sake of earning in-game currency, level bonuses, and skill points. It makes no sense at all."

The capsule doors opened and Julie spotted Laura and Don waiting by the freight lift tube at the next spoke ring further up the deck. She shifted from speaking out loud to subvocalizing and began walking across the largely empty factory floor.

"So the Wanderers are willing to work as long as they're playing a game?" Julie asked. "That's one of the weirdest—hey, you changed the subject on me. What happened to answering my question about how Dollnicks teach engineering?"

"Learning the names of spaceship parts and how they fit together isn't exactly engineering," Flower said after another hesitation. "Do you remember what the Zarent chief engineer told you about their little apprentices and Sharf two-man traders? It's the same with Dollnicks, though we use colony ship models."

Julie stopped short, and when she started walking again, her stride was stiffer than before. "You're saying I just spent weeks struggling to do something that Dollnick children learn on their own before they even start their formal schooling."

"Don't be angry, Julie. If you had attended a nursery school where there were scale models of spaceships to play with, I'm sure you would have mastered the fundamentals in no time. It's not a competition, you know."

"Isn't it? You're always telling me that interspecies business competition is a substitute for war."

"The Zarents will be arriving in thirty seconds."

"We'll finish this later," Julie said, and then jogged the rest of the way to the freight lift tube.

She barely had time to greet Laura and Don before the doors slid open and a half-dozen Zarents on unicycles pedaled out. They were accompanied by twice their number of four-armed maintenance bots that were a bit smaller and blockier than Flower's standard model, but despite the obsolete design, they were as shiny and free of dings as if they had just been manufactured.

"Greetings," the chief engineer said, tilting his unicycle towards the reception committee. "Flower invited us to test a few of the bots she's reconditioned while we help you put together your assembly line."

"Thank you for volunteering your time," Laura said.

"We did a barter deal," the Zarent informed her honestly. "And I want to congratulate you on the adequacy of the work you performed on the Miklat."

"Uh, thank you," Laura said, doing a little head bob in response to the Zarent's tilt. "None of us had any experience working on old Dollnick colony ships so we just did what Flower told us."

"The ability to follow instructions is the first rotation on the path to enlightenment," the chief engineer told them. "The lift tube capsule will be returning with more of my engineering staff and another batch of bots in a few minutes, so why don't you show us where you want the assembly line."

"Don't you need to see all of the machinery first?" Don asked.

"We'll sort it out as we go. Flower provided us with the seller's imaging of the assembly line before it was broken down for shipping. The Sharf practice a form of just-in-time production where each station on the assembly line is responsible for manufacturing the parts it contributes to the finished product."

"Do you mean that the machines that stamp out hull parts are located right next to the assembly line station where they're welded together?" Don asked. "I worked on an assembly line in a manufactured home factory one winter, but all of the parts and subassemblies arrived on trucks from other locations."

"Sounds terribly inefficient," the Zarent said. He pivoted on his unicycle to look in the direction that one of his engineers was pointing with a tentacle. "Fourth Engineer Miklat tells me that the white tape on the deck corresponds to the rough dimensions of the assembly line in the Sharf imagery."

"Don and I used those images for the layout, but we aren't very confident in the results," Laura said. "Our next step was going to be arranging all of the parts we have—" she waved her arm at the mounds of Sharf machine components surrounding the lift tube, "—in accordance to where they appear in the pictures, but then Flower decided our time would be better spent learning something about repair work on the Miklat."

"I approve of your strategy and I'm saddened that you were unable to pursue it while engaging in work that we left undone," the Zarent said, and the whole group of engineers dipped their unicycles in apology. "Now, which end do you want the ships to come off?"

"We hadn't gotten that far yet. To tell you the truth, we're a little worried about whether the finished ships will even fit the vertical space in here."

"But we assumed Flower already knows they will or she wouldn't be doing any of this," Don added.

Everybody turned to look at Julie.

"Just a minute." She pointed at her ear and subvoced, "What do I tell them?"

"The ships will come off the assembly line lying on their sides, and there's ample room between decks," Flower replied. "We discussed all of this last week and you said you understood."

"I was trying to figure out how the fuel pack connected to the main drive in the scale model and I was just agreeing so you'd stop distracting me," Julie subvoced back, and then continued out loud. "Flower says that you'll assemble the ships lying on their sides."

"But unless there are different capsules for the freight lift tubes than the ones we've been using to deliver cabins to the writers colony, we'll never get the finished ships out of here without cutting them in half," Don said. "Is there a larger capacity lift tube, or an empty shaft somewhere else on the deck?"

"All of the decks have full-height exterior hatches at the midpoints between the spokes," Julie said, dredging her memory for details of the plan Flower had laid out. "That's why if you look at a colony ship end on, even if the transparent parts of the hull are all lit up from the inside, you'll see dark lines in the same pattern as the spokes."

"So are we going to have to evacuate the deck every time we're ready to launch a ship?" Laura asked.

"Flower has an atmosphere retention field in place around her whole structure, and she'll have a portable backup field that functions like an airlock installed before the first launch. So I guess it makes sense to have the finished ships come off the assembly line as near to the end of the ship as possible."

"In line with the midpoint between spokes," the chief engineer added. "That's exactly where I would have put it myself for structural reasons. So let me and my crew bot up and we'll get started."

"Bot up?" Don asked.

"In designing us, the Farlings had to make many tradeoffs, and one of them was giving us a small form factor so we can work in geometrically complex spaces. While we are much stronger than Humans on a size-adjusted basis, moving massive objects with tentacle power alone is not our specialty. We all practice with servomechanisms from a young age, and Flower has graciously programmed these bots with a servo-mode."

The Zarents set down their unicycles, and then moving on their tentacles, approached and mounted the floating bots. What Julie had taken to be the blocky external battery of a previous generation actually unfolded into a servo controller. The little aliens slipped into the saddles and inserted a tentacle into each of eight flexible tubes. Then they performed some calibration exercises, matching the movement of the mounted bot's arms to that of their individual tentacles, and then repeated the calibration process for a companion bot without a rider.

"Eight tentacles to fully control two bots," Don said, looking envious. "Pretty slick. But how can you see what the second bot is doing?"

"In addition to telepathy, we have a biological interface for electromagnetic radiation in the useful part of the communications spectrum," the chief engineer explained. "Flower has equipped the bots with transceivers that operate in our sweet spot."

Six more Zarents accompanied by a dozen bots emerged from the lift tube, and this group immediately fanned out among the mounds of Sharf equipment.

"I've instructed my junior engineering staff to start putting together the basic magnetic levitation conveyer system that the assembly line is built around," the chief engineer continued. "My team will begin building the manufacturing stations." He seemed just as comfortable riding a floating bot as he had been pedaling his unicycle, and Julie found herself having to break the occasional step to keep up.

"Will we be getting in the way if we watch?" Laura asked.

"Not at all," the Zarent assured her. "I only hope you aren't so bored that you fall asleep. When moving and assembling massive pieces of machinery, the secret is to go slowly."

"We had an expression in the building trade—measure twice, cut once," Don said. "We still ended up with a lot of waste. Do the Zarents have any sayings like that?"

"If at first you don't succeed, your initial plan was defective," the chief engineer recited in a sing-song through his speaking device. "We're trained from an early age not to waste our efforts in bumbling towards a solution."

After that, the three humans hung back and watched the twenty-four bots controlled by the twelve Zarent engineers as they deftly began fitting together the components of the assembly line. Julie witnessed the two bots under the chief engineer's control joining the halves of what looked like some sort of motor that had metal alignment dowels as long as her thumbs protruding from one side of the casting. No last-minute adjustments were necessary—the bots approached each other with the heavy motor halves held firmly in four arms, and the alignment dowels slid right into the holes.

"I couldn't do that with a single bolt and a washer in one try," Don muttered to the two women. "I hope operating this equipment doesn't require that level of hand-eye coordination."

"Don't worry about it," a scratchy voice behind them said, and they turned to see that the Sharf spy had joined them. "The Zarents are in a class of their own when it comes to fine control over their appendages."

"Yaem," Julie greeted the skeletal alien. "What are you doing here?"

"Dropping off this tab with my translation of the operating instructions for the assembly line. Flower supplied the tab so I don't need it back."

"You did the translation yourself? I thought Flower only needed your help with the old engineer's handwriting."

"It was no more work to do both at the same time, and it gave me a chance to improve my technical Humanese," Yaem said. "It's odd how your species has a different vocabulary for each specialty rather than using the same words for everything. I suppose it has to do with professional guilds protecting their turf."

"But different professions require different vocabularies," Laura protested. "I grew up working in my father's shipyard, and my friends used to interrupt me all the time to ask what words meant because they just didn't encounter them in their own lives. Even the names of the tools were all foreign to them."

"It's understandable for unique tools and components to require proper names, but it's another thing to use parallel words to describe the same characteristic or action," Yaem said. "M793qK once complained to me that when he had to write up a medical case history for a legal action back on Earth, he needed to substitute words from a dead language to get the authorities to take him seriously." The Sharf's eyestalks suddenly stretched, and Julie turned to see what looked like a swarm of bots bringing together the pieces of a large machine. "That looks dangerous," Yaem commented.

"Some type of progressive stamping machine, I think," Don said. "I've been reading up on metal forming, and you can't stamp complex shapes in a single operation. Even heavy sheet metal can rip like paper or get stretched too thin in the wrong places."

"I'll drop in and take a look when it's all set up, but I've got to get back to WandererCon," Yaem said.

Julie grabbed the skeletal alien's arm. "You're kidding me, right?"

"It's not an official con, just what I'm calling it," the Sharf said. "Flower is pulling out all the stops to keep the Wanderers occupied, and it turns out that they're willing to attend entertainment-themed panel discussions, even if it's just to heckle the Human experts. Guess who got stuck coming up with a program?"

"Better you than me," Julie said, releasing the arm.

"And I hope you're capturing images of the assembly process so you'll know how everything went together after the Zarents are gone," Yaem said over his shoulder on his way to the exit. "You never know when information like that may come in handy."

"Oh, fudge," Laura said and looked at Don, who shrugged. "Julie?"

"I didn't even think of it," Julie admitted and pointed at her ear. "Is there any chance you're recording all of this, Flower?" she subvoced.

"Yes," the ship's AI replied. "I have optical cameras installed throughout the manufacturing space for quality control and safety enforcement. Watching the Zarent engineers working is a genuine treat. Once the assembly line is up and running, I'll send all of the video to the Grenouthian director and ask him to create a documentary about the birth of Flower Shipyards. It could turn into a major source of free publicity. Please pay close attention and ask questions today because the director will likely want to conduct interviews for a voiceover to go with the video."

"Flower has it," Julie told Laura and Don. "And she wants us to pay attention and ask the Zarents questions so we can get a documentary out of this and she can use it to generate sales leads."

"I'll follow around the engineers setting up the basic assembly line," Don volunteered. "I'm more of a structural guy than a machine guy."

"I'm going over there," Laura said, pointing at where the largest machine was coming together not far from where they stood. "I think that one is some kind of automated welding rig that fabricates a hull from stamped pieces."

"I guess I'll stick with the chief engineer," Julie said, and then subvoced, "How much of this assembly line is automated? If Laura is right, it sounds like the machines do most of the work."

"The chassis fabrication is largely automated, but the machines require attendants," Flower replied. "Mass production of hulls for small ships is one of the few manufacturing activities that nobody tries—oh, not again."

"What's wrong?"

"I'll be right back."

Julie spent the next five minutes jogging around after the chief engineer and his pair of robots before Flower spoke again. "While I was busy watching the Zarents work, the Wanderers cleaned out another dungeon. I'm going to have to stop recycling stories copied from the professional LARPing league and start making up my own. It's been almost like the players are using cheat codes."

Sixteen

Bill followed Flower's directions to the Human Empire's headquarters and was surprised to find the waiting area full of aliens. He thought he had walked into the wrong office and was about to leave when he noticed a Drazen waving his tentacle and realized that it was Jorb. It took another minute just to work his way through the crush, but he eventually made it to where several of the spies from the cafeteria had formed a cordon in front of a closed door.

"What's going on?" Bill asked. "Flower told me this is the Human Empire's headquarters and that Samuel needed my help with something."

"You're her new Human food expert, and the negotiator for the Wanderers is insisting on dealing exclusively with Humans."

"Harry knows more about food than I ever will," Bill protested. "I've only been working part-time in the research kitchen for a year."

"Harry stormed out," Lume said, adding a mirthful whistle even while he corralled a Wanderer who was trying to slip into Samuel's office. "His wife, Irene, works as a greeter at the amusement park and bazaar. It seems that Wanderers have been tormenting her with questions about how to get to places that are right in front of them."

"Huh?"

"It's the Wanderer way of making a person out to be a sucker," the Dollnick explained. "Their goal is to get somebody to take the request for directions seriously."

"Like if you asked Lume right now how to get to Samuel's office," Razood chimed in. "Harry says that his wife likes to think the best of people but that leaves her vulnerable to these sorts of pranks. Samuel asked him here to explain the best way to store Harry's Fruitcakes for the maximum shelf life, but when the negotiator laughed at Irene's troubles, Harry got mad and left."

"I guess I would have left too," Bill said. "But do they really need me to explain how to store an alcohol-soaked fruitcake? We include instructions in the box."

"It's their way of doing business," Jorb said. "They talk and talk until you can't keep track of what's been said, and then they pounce. Be careful in there."

Bill took a step towards the door and then halted. "But what are you guys and all of those aliens doing here?"

"Even though the Humans on the Miklat made up just a couple percent of the population, the other species all decided to join their negotiations. They must have found out Samuel is so new at this that he got his job title from a reporter just a few weeks ago."

"What does that mean, joining their negotiations?"

"It's a standard tunnel network procedure," Lume explained. "Whenever multiple species are involved in multiparty negotiations, they have the option to choose a single representative to settle the matter according to the laws and practice of that species. Typically the Wanderers would have given that responsibility to their most populous subgroup, but they went with their senior Human because they judge Samuel and the Human Empire to be the softest target."

"Then I'm not sure I want to go in there," Bill said. "I could say the wrong thing and cost everybody a fortune."

"Vivian is in there too and she'll stop you before you can do any damage," Jorb said. "Just don't make any promises of any kind and no harm can come of talking."

The office door slid open and an old man stepped out, closely followed by a middle-aged woman who apparently served as his aide. As soon as he appeared, the alien Wanderers all started making noise, stamping their feet, slapping their bellies, and generally acting like rowdy fans at a sporting event. The old man acknowledged his supporters and then set off across the room, his aide supporting his elbow.

"What's happening now?" Bill asked.

"Bathroom break," Lume told him. "All of us think it's strange how old Humans revert to infancy when it comes to their capacity to hold bodily fluids. He should probably go see M793qK."

"It's a good time for you to go in," Razood said and gave his former apprentice a gentle push towards the office door. "Tell Samuel to stay strong."

Vivian greeted him as he entered. "Bill. It's good to see a friendly face."

"Yes, come in," Samuel said, motioning with his hand. "Sit next to Vivian."

"I was just going to tell them about the best way to preserve fruitcakes and get out of your hair," Bill said.

"No, you have to stay," Vivian told him. "We need every advantage we can get and these Wanderers must spend half of their lives negotiating with each other. Ronald is a tough customer."

"With you here, we'll have them outnumbered," Samuel explained. "It's a psychological advantage, you don't even have to say anything. Just try to look interested and nod your head from time to time."

"How about the fruitcakes?" Bill asked.

"That was just a delaying tactic on Ronald's part and he's already moved on from it. We've been negotiating for three hours already and I haven't been able to pin him down on what he wants. It's incredibly frustrating."

"If he won't tell you what he wants, why is he even here?"

"To get the maximum he can," Vivian explained. "The Wanderers practice a form of negotiation where they try to get the other party, the Human Empire in this case, to make the first offer. Then Ronald will treat that as the starting point and start piling on demands."

"So my job is to get him to tell me what he wants first, without letting on what we're willing to give him," Samuel said.

Bill glanced at the door to make sure it was still closed and asked, "What are you willing to give him?"

"I don't have anything to give. It comes down to what Flower is willing to pay, but the Wanderers won't negotiate with artificial intelligence. The crazy thing is that it's—"

The door slid open and Ronald shuffled back in, accompanied by his aide and a young man who looked like he spent eight hours a day working out in a gym.

"You added somebody, I get to add somebody," the old Wanderer said. "It's only fair."

"I can leave," Bill offered, jumping up.

"Suit yourself, but my athletic supporter remains," Ronald said, and gave a snort. "So where were we, young McAllister?"

"My title is First Administrator," Samuel told him for what felt like the fiftieth time.

"I once met a First Among Equals, as Horten pirate chiefs call themselves. A very colorful gentleman. He had a tattoo of a giant—"

"You told that story two hours ago and I didn't appreciate it the first time," Vivian interrupted. "Perhaps you're getting tired and you want to call it a day."

"Oh, no," Ronald said. "I haven't even hit my stride yet. Why we storytellers have contests that go on weeks at a time. At a recent gathering on the Miklat, I placed second only to the senior Verlock storyteller in the just-shoot-me category."

"Excuse me?" Samuel asked.

"You know, a competition to tell pointless stories that go on forever until the audience is ready to put an end to their own lives to escape. I once bored a Frunge into a catatonic state resembling petrification."

"I don't understand how bringing about my paralysis will help you get what you want. In fact, if I die, the only official representative of the Human Empire left to negotiate with you will be my wife, and I doubt she'll be any more sympathetic to your cause."

"I won't be," Vivian promised grimly.

"You said you could get us a new gym," the muscular young Wanderer spoke up suddenly. "The Miklat was the only ship in the mob without the variable magnetic monopole technology that can create any resistance down to the weight of a sodium atom. I was too embarrassed to compete at other mob's pose-downs because their lifters all laughed at me for training with free weights."

"Now there's something I'm sure we can help you with," Samuel jumped in before the old storyteller could react. "One of our goals for the next century is to set up a ministry of sports to represent humanity at inter-species competitions. I'd like to hear your ideas about—"

"Out!" Ronald bellowed at the young athlete. Then he pointed at Bill and added, "You go with him."

"Not so fast," Vivian said. "You just told us that your additional negotiator could stay even if Bill left, so the same must apply for our side."

"I'll bring somebody else in," the Wanderer said and began whispering instructions to his aide.

"I don't think I can allow that," Samuel told him, pushing his newfound advantage. "If a gym kitted out with Verlock technology is your only demand for returning to the Miklat, we'll get right on it. Vivian, can you check into pricing for exercise equipment?"

"Now hold it right there," Ronald said, his folksy manner suddenly replaced with steely resolve. "We're talking about the outfitting and provisioning of a home for almost twenty-thousand inhabitants from a dozen species and you're trying to buy me off with a gym? We haven't even discussed this erroneous idea the Zarents seem to have about the ownership of the Miklat."

"I don't understand what you mean. You abandoned the ship and it was granted to Flower as salvage under tunnel network law. Flower chose to barter it to the Zarents in return for help with an engineering project of her own. The status of the Miklat isn't on the table."

"Then we have nothing to talk about," Ronald declared, rising from his chair.

"I guess not," Samuel said, picking up a tab from his desk and pretending to be absorbed in its contents.

"Don't let the door hit you and your friends on the way out," Vivian called after them.

After the three Wanderers left the office, Bill asked, "What just happened? The last thing I heard, Flower was so desperate to get rid of them that she was considering Jorb's idea to force them off the ship with bots."

"This is the third time Ronald's walked out of the negotiations this morning," Vivian said. "It's getting rather monotonous, actually. Is he doing anything different this time, Flower?"

"He's going over to talk with the representatives from the other species again. The former captain is asking him how it's going, and he's saying that he has you eating out of the palm of his hand. Now they're talking about plans for a victory party, and the Frunge is saying something about returning to the mob in time for—this is interesting."

"What's interesting?" Samuel asked.

"They weren't kicked out of the mob after all. This whole thing was a ploy to get their ship fixed up by requiring a rescue. They were willing to risk losing the Miklat as salvage because they just assumed that getting the ship back would be a necessary part of any deal to get rid of them."

"But we can't return the ship since you already gave it to the Zarents," Bill said.

"Exactly. We've broken their playbook."

"What else are they saying?" Vivian asked.

"Ronald asked about lunch, and the Drazen suggested ordering pizza from the food court. Then they started discussing toppings, and the Verlock wants his with the crust burned. Now they're arguing over whose turn it is to pay, and Ronald is telling them to charge everything to the Human Empire headquarters."

"They can't do that," Samuel said, jumping up.

"Let it go, Sam," Vivian said. "We'll just confiscate one of the pizzas when it gets here."

"Are you sure you want me to stay?" Bill asked.

"Absolutely. We weren't making any progress at all before you arrived."

"And you're making progress now?"

"We have him on the run with the gym thing," Vivian said. "When he comes back in, I bet he puts a real proposal on the table for the first time."

"This isn't like any of the negotiation workshops I took at the Open University, or anything my mom ever told me about either," Samuel said, sinking back into his seat. "The only part of it I understand is why the other species picked Ronald to represent them."

"He seems like a tough negotiator," Bill said.

"Yes, but some of those aliens live more than ten times as long as we do and have more experience than Ronald or I ever will. The reason they chose him to do the negotiating is that they're accustomed to running affinity scheme extortion rackets going after their own species, but there aren't enough aliens living on board Flower to extort anything worthwhile. For example, the Miklat carried thousands of Vergallian Wanderers, but I doubt Flower has even fifty living on board. Even if Flower's Vergallians coughed up a hundred creds each, it wouldn't buy the Miklat's Vergallians lunch."

"It's less like diplomacy than a business deal," Vivian said. "The Wanderers know they can't stay on board forever, but they want to get the maximum for leaving. And they won't negotiate directly with Flower because she's artificial intelligence."

"And smarter than they are," Samuel added.

"Could you get a neutral third party to help, like a judge or something?" Bill asked.

"Too risky. The Wanderers are experts at bribery."

The door slid open and Ronald returned with his aide. The weightlifter was conspicuous by his absence.

"All right," the old Wanderer said. "Lunch will be here soon, but I'd like to get this little negotiation out of the way first, so why don't you put your cards on the table?"

"Me?" Samuel said, affecting an innocent look. "I don't hold any cards. I still don't have a clue what exactly it is you expect me to do for you."

"Not you as an individual, you as the embodiment of the Human Empire. As the First whatever-you-called-yourself, you are our only official rep—"

"I keep telling you that I'm not," Samuel interrupted. "You can't just declare yourself a member of somebody else's empire and expect them to go along with it. Sure, you're human, but there are billions of humans roaming around out here, and less than twenty percent of them live in the sovereign human communities that make up the initial membership of the Human Empire. And I've explained a hundred times that the empire hasn't even entered the planning stage yet. We're still working on the broad outlines."

Ronald thumped the top of the expensive desk. "Nice office furniture for a broad outline."

"My wife paid for it out of her own pocket."

"Then I believe the first thing we need to clear up is this misconception of yours that you don't represent us," the Wanderer said. "I just finished discussing the details with my colleagues and we've agreed to declare the Miklat a sovereign human community."

"You can't," Samuel said, resisting the urge to bury his face in his hands. "Humans make up less than two percent of the Miklat's population."

"As is the case on many open worlds with sovereign human communities."

"That's different. Those are planets. The Miklat is just a ship."

Ronald's aide, who had been thumbing her way through something on a tab during this exchange, showed the results to her principle, who broke into a wide smile. "Actually, under the Wanderer Exclusion Amendment to the tunnel network treaty, our mobs were granted the status of rogue planets."

"Doesn't change a thing," Samuel insisted. "Even Flower had to go through an application process to become a member of the Conference of Sovereign Human Communities, and currently, that's the only path to getting on the Human Empire list. Besides, I don't believe for a minute that you really want to join our empire, or any other empire. You're just grasping at straws that will make it harder to kick you off Flower."

"So you admit you want to evict us from our rightful refuge," Ronald said triumphantly.

"Of course we want you to leave, that's what this is all about. Did you think I was trying to sell you a subscription to the Galactic Free Press?"

"I already get the free edition with the advertising, thank you very much. So now that you've finally shown your cards—"

"Which you've known all along," Vivian interjected.

"—let me tell you the minimum I'm willing to accept to return to the Miklat."

"Please do," Samuel said.

The door slid open and Lume stuck his head in the office. "Pizza's here and it's going fast. Do you want me to grab you anything?"

"There should be a party-sized Mediterranean Special earmarked for the negotiating room," Ronald said. "Unless one of you objects?" he added, looking at Samuel, Vivian, and Bill in turn. "Excellent. Let's take a brief lunch break, and I'm sure everything will look brighter on a full stomach."

Somebody handed Lume a pizza box the size of a small table, and he relayed it to Ronald's aide, who placed it on Samuel's desk. She opened the box, removed slices for her boss and herself, and then closed the lid, keeping her free hand on the top.

"What are you trying to pull now?" Vivian demanded. "We know you charged that pizza to the Human Empire, and there's enough in that box for ten people."

"Wait a sec, Viv," Samuel said, and placed his own hand on top of the box, next to the aide's. "I think we agreed to make an effort to wrap this negotiation up before lunch. I realize that you are a master storyteller, Ronald, and I concede that you can talk us all into a coma, but I don't see how that moves things forward. As one human being to another, I'm asking you, please, just tell me what you want."

"Isn't it obvious?" the old man said. "A storyteller is judged by the size of his audience, and humans were so outnumbered by the other species on the Miklat that my place was permanently at the foot of the table."

"So you want a way to show the aliens that people respect your abilities," Samuel said. "I'm sure we could come up with something. How would a theatre with an audience of five thousand strike you?"

"I was thinking more along the lines of publishing contracts for all of the senior story tellers," he said with a sly glance in Vivian's direction.

"Oh, no," she responded. "I don't know where you're getting your information from, but my mother only publishes alien romances in translation."

"Then I guess I'll have to bore you into a coma, assuming you don't starve first."

"Wait," Bill said, his eyes on the pizza box. "My fiancée is apprenticed to a famous author who helped start a writers colony on board. I'll bet they know lots of publishers."

"I've heard of engagements that drag on forever and nothing ever comes of them," Ronald said dismissively. "How do I know this alleged fiancée is committed enough to use her connections to help you?"

"Help me? She'd be helping you. I'm going to spend the rest of my life with Julie and the only reason we aren't already married is because I just started at the Open University and she has a new job working for Flower full time."

"I'm not interested in some deal where I maybe hear back from you next week. When will you talk to her?"

"As soon as I get home. Julie lives across the hall from me, and if she's working late and I fall asleep, the worst case is that I'll see her for our morning calisthenics."

"If you moved in together I wouldn't be stuck waiting," Roland grumbled. He lifted his chin at his assistant, who took her hand off the top of the box and lifted the lid. "I believe we're finally making progress."

Seventeen

"Could you give me a hand with this, Jack?" Maureen asked the president of the independent living cooperative. "These overhead compartments were designed for Dollnicks and I can't even reach the touch panel."

Jack jumped up from his seat and stood on his toes to trigger the overhead compartment to open. Maureen handed him the flat, rectangular parcel, and he slid it in, hoping he'd be able to reach the edge to pull it out again.

"Seems like a lot of work to go to for a three-minute trip," Harry commented from his seat on the other side of the shuttle's aisle. "You couldn't fold whatever it is and fit it under the seat? That's where Irene stows the camera she borrows from the Grenouthian director to document our trips."

"It's a bronze plaque," Maureen explained. "We'll take a group picture when we're done and put it in next year's brochure for Flower's Paradise. Maybe even on the cover."

"Where did you get a bronze plaque made?" Harry asked.

"Razood, the blacksmith in Colonial Jeevesburg, did it for the cost of materials. He said he hadn't worked in bronze since the Frunge equivalent of high school and it brought back memories." She sat down next to Harry, raised the footrest intended for Dollnick children, and fastened her safety restraints. "It seems like months since we went on a group outing."

"That's because everywhere we've stopped this circuit has been refusing to let us land for fear that some Wanderers would sneak onto their worlds or habitats," Jack said. "I'm just glad that our new members see the humor of the situation rather than accusing us of false advertising."

"Welcome to Flower's Transportation Services," the Dollnick AI announced over the shuttle's public address system. "Our trip to the Miklat today will take two minutes and fourteen seconds. I will be accelerating all the way, except for the time it takes me to flip at the midpoint, but weightlessness will last for less than five seconds. Please remain in your seats for the duration."

"Why do I always feel like I need to use the bathroom when she makes one of those announcements?" Harry whispered to his wife as the shuttle left the docking bay at Flower's core.

"It's psychological," Irene said. "Just be glad it's not like taking a suborbital flight back on Earth where we had to sit in the plane on the tarmac forever before taking off or after landing. I never understood why they do that."

"We only flew the two times, for our honeymoon and on our twentieth anniversary, so maybe we just got unlucky," Harry said. He leaned forward a bit to speak around his wife. "Dave. You used to fly all the time. Was sitting on the ground for hours before the flight normal?"

"A few decades ago, we probably spent more time on the ground than in the air, though it depended on the airport," the former salesman replied. "Sometimes there were mechanical problems or issues with the catering or cleaning crews, but a lot of delays were caused by weather. When planes are coming from all over, a thunderstorm a thousand miles away can mess up everybody's flight schedules because disruptions cascade through the whole system. These days delays of any kind are really rare."

"What changed?" Irene asked.

"Alien technology," Dave explained. "The airports started buying the same sorts of systems that the advanced species use for their suborbital flights, and then somebody told me they contracted with the AI who handles the tunnel network traffic for Earth to do all of the flight scheduling for the whole planet."

"A Stryx is scheduling Earth's air traffic?" Harry asked in disbelief.

"Not a Stryx, one of the AI's that works for them managing tunnel network exits," Dave said. "You know that artificial intelligences have to earn a living just like everybody else, at least if they want spending money."

"Wooooo-hooooo!" a chorus of voices cried during the brief Zero-G flip, the unofficial battle cry of independent living cooperative outings.

"I talked to Dewey about it once, and he said that traffic control is considered a plum assignment by AI because it combines responsibility with problem-solving," Dave continued. "The more complicated the job, the more they enjoy it."

"You seem very chipper today," Irene observed. "Didn't you say something at breakfast about Flower insisting that you get a check-up before letting you come on this field trip?"

"M793qK says that thanks to him, I now have the body of a sixty-nine-year-old," Dave said proudly. "When I had my first evaluation when I joined the cooperative, he said I had the body of an eighty-six-year-old."

"And you're what? Seventy-eight?" Harry asked.

"I'm going with sixty-nine from now on. The doc says that birthdays are irrelevant, he doesn't even know his. The important thing is the age of your body and I'm going to start using the new number. If I stick with the diet and the exercise, I might even get back to being middle-aged."

"Did M793qK tell you that?" Irene asked.

"No, and he said I was old and foolish if I thought that was the case, but I've always believed it's important to set goals."

"Thank you for choosing Flower's Transportation Services," the Dollnick AI announced over the public address system. "We hope you had a pleasant trip and that you enjoy your outing. Please remember that the Miklat is undergoing repairs, so no jumping in the lift tube capsules."

"That sounded a bit ominous," Irene said to Harry as they undid their safety restraints and folded up the footrests. "Do you need to use the bathroom before we disembark?"

"No, I'm fine now. You were right, it's psychological."

Jack stood by the shuttle's front exit with his hands raised and called out, "All right, everybody. You know the drill. We'll be handing out location bracelets as you disembark so that Flower will be able to find you if you wander off and get lost, but please practice the buddy system and it won't become an issue. The Zarents have asked us to limit the number of passengers per lift tube capsule to eight, so it's going to take a while for all three hundred and twenty-four of us to get up to the ag deck. If you have any problems finding the right place, Flower is monitoring the lift tube system, so just ask for her by name and she'll take over from the Miklat's speech recognition controller."

"Do we get gloves?" somebody called out. "I didn't bring any."

"Everything we need is already waiting for us on the ag deck," Jack told them. "And make sure your magnetic cleats are enabled because we weigh even less here than on Flower's docking deck."

After all of the cooperative members filed out of the shuttle, took a bracelet, and headed for the lift tubes, Jack found Maureen waiting with Nancy.

"Didn't you forget something?" Maureen asked.

"Oh, sorry," Jack said and reentered the shuttle to retrieve the plaque. After opening the overhead bin, he couldn't reach the package, which had slid further back. He took a quick look around to make sure nobody was watching and then carefully climbed onto the seat and reclaimed the prize.

"Thank you," Maureen said, accepting the package back from Jack. "The plaque is lighter here than it was on Flower, but I don't understand why. I thought the two ships were spinning at the same rate."

"They are, but the Miklat's interior dimensions are all smaller than Flower's," Nancy explained. "A smaller core radius means less angular acceleration and lower weight."

"So even at the outermost deck, there won't be anywhere near Earth's gravity?"

"The Miklat's inhabitants are practically all aliens," Jack said. "Earth weight isn't their ideal, though most of the tunnel network species are comfortable within a fairly close range. Both of the Dollnick ag worlds I worked on were around ninety percent of Earth normal, but I've heard that the Verlocks prefer something closer to a hundred and twenty percent."

"And the Zarents will increase the rotation rate after Flower cuts them loose," Nancy added as they joined the line for the lift tubes. "That the two ships are spinning at the same speed is just an artifact of the Dollnick towing system."

"I know that you were a teacher, but how do you understand so much about space engineering?" Maureen asked.

"I was curious, so I checked with Flower," Nancy said. "Learning is all about curiosity in the end. My favorite students were the ones who asked the questions I couldn't answer."

"That's one of the things that attracted me to her," Jack said, placing an arm around his petite wife and pulling her closer. "There's not a hint of insecurity about Nancy."

It took nearly twenty minutes for the group from Flower's Paradise to reassemble on the ag deck where a Zarent on a floating sled guided them to a freshly plowed area. Long tubes of a black material that might have been plastic ran in straight lines, like furrows, their lengths broken at regular intervals by a loop. Several of Flower's maintenance bots were just finishing breaking out what looked like a forest of seedlings from shipping containers, along with large boxes of gloves and trowels.

Irene guided the floating immersive camera with the practiced hand motions she had developed in over a year of acting as the cooperative's cameraman. In addition to capturing images of all of the retirees who had volunteered to plant trees for the Wanderers, she made sure to get a good shot of the Zarent who introduced herself as Chief Agronomist Miklat.

Supervising a crew planting seedlings was a job that Jack was eminently qualified for, though he had never before dealt with a group of laborers whose minimum age was sixty-five. Flower had supplied five thousand seedlings, including apples, peaches, pears, plums, and oranges, and despite the occasional complaint about creaky knees, it took less than four hours for the three hundred plus volunteers to get the little trees all planted and the pots stacked up for return.

"Don't we have to water them right away?" somebody asked.

"Those loops in the tubing where we planted all the seedlings aren't just there for spacing, it's Dollnick drip irrigation," Jack explained. "The reason I had you position the seedlings all the way to the side of the loop near the main is because there's a secondary system optimized for watering new plants. As they grow into trees, the trunks will self-center the loops, and the main system that pumps through the large outer tube will take over."

"Everybody gather together around the plaque so Irene can get some good images of us," Maureen called out in a loud voice. "No, don't take your gloves off or straighten up your clothes. It's better that we all look like we've been working. And remember to smile."

"What's it say on that plaque anyway?" Harry called from the edge of the group where he'd ended up.

"This orchard planted by the volunteers from Flower's Paradise with fruit tree seedlings donated by Flower Agricultural Services as a gift to the Miklat," Maureen recited from memory.

"Come on everybody, smile," Irene coaxed them.

"We could all say 'cheese,'" Jack suggested.

"Or 'catering,'" Harry said, pointing to where Flower's maintenance bots were now setting up tables.

"Isn't it going to take years before these trees produce any fruit?" one of the volunteers asked Jack. "What are the Wanderers going to eat until then, and what have they been living on until now?"

"You're right that fruit trees take a few years to mature, but keep in mind that we can only see a tiny fraction of this ag deck from where we're standing, and there may be more than one," Jack said.

"And there were only twenty thousand Wanderers on the Miklat when they abandoned ship," Nancy added. "According to Flower, the capacity of this generation of colony ships was a tenth of her own, but that's still a half a million Dollnicks, so they were running under four percent capacity. That means if just four percent of the ag deck space was producing, they could have gotten by without problems."

Under Maureen's direction, Irene captured enough video for a whole series of commercials, and then the hungry retirees all descended on the picnic lunch. Bill arrived and began setting up a table at the end of the row with test products from the All Species Cookbook, and some of the more adventurous retirees who had already eaten their fill of sandwiches and fresh fruit queued up to see what was on offer.

"Why do you have nose plugs in?" Harry asked his assistant, whose nostrils were clearly stuffed with filtering devices.

"The smell made me sick," Bill admitted in a nasal tone. "I don't understand how people can eat this stuff."

"With crackers," said a grey-haired woman who neither of them recognized. She took the silver cheese knife from the platter and cut herself a thick chunk of the Limburger, then smeared it on the whole-wheat cracker. "Are you sure you won't try it?" she asked playfully, extending it to Bill.

"I don't get paid enough for this," he said, ducking away. "I should have run as soon as M793qK started explaining the stinky scale all the aliens use."

"That's a new one to me," Harry said. "Where does the Limburger rate?"

"He said it's a ninety-seven, but the scale goes from sixty-four to a hundred and twenty," Bill said. "Why can't the aliens start all of their scales at zero like normal people?"

"This is yummy," the grey-haired woman said, loading another cracker. "What else do you have?"

Bill couldn't help grimacing while removing a large piece of prickly fruit from a cooler. "It's called durian, and it smells so bad that M793qK said even Drazen Foods won't export it."

"That doesn't sound very likely," Harry said. "The Drazens love strong tastes and odors."

"They probably didn't want it in their facility because they worry about the dogs," Nancy said, coming up to watch the fruit-cutting operation. "I toured the main Drazen Foods factory on Earth, which is practically a city in itself, and they also have a perfume operation with dogs doing the quality control. One of their biggest exports is hot peppers, and the dogs won't go near that building because their noses are so sensitive."

"Watch what you're doing or you'll cut off a finger," Harry barked at Bill when the young man attempted to avert his head while cutting open the fruit. "Oh, that is pungent."

"This is my lucky day," the grey-haired woman said. "How are you serving it?"

Bill reached back into the cooler and pulled out a large jar of tongue depressors. "I didn't really know what it goes with, but Flower said that the pulp is creamy, and the Doc gave me these to use as one-time spoons."

The woman took a tongue depressor, loaded it with the yellowish pulp, and closed her eyes after licking it clean. "It tastes like custard, with a hint of almonds and cream cheese."

Nancy scooped out a sample with a tongue depressor, flinched at the smell, but took a small taste. "This is lovely," she said. "I wonder if Flower could grow it?"

"I hope not," Bill said. "When I asked her if it was really from Earth, she checked our historical records and found that there were news stories about countries banning this fruit from public transportation and hotels because the odor was so offensive."

A mob of seniors attracted by the smell descended on the table, and five minutes later, the grey-haired woman was complaining, "There wasn't enough actual fruit. The seeds are enormous, and there's more rind than pulp."

"Where would you put it on the stinky scale?" Bill asked, swiping his tab awake and navigating to the feedback form.

"Maybe a hundred and ten?"

"How about the Limburger?"

"Around a hundred."

"You have Limburger too?" one of the newcomers asked. "I'm surprised I didn't smell it."

"That's because the durian overpowers it unless you're up close," Harry said. "Do you have anything else in the cooler, Bill? I'm not a big fan of stinky cheese or fruit that smells like something died."

"There are a couple tins of some fish that M793qK told me not to open until I got here."

"Caviar?" somebody asked hopefully.

Bill pulled out the can and struggled to read the label. "Surströmming, but I don't know if I'm pronouncing the two dots over the 'O' correctly."

"It looks Swedish to me, and I'm not sure how they pronounce umlauts," Nancy said.

"Bring it on," the grey-haired woman said, arming herself with a cracker.

"Flower said that it's fermented herring, and they add just enough salt to keep it from rotting," Bill warned his audience. He peeled the foil off the top of the tin, and even with his nose plugs, he had to swallow back his bile.

"That's foul," Harry said, backing away from the table. "I think we have a new winner."

"If that's not a hundred and twenty on the stinky scale, I can't imagine what is," Nancy said.

"Let me try it," the grey-haired woman said, and loading some herring onto her cracker, took a small bite. "Well, maybe it's an acquired taste."

Irene worked her way around the back of the tables, guiding the borrowed floating immersive camera ahead of her. "I'm sure this will make a really interesting tidbit for some future promo," she said. "Do you have another one of those fruits, Bill?"

"Unfortunately," he said, reaching back in the cooler chest. "I was hoping that nobody would ask."

"Look on the bright side," Harry told him. "At least there aren't any Wanderers grabbing things and insisting you pay to get their opinions. I hope that M793qK reimbursed you for that time."

"I didn't ask him," Bill said, steeling himself to cut open the second durian. "He was so impressed with me for the precise ratings I got from those three Wanderer women that I didn't want to spoil it."

"Maybe you can bring something home to Julie. Women have surprisingly strong stomachs."

"I don't think she would like any of this stuff," Bill said as the seniors armed with tongue depressors descended on the two halves of the stinky fruit. "She eats pretty much the same foods as I do."

"Maybe you should check with her," Harry suggested. "If you had asked me five years ago whether Irene would ever be willing to live on a giant spaceship and eat meals in a cafeteria with a four-armed robot running the steam table, I don't have to tell you what my answer would have been."

"Well, I guess it's not like anybody else is going to eat this stuff," Bill said, transferring the remaining cans of Surströmming to his belt pouch. "If she reacts like I think she will, I can always bring them into the alien cafeteria and put them in the giveaway bin."

Eighteen

"Some empire, that you can't even get a couple of washed-up authors to come and meet us at your headquarters," Ronald grumbled. "I was getting used to this office."

"I thought that visiting their colony for semi-retired writers would make for a nice change of scenery, and it's just a short trip in the lift tube," Samuel said. "I didn't know you would be bringing all of the other senior storytellers with you today. What happened to your assistant?"

"My assistant didn't want to lose her place in line to get into a LARPing studio, and my colleagues insisted on coming when they found out I would be meeting with the author of the *Galactic War College* series."

"They read science fiction from Earth?"

Ronald snorted in derision. "We're storytellers, we don't read unless we have to. But Mr. Harstang was the featured speaker at WandererCon last week and he showed some episodes from the immersive adaptation of *Galactic War College*. It was terrible, of course, and we all had a good laugh at the ridiculous space battles. But it got us thinking that if this hack can have his stories made into an immersive series, why not us?"

"If you want his help, you may want to phrase that a little differently when we meet him," Samuel said. "Vivian and Julie are already at the writers colony to help with the catering setup. We can leave as soon as the other storytellers are finished with—what is it they're doing?"

Ronald turned and looked out the open office door at the group of elderly aliens sitting on the floor in a circle. "Gambling," he said in disgust. "Whoever taught those reprobates how to play Texas Hold'em should be drawn and quartered."

"Not a fan of poker?" Samuel asked.

"I can't read the Verlock or the Dollnick," the old man complained. "They keep inventing fake tells, you know what I mean? They trick me into believing that a twitchy eye means they're bluffing and then they drop the hammer. I should know better than to play cards with aliens who have been at it since Columbus sailed the ocean blue."

"How about we let them play out this hand and then we'll get going?"

"They can drag the bidding round for a single card out for five minutes with all their table talk so I'll just speed things up." The storyteller sauntered around the group and stopped behind the Frunge, who happened to be inspecting his hole cards. Ronald winked at Samuel, and then held up both hands, each showing three fingers. There was already a pair of threes showing in the community cards, and the rest of the players immediately folded. The disappointed Frunge carefully mixed his own pair of threes into the discards and then he swept up the antes.

"If you're all ready, we'll be heading down to the ag deck where the writers colony is located," Samuel said.

"Makes sense they'd be living with the cows since that *Galactic War College* anime we saw was manure," the Drazen cracked, and the other storytellers joined a short round of laughter. "I would have asked Yaem for my money back after the screening, but we didn't pay to get in, so I was stuck."

"We should be negotiating our return to the Miklat with Yaem," the elderly Dollnick said. "We probably could have gotten a free lifetime supply of anime out of it."

"These authors of yours better come across with the goods," the Frunge grumbled at Samuel. "I'm getting tired of your crazy ship's AI blasting me out of bed with that infernal Dollnick opera every morning. I don't understand how anybody can live here."

"The fresh fruit and produce are excellent," the heavily tattooed Horten woman said. "But I have to admit that being around all of those industrious humans dressed up like aliens gets to be depressing after a while. It seems they've been brainwashed into believing that work is the path to enlightenment."

"Humans enjoy working," Samuel said as he led the group out of the Human Empire headquarters. "So did all of the aliens I grew up around on Union Station. In fact, most of them thought that we were the lazy ones."

"Why did you turn right?" the Drazen storyteller demanded.

"Our headquarters is exactly opposite the lift tube doors on the other side of the spoke so the distance is the same either way."

"That's why I'm asking. Why didn't you go left?"

Samuel shrugged. "We can return and head around the other way if it means that much to you. I just want to get this over with."

Ronald stepped up close to Samuel while they waited for the capsule to arrive, and whispered in his ear, "That advice you gave me earlier about talking politely with Mr.

Harstang? You may want to keep it in mind when addressing my colleagues."

"I'm just getting worn out by all of this. I appreciate that it's good practice for me—well, practice at any rate—but the Wanderers are not members of the Human Empire, nor do I believe any of the humans among you would join if invited. Maybe it's because I started in space engineering at the Open University before transferring to the diplomatic track, but I like problems that I can solve. You people—"

"Welcome to the real galaxy, kid," the Frunge storyteller interrupted as the whole group squeezed into the lift tube capsule. "If diplomacy was easy, everybody would be doing it, and then the arms manufacturers would all be out of business."

"That reminds me of the time we were harvesting abandoned supplies from the rear lines of the Butterri Conflict," Ronald said. "The captain refused to load any of the ammunition, but I checked the prices later and we could have made a killing."

"Ammunition is dangerous," the Verlock lectured ponderously. "You start by selling it, you end by needing it yourself."

"Yeah, and those retreating Butterri forces would have eventually hunted us down if we took their ammo," the Drazen said. "You have to know who you're dealing with and act accordingly."

"So it wasn't really abandoned?" Samuel asked.

"The only universal truth about war is that it's full of waste," the elderly Horten woman said. "Whether the particular supplies we harvested would ever have been utilized by the Butterri is open to debate. It's entirely possible that they bought everything back from us on the war surplus market."

"I guess I just don't understand business," Samuel said as the doors slid open on a pastoral scene. "We're meeting everybody at the dining pavilion."

"The apple and peach trees are blossoming," the Drazen said, sniffing the air. "I'll have to take a walk in the orchards after this is over. I miss the fruit trees we had on the Miklat when I first joined."

"What happened to them?" Samuel asked.

"It's trickier than you might think to maintain orchards on a spaceship. Somebody has to take care of the pollinating insects, start seedlings to replace aging trees, and simulate seasons through changes in lighting and temperature or the trees will never flower. The Zarents did their best, but they were stretched too thin trying to hold the Miklat together, and something had to give."

"Like both the primary and secondary piles," the Verlock put in.

"There he is," Ronald said, spotting Geoffrey talking to Julie as the girl laid out place settings on a picnic table. "Everybody remember not to tell him what we really thought of his pathetic stories. We should probably find something to compliment."

"If I had to choose between reading him or the old broad who wrote the sexy paranormal books, I'd take her every time," the Dollnick said. "At least her stories were believable."

"You find werewolves and bear-shifters more realistic than military science fiction?" Samuel couldn't help asking.

"Not military science fiction per se," the Dollnick storyteller replied. "Just military science fiction in which a ragtag bunch of Humans in an obsolete warship out-think and out-fight superior aliens. Our own military science fiction is excellent, and both the Drazens and Hortens do a reasonable job."

"Sam," Vivian called from where she was struggling with the panel on a floating catering cart. "Come and help me with this."

He gestured for the delegation of Wanderer storytellers to seat themselves at the picnic tables and went to his wife. "Is the latch stuck?"

"No, I faked it to talk to you so that I wouldn't have to ping your implant while you were with the Wanderers. Geoffrey explained to me that his old publishers weren't very happy with him after his attorney got through with recovering his rights because they'd paid cash for them when his so-called family had him committed. Bianca the Sixth is only writing children's books these days, and she said her publisher asked her years ago to please stop submitting works from other authors she knew."

"How about the next Bianca, the one Julie is apprenticed to?"

"She's headlining a writers retreat at a nature preserve on Earth and we couldn't reach her over the Stryxnet. Besides, I finally heard back from EarthCent Intelligence this morning and their Wanderers analyst said that the storytellers don't perform romances, at least not in the sense of romance books."

"So this is all going to be another waste of time," Samuel said in exasperation.

"Not necessarily. Geoffrey and Bianca said that several of the storytellers approached them secretly at WandererCon when none of the others were watching. It turns out they're only interested in publishing books because they think it's the easiest way to break into immersives and anime. So Flower is holding the

Grenouthian director in reserve, and if we don't make any progress, she's willing to produce a series pilot about storytellers if that will get the Wanderers off the ship."

"I'm not sure they'll want to be in business with Flower. They all hate how she tries to get them to abide by the ship's rules."

"From what Geoffrey has told me about the entertainment industry, Flower is a pushover compared to the average executive producer. I'll bet you the Wanderers have figured that out already or they wouldn't still be here."

"All right, we'll play it by ear. I better get over there before they take out the cards again or we'll be here all day."

"—not even millions?" the Dollnick storyteller was asking Geoffrey when Samuel took the end seat on the picnic table bench.

"My biggest advance was two hundred and fifty thousand eBucks, call it fifty thousand creds, and that was for a trilogy," Geoffrey said. "What's more, if those books had been picked up by a studio, the publisher would have gotten fifty percent."

"What a rip-off," Ronald said. "If that's the kind of deal we can expect, we'd be better off doing that self-publishing you talked about. It sounded dead easy."

"Easy to publish, hard to find readers," Geoffrey told him. "You'll all be new names to the English-speaking market, and the immersive studios aren't going to be impressed just because you can point to an eBook in some catalog that nobody is downloading. This idea you have of quickly becoming famous as authors and then getting deluged in offers from immersive or anime studios just isn't realistic."

"Then where do all the new shows come from?"

"Studios want scripts from writers who know about immersive production methods and tailor their stories to the media. On the rare occasion that they buy a bestselling book to turn it into an immersive, they get a team of screenwriters to do the adaptation. Even if the original author is a part of that, he rarely has any control."

"You mean the other writers can make alterations to the story without the author's approval?" the Frunge storyteller demanded.

"Alterations? They can even change the ending or include new material wholesale," Geoffrey said. "Did any of you stay awake long enough to see the battle scene from my *Galactic War College* series where the heroine escapes by diving her ship into a black hole? That whole sequence was made up by the producer's eight-year-old son. I didn't even know it was included until the final version came out."

The alien storytellers all looked at each other for a long moment, and then the Verlock said, "We can live with scientific inaccuracy. When can you start?"

"Excuse me?" Geoffrey said, setting down the fork he had just picked up. "Start what?"

"Writing scripts," Ronald told him. "None of us have ever worked with the format. I stole a book from your library, *Screenwriting for Humans*, but it all seemed very tedious. What do any of us know about camera placements or dissolves? I got as far as the difference between establishing-shots and slow-pans before I gave up."

"We'll tell you our ideas and you could flesh out the details in return for a piece of the action," the Drazen storyteller offered. "How about ten percent? That seems fair for what's basically secretarial work. After all, it's the ideas that really matter."

Bianca began to choke on her salad, and Julie hurried over to thump her gently on the back and give her a glass of water.

"Is that really what you think?" Geoffrey asked. "I've been in the business for almost fifty years, and while I know that's not a long time for most of you, it's more than half a lifetime for us," he said, sweeping a hand to take in Bianca and Ronald. "Ideas aren't worth their weight in electrons. You have to be able to craft something that an audience can relate to, something that inspires or entertains."

"Everything starts with an idea," the Verlock said.

"If you're looking for a ghostwriter to get your stories down on paper, there are a couple of writers in our colony who might be willing to do some creative transcribing in return for an hourly wage. But you won't find screenwriters anywhere in this galaxy willing to write scripts for you on the speculation of receiving ten percent of your take if you ever find a buyer."

Ronald glared at Samuel. "You said this was all set up!"

"I said the meeting was set up. I had no idea what you planned to get out of it, and I certainly didn't expect you to ask Mr. Harstang to write a script for you."

"Scripts. Plural. We have lots of stories."

"Listen," Bianca said, joining the conversation for the first time. "I've been attending your open storytelling sessions out of curiosity and most of your performances with all of the descriptions aren't that far from being anime scripts. But I'm sure I don't have to tell you that for business reasons the studios all want to do series. The question I have is, do any of you tell stories that reuse the same characters and settings, or are they all one-offs loosely based on actual events?"

"I would have noticed if you attended any of our storytelling sessions," the Dollnick said skeptically. "I have an excellent memory, and the only Humans who showed up were cosplayers."

"I came as a jaguar shifter," Bianca said. "I like to keep in practice."

"The predatory feline with the twitchy tail? Then you heard me tell the story about the wayward prince and the Terregram mage. There are thousands of *Wayward Prince* stories in the Dollnick Wanderer canon, and most of them are bloody."

"Bloody is good," Geoffrey said. "Are there any issues with the rights?"

"Hold on a second," the Drazen said. "Anybody can bleed, but if you're looking for continuity and thrills, our *Rogue Consortium* stories are known for their realistic depictions of industrial espionage, betrayal, and murder on a planetary scale."

"They should be, considering the plots are all copied from our famous *Business Pirates* tales," the Horten storyteller said.

"What could be more exciting than our *Travelling Blacksmith* saga?" the Frunge demanded. "We've been telling those stories for over a million years. There's nothing that can't be fixed with a big enough hammer."

"I came in too late to hear your whole story, but I was taken by the ending," Bianca said, directing her words at the Verlock who was sitting across from her. "It's the first time I remember hearing a dramatic story where the hero wins by solving a mathematical equation."

"I know many such exciting tales," the Verlock said, his enthusiasm apparent despite his slow speaking cadence. "Would you like to hear one now?"

"No!" the other storytellers all shouted as one.

"When you get back to the Miklat, why don't you spend some time writing up, or, uh, dictating a selection of stories that would work well in serialization, and I'll send them around to the industry people I know," Geoffrey offered.

"That sounds an awful lot like work," Ronald said, pulling a face. "How about if we dug up recordings of our previous performances and you pick out the ones with the best commercial potential?"

"I think we have them," Flower spoke suddenly over Julie's implant. "Get in there and tell them that the Grenouthian director is on the way with an offer. Make something up about how enthusiastic he is."

Julie cleared her voice and announced, "I've been informed that the Grenouthian director who manages Flower Studios has heard about your wealth of material and is on his way here to talk about a potential series. He's a big fan of the *Wanderer Mob* anime series that was up against *Everyday Superheroes* in the awards last year."

"Bah, that's basically a children's show," the Dollnick said. "Who cares about little Zarents riding around on unicycles trying to keep the mob's ships from exploding. We're talking about real drama, with evil entities and battle scenes that will make your feathered crest stand on end."

"Yes, I'm sure that's exactly what the director is looking for," Julie said, hoping that Flower was keeping the Grenouthian updated. "I think—"

"Now let's slow things down for a moment," Ronald interrupted. "Dangling an anime series in front of us is all well and good, but we still have to deliver something for our followers."

"Unfortunately, he has a point," the Drazen storyteller said. "If we were talking about an immersive, we could offer our compatriots roles as extras, but that won't work with anime."

"I've never seen everybody so willing to stand in line as they have been for those LARPing studios," the Dollnick said. "If we took those with us..."

"They aren't mine to give," Samuel protested, but the Wanderers ignored him.

"That might work," the Verlock said. "We should probably put it to a vote."

"And some cash payment, even if it's just twenty or thirty creds a head," the Dollnick said.

"Yes, a cash payment is essential," Ronald agreed.

"What about the Zarents?" the Horten asked. "We can't have them lording it over us or we'll be the laughing stock of the mobs."

"Our mob will treat us like returning heroes if we have those LARPing studios on board," the Drazen said confidently.

"So we'll put it to a vote and get back to you with our final demands," Ronald said to Samuel and rose to his feet. "I want to make sure everything is on track for the Break Rock dance. It's about time we made some money out of our trip."

"Where are you going?" the old Dollnick demanded. "I'll admit you've done a fine job negotiating for us to this point but you need to learn patience. We're going to wait and hear what the Grenouthian director has to say. He's award-winning, you know."

"Humans," the Verlock said. "We've been on Flower less than a cycle and he's rushing to close the deal. I've never been involved in such fast negotiations in my life."

Samuel bit back a groan and plastered on a smile.

Nineteen

"Thank you, Teacher," Julie said to the Drazen choir mistress at the end of her singing lesson. "I always feel better when I leave here."

"Did you mean that as a compliment?" Rinka asked. "Humanese needs to evolve a conjugation that expresses intent."

"I meant that your lessons fill me with joy, not that leaving makes me feel better."

"I'm sure it's the act of singing that fills you with joy as opposed to my corrections. Are you and Bill coming to the Break Rock dance tonight?"

"Are they letting us visit the habitat?" Julie asked. "I've gotten so used to the open worlds refusing to allow Flower's shuttles to land that I've almost forgotten that we ever left the ship."

"Break Rock didn't put any restrictions on visitors, but that's because it's run by Humans. Jorb told me that a few Wanderers went over for a look and they came scurrying right back again. But the dance is here, on the Con deck. The Wanderers are putting it on for the guests from Break Rock."

"What?"

"You have to buy tickets," Rinka explained. "I told Jorb to get an extra pair just in case they sell out. I've never been to a Wanderer dance but they're sort of legendary among the clubbing crowd. When a mob stops at a Stryx station, most of the traffic is to their dance hall."

"How many people can they possibly fit in one dance?" Julie asked.

"Here, I don't know. I suppose it depends on how much space Flower lets them have, but mobs usually dedicate a whole ship to dancing and music. It's sort of their thing."

"With all the grief they've given Flower, I'm not sure I should go. It feels kind of like consorting with the enemy."

"Putting on live entertainment events is the closest the Wanderers come to doing anything constructive so I'm sure she approves," Rinka said. "Besides, it's an excuse to dress up."

"All right. What time is it? I'll have to tell Bill, and maybe we can meet somewhere and all go together. It feels like I haven't seen him outside of work in weeks."

"The Wanderers are fond of around-the-clock parties so it doesn't really have a start time," Rinka said. "Why don't you ping me after you talk to Bill? And you should make sure Samuel and Vivian know about it. Maybe it would help with their negotiations."

"Will do," Julie said and headed back to work. Something seemed off when she arrived at her office and it actually took her a few seconds to realize what it was. "What happened to my scale model?" she asked out loud.

"It wasn't a challenge for you anymore so I had it removed," Flower said. "There's a point at which putting a puzzle together faster and faster doesn't teach you anything new."

"Did you have it taken back to the shipyard to train the workers?" When no answer was forthcoming, Julie glared up at the ceiling. "Okay, what is it you're trying to hide from me this time?"

"I wasn't pausing intentionally. There's a Verlock mage working on a powerful incantation in my second LARPing studio at the same time that a Wanderer raiding party is staging a night attack in my first LARPing studio. I just got busy for a moment."

"And..."

"I had the scale model brought to the Big Boots kindergarten, the one that Pyun Em is attending, though if I had my way, she'd be in sixth grade by now."

"You're talking about the captain and Lynx's little girl? She can't even be six years old."

"What does age have to do with academic attainments?" Flower said. "At least this way she'll learn something more useful than building towers with foam blocks."

"Are you going to send the kindergarten the manual?" Julie couldn't restrain herself from asking.

"That would be a bit much for the age group. What are you going to wear to the dance?"

"A dress. Are you a fashion consultant now?"

"You've been working so hard lately that I decided to give you a bonus," Flower said. "It's a gift certificate to Royal Outfitters."

"The Vergallian fashion chain? All of their stuff costs a fortune and it's designed for women who don't eat."

"That's just the models in the advertisements. They'd go out of business if they only sold to women who fit in sub-zero sizes. Why don't you take the rest of the afternoon off and pick something out?"

Julie hesitated. "Is there something more to this that I'm missing? You're not going to ask me to seduce some Wanderer chief, are you?"

"If I thought seduction would get them off the ship I would have sent Avisia, the Vergallian intelligence agent who runs the finishing school. And hurry up or they won't have time to make alterations."

"Can you ping Bill for me?"

"I'm putting him through, but don't talk long because he's busy," Flower said.

"Julie?" Bill's voice asked in her head.

"We're invited to a dance with Jorb and Rinka later. I'll ping Vivian and ask her to tell Samuel."

"I'll tell Jorb as soon as we get killed. I'm kind of in the middle of a battle with orcs."

"Sorry. We'll talk later," Julie said and broke the connection. "Sounds like you finally got them a turn in the LARPing studio, Flower."

"I snuck them in the service entrance under the guise of doing maintenance, and they're pretending to be self-aware non-player characters. The Wanderer raid they joined just ran into an orc ambush."

"Doesn't that mean that you ambushed them? So you can stop."

"Aside from the moral hazard inherent in favoring one group of players over another, if I let them win I'll have to create a new dungeon, and I'm running out of ideas," Flower said.

"Can't you just ask some of the gamers from Bits to help?"

"They've been joining with the Wanderers to get playing time. Humans are so far behind the other species at everything that I never realized how competitive you are at gaming."

"Doesn't that make the information from the Bitters even more valuable?"

"If they would share it with me, but when I said they're competitive, I meant that they want to win at all costs," Flower said. "Zick supplied me with a dungeon design that he claimed would stand up against assaults for weeks. Then he walked right through because he knew all the tricks."

"Oh, that's pretty low," Julie said.

"And the worst part is that he got so much legendary and epic gear from looting the dungeon boss that I'd be hard put to kill him now if my life depended on it."

"Uh, Flower? You're not getting addicted to LARPing yourself, are you? I mean, it's just a made-up game, right?" The lift tube capsule door closed and it started off on its own accord. When there wasn't any answer, she asked, "Are you busy again?"

"Sorry, I got caught up in something, but it's all taken care of," Flower said, sounding rather smug.

"You didn't kill Bill, did you?"

"He knew what he was getting into when he joined the raid, and it's not like I targeted him in particular."

"What did you do to them?" Julie demanded.

"Dragon," Flower said as if that explained everything. "I borrowed the construct from my mentor."

"You got a holographic dragon from the Stryx?"

"It's not like I could have whipped up a better one myself, and there's no sense in reinventing the wheel. Plus, dragons are nearly impervious to magical attacks, so I'm sending it against the Verlock mage in the other LARPing studio as we speak."

"Is that fair?" Julie asked as the capsule door slid open on a corridor with a small number of luxury shops that the ship's population and visitors could support. "What can players do against a dragon?"

"Not much, especially when they're caught unprepared," Flower reported happily. "Scratch one Verlock mage."

"So is that it? Everybody will stop playing now?"

"It doesn't work that way. I can't just throw the dragon against every adventurer, and all magic has a cost involved. In the case of dragons, it's eating and sleeping, which means that from now on, I'll have to be on guard against poisoned sheep carcasses and heroes sneaking into the lair. Besides, it's a loan, not a gift, so I have to be extra careful."

"I thought it was just a copy of computer code that your mentor sent you over the Stryxnet," Julie said.

"Not to sound mysterious but it's more complicated than that. Have you ever considered dusk?"

"Huh? Is that a philosophical question? Not since I've been living on board, anyway."

"I'm talking about the color, for a dress," Flower said. "Let's try to stay on mission."

"I've never even heard of it." Julie stopped to look at the latest fashions in the display window of the Vergallian boutique. "Is it a Dollnick color?"

"It's a sort of light purple. The SBJ Fashions catalog describes it as 'dusty purple', but other than the vowels, I don't see the connection."

"I was thinking of something in blue."

"Everybody wears blue. I've been keeping an eye on the early arrivals to the Break Rock dance and forty percent of the women are wearing blue."

"How about red?"

"Twenty-two percent."

"White?"

"Perfect," Flower said. "I'll arrange for the captain to come and you and Bill can finally get married."

"Alright, already. I'll look at dusk if they have it, but only because you're buying."

Before Julie had taken three steps into the boutique, an elegantly dressed Vergallian man materialized at her side. "Is this your first time visiting us?" he asked. "I'm sure I would have remembered you, but I am absent on a regular basis to attend the fashion shows. If you've been here before you must have dealt with one of the assistants."

"I've never been here," Julie told him. "Flower said she was giving me a gift certificate and—"

"Hold that thought," the Vergallian said and called over his shoulder. "Batya, Bandia. We have a special customer."

By the time Julie escaped from the boutique two hours later, she felt like she had worked a double shift and was worried that she wouldn't have any energy left for dancing.

"Go home and take a nap," Flower advised without being asked. "I'll wake you when Bill is dressed and ready to go."

"Did you give him the afternoon off as well?"

"I would have, but M793qK grabbed him as soon as he got out of the LARPing studio. They're performing safety testing on a dozen brands of microwave popcorn."

"To see whether people get burned by the steam or hot air when they open the bags?" Julie asked. "I always hated microwave popcorn for that reason."

"There's a specific warning on the bags, so getting burned would fall under the tunnel network consumer goods treaty definition of operator failure," Flower said. "He's inspecting for the unpopped and partially popped kernels, which are a safety hazard, especially for older teeth. Of course, the Verlocks would pay extra for hot unpopped kernels, especially if they're heavily salted, but they aren't the target market."

"I hope M793qK isn't making Bill eat a dozen bags of popcorn."

"They're using a device the Farling borrowed from one of the carnival vendors to separate the fully-popped corn from the failures. Bill's job is assigning the partially popped kernels to one of three categories, depending on the degree to which they opened, and then he has to count the results for reporting."

"I guess it's sort of related to his Open University studies then," Julie said, waving a hand over the entry pad next to the door to enter her cabin. "I didn't realize that separating the kernels was something those carnival poppers could do."

"The machine M793qK borrowed was designed for lotteries that used numbered ping pong balls," Flower explained. "Forced air systems are ideal for separating materials by their weight and aerodynamic properties. I use air separation in my recycling facility."

"This place is turning into an asylum and I don't mean that with positive intent. And it's going to take me twenty minutes to get into this dress and fix my hair, so you better wake me when he gets off work."

Four hours later, Bill finally convinced Julie to let him rest his feet for a minute, and she spotted Vivian and Samuel taking a breather at the same time. Jorb made a move to follow, but Rinka hooked him around the neck with her tentacle and kept him on the dance floor.

"You guys are really, really good," Bill said to Samuel. "You look like something out of the immersives when you're doing those ballroom numbers. If you stay on board, I'll bet Flower drafts you as stand-ins to provide scaffolding."

"What's that?" Samuel asked.

"A way to get you to act in her anime productions without paying you as principal animation actors."

"It sounds like fun," Vivian said. "And I love your dress, Julie. That color works so well for you. What is it called?"

"Dusk," Samuel answered before Julie could speak. "My sister used to make me test her on color swatch recognition when she was attending the fashion design program at the Open University. I can identify like two dozen shades of white."

Julie looked at him skeptically. "White is white. Isn't it another color by definition as soon as you put something else in?"

"Not in the fashion industry," he said, and began ticking off shades on his fingers. "There's snow, and ivory, and ghost white, and beige—"

"Enough, Sam," Vivian interrupted. "You said if I let you take a break you'd buy me champagne."

"Champagne is a shade of white too," Samuel told her triumphantly. "Come on, Bill. You can help me carry. I don't think I could manage a tray in this crowd, so two glasses is my limit."

"It's funny," Julie said to her friend as the young men headed off. "I never thought I'd end up feeling sorry for anybody who can't balance a tray of glasses with one hand while moving through a crowd. I guess it's my only real superhero skill."

"You and Bill are coming along nicely at couples dancing," Vivian said. "I can't believe that Jorb only started teaching him a couple of months ago."

"We have your wedding to thank for that." Julie lowered her voice and asked, "How are things coming with the Wanderer negotiations?"

"Ronald has been driving Sam nuts with details over how many people should be at the next meeting, the heights of the chairs, and what flavors of juice should be served. I think he's delaying for the sake of delaying to please the other aliens. Sam says that patience and actually listening to the other side's demands are the least expensive concessions you can make in any negotiation, but Drazen Intelligence taught me the direct method."

"What's that?"

"You know, discover your enemy's weak points and threaten them."

"Oh. I'm not sure the Wanderers have any weaknesses, or rather, they've turned their weakness into their strength," Julie said. "I've been thinking about them a lot since it's part of my job now. I even tried to research the last mob visit to Union Station in the archives of the Galactic Free Press, but I guess it was edited out because I couldn't find anything."

"The mob came to Union Station before Aunt Chastity started the paper," Vivian explained. "In fact, my aunt eloped with a Wanderer, and she got the whole idea for starting a virtual newspaper when they visited Earth during their honeymoon."

"Your aunt married a Wanderer!"

"It's not like laziness is a communicable disease, whatever the aliens think. And Marcus is the one who coached me and Samuel in Vergallian ballroom dancing."

"What's it really like, being married?" Julie asked suddenly. "I've never really known anybody our age who was."

"It's great," Vivian said, breaking into a wide smile. "During all those years we were dating, Sam could get up to all sorts of stuff at home and I wouldn't ever hear about it. Now that we live together, I always know what he's doing without having to spy on him."

"I never thought of that. Not the spying, I mean, but the fact that I'd get to spend some time with Bill every day, even if we're just sleeping. Flower has been working us both so hard since the Wanderers got here that I see less of Bill than I did before we were engaged. I learned a lot about cooking when I worked at the diner, but I just can't be bothered to make meals for myself. I end up living on take-out when Bill's busy with work."

"I couldn't cook my way out of a paper bag," Vivian admitted. "I'd like to take a course, but somebody might figure out that my twin brother is the celebrity chef of *Stone Soup* and tip off the Grenouthian network. They love doing stories about anything that makes Humans look silly because it ties into all of their comedy-documentaries."

"Here you go," Bill said, handing each of the women a glass of champagne. "The Wanderers may be allergic to work, but it doesn't extend to bartending. Can you believe they were charging three creds a glass? That's like fifteen e-bucks back on Earth."

"What happened to Sam?" Vivian asked.

"He ran into the storyteller's assistant, I don't know her name, and she had a list of final demands for the meeting to go over. She said it would only take a minute."

"I'm getting nervous about attending the meeting now, but Flower insists that it will be educational," Julie said.

"The one I got dragged into wasn't that bad," Bill said. "Someday I'm going to have to negotiate for myself in business, and I guess I always thought it was about figuring out what's fair so the other side would agree. But I'm learning that you have to watch out for your own interests in business because you can't count on the other guys to do it for you. If you start off by offering a fair deal, they'll just chip away at it until you're left working for free."

"And the rest is commentary," Vivian said.

Twenty

"This box—" M793qK paused dramatically and pointed at the container he had deposited at the front of the cafeteria "—is where Bill will put the food samples that are leftover after we complete the necessary certification testing for the All Species Cookbook. I will tolerate no further depredations on the samples stored in the kitchen."

"But the old Humans in the independent living cooperative eat all the good stuff," Avisia protested. "I haven't had a truffle in weeks."

"You don't see Brynlan complaining, do you?" the Farling demanded, motioning towards the Verlock spy.

"That's because he's the only one who can eat any of those high crunch-factor foods without soaking them in water for three days."

"Other than the ramen noodles, you can keep it all," the Grenouthian director said dismissively. "I'll take the Human produce that Flower grows on her ag decks over any of those processed foods you all go crazy over."

"Couldn't you just contact the makers and tell them you need more samples for testing?" Jorb asked the Farling. "If you can get me some more of those bar-b-que chips, I can make it worth your while."

"I doubt that very much," M793qK said. "This is your final warning. I've added my own security measures to

Flower's kitchen cabinets. Stay out of the samples or you'll be needing my services as a physician. Understood?"

"Speaking of medical services, how are your Zarent patients?" Razood asked.

"All recovering nicely," the Farling said, and his demeanor went from that of an alpha predator staking out territory to surprisingly tender for a beetle-like alien twice the bulk of an average man. "I have to admit that Flower's offer to give them a permanent refuge in her core took me by surprise. It will be nice having access to sentients capable of carrying on an intelligent conversation about the universe, present company excepted, of course."

"Of course," Brynlan echoed.

"I can't believe Flower is planning to give up both LARPing studios to get rid of the Wanderers," Jorb said, his tentacle rising in anger. "It's not that they can't be replaced, it's the principle of the thing."

"Wanderers don't have principles," the Grenouthian director said, breaking a carrot in half to inspect the core. "Do you think I'm looking forward to making an anime special about a bunch of old storytellers?"

"I thought they were going to submit some ideas based on the serial stories they tell and you were going to see if some of your staff scriptwriters could make anything of them."

"That's what I had planned, but when we started negotiating, they held out for the addition of a special broadcast featuring interviews with all of them talking about their craft. I cleared my schedule for the day after tomorrow to just get it over with—otherwise, we'd still be arguing over whose turn it was to talk."

"Running a con for the Wanderers just about destroyed my faith in fandom," Yaem said, taking his place at the table. "I had to empty the complaints box twice a day because they kept stuffing it with notes about the quality and quantity of the anime."

"You mean like the old restaurant joke?" Jorb asked. "The food is terrible and the portions are too small?"

"Exactly. The Wanderers seem to believe that it gets funnier with the retelling."

Bill came out of the kitchen without his apron and said, "Harry will be bringing out dessert in a minute. The Wanderers have invoked some obscure protocol about attendance and Samuel needs me to sit in on this afternoon's negotiations since I was at an earlier session."

"Did you eat anything yourself?" Razood asked. "You've seen how negotiations with the Wanderers can drag on."

"Samuel is going to order pizza after the first hour and try to leverage the toppings for an advantage. See you guys later."

When Bill reached the Human Empire's headquarters, he saw that the Wanderer delegation was limited to the senior storytellers without their usual assistants and hangers-on. Rather than Ronald and a few others cramming into Samuel's office, the meeting had been moved to the conference room, and Julie was handing around juice and cookies. Vivian waved for Bill to come over and sit in the empty chair next to her, and as soon as Julie finished serving the aliens, she took the last seat.

"All right," Samuel said. "Let me state for the record that in the interest of getting this over with, the Human Empire waives our right to bring four more negotiators to our side of the table. I've reviewed all of your demands, and not to put too fine a point on it, I give up."

"You concede?" Ronald asked, rubbing his hands together. "Excellent. We'll expect the cash payment before we—"

"I'm sorry," Samuel interrupted. "I'm afraid there's been a misunderstanding. I only concede that I'm in over my head trying to negotiate with someone so much older and wiser than myself so I'm giving up on trying."

"But then we'll stay here forever," the Horten storyteller said in a threatening voice. "Flower won't be able to carry out her mission if the governments at the open worlds where she stops refuse to allow anybody to disembark."

"I didn't say the Human Empire was giving up, this is a personal failing on my part. Maybe a new negotiator with female intuition will be able to figure out what it is you really want."

"Ah, so I'll be negotiating with your wife from now on," Ronald said, turning his attention to Vivian. "In the spirit of cooperation, I'm willing to let you choose one item from our final demands to reopen for further consideration."

"Excluding the cash payment," the Drazen storyteller put in.

"Not me," Vivian said and pointed up at a corner of the office.

"Flower?" Ronald asked. "I'm afraid that won't do at all. We don't negotiate deals with artificial intelligence."

"The replacement negotiator will be the Human Empire's mentor, who is scheduled to arrive tomorrow from the general direction Vivian is indicating," Samuel said. "I don't have to tell you how humiliating it is for me to fail at my first major diplomatic challenge, but I'm confident that when our mentor gets here she'll be able to resolve everything without further delay."

"You called for your mommy?" the Dollnick storyteller asked in a mocking voice. "I suppose we should be honored that the famous Union Station ambassador is coming to meet us."

"Not my mother," Samuel said. "I thought you knew that our mentor is the granddaughter of the Cayl emperor, and she—"

"Ca-Ca-Ca-Cayl?" the Verlock storyteller stuttered, half rising from his chair. "Co-co-co-coming here?"

"With her royal escort," Samuel confirmed. "I'm not an expert in Cayl etiquette, but I'm planning on two columns of warriors and their hounds at the official reception."

"Ca-Ca-Ca-Cayl hounds?" The Frunge rose from his seat and fled for the door.

"He said tomorrow," the Drazen shouted after the old storyteller, who moved remarkably quickly for his advanced age. Then he turned back to Samuel and asked in an artificially cheerful voice, "Around what time tomorrow?"

"The message said to expect them at nine, but I'm not sure whose clock that's on," Samuel said apologetically. "I'll ask Flower to transmit a copy of your demands to the Cayl forces over the Stryxnet so our mentor can be up to speed when she arrives, and—"

"Don't be so hasty," the Verlock interrupted at nearly triple his usual talking speed. "Why would we bother the Cayl emperor's granddaughter over such a small matter? Surely we can work this out and be on our way so as not to spoil her reception."

"Before nine," the Dollnick added.

"Well," Samuel said. "It's not that your demands were unexpected, just that they exceeded our ability to pay. For example, the five hundred thousand creds..."

"We could manage with four hundred thousand," Ronald said, looking towards the other Wanderers for approval.

"I don't have any funds to dispose of myself, but Flower is willing to go fifty."

"Fifty creds?"

"Fifty thousand."

"Oh," Ronald said. "That still comes to a couple of creds a head. Does anybody object?"

"Hurry up," the Drazen said. "I've got packing to do."

"And Flower can't withdraw the Zarent's ownership of the Miklat as it's already been registered, so they would have to be the ones to make any decisions there," Samuel said apologetically.

"I've been thinking about that, and it could work out in our favor," the Horten storyteller said. "The Zarents were always pestering us for maintenance costs because it was our ship, but if it's their ship..."

"Excellent point," the Verlock said. "I won't be surprised if the other ships in the mob follow in our footsteps."

"So if the rest is acceptable," the Drazen insinuated, half rising from his chair and measuring the distance to the exit with his eyes.

"Your demand for both of Flower's LARPing studios made perfect sense to me, seeing how your people have practically monopolized them since they opened," Samuel continued. "But I have no experience in military matters, and I'm a little worried about how we're going to keep two columns of Cayl warriors—"

"And their hounds," Vivian interjected.

"—occupied so they don't feel the need to go looking for more corporeal enemies to fight. I hear that they're very keen on tracking ships through jump space."

"One LARPing studio is probably more than we can handle without an advanced AI to manage the gameplay," the Drazen storyteller said hastily. "And considering all of the wonderful work that your volunteers did with the new ag deck plantings on the Miklat and such, I think we can just let the rest of our demands go for this time. Ronald?"

"If that's what everybody else wants, who am I to go against you?" Ronald conceded without hesitation.

"So if you could impose on your daughter's calligraphy skills to create a contract, we could hold a signing at our mentor's official reception," Samuel said enthusiastically.

"I'd love to oblige you, but something has come up and we really must be moving," Ronald said as another of the storytellers slunk out the door behind him. "I think a handshake should suffice between men of honor. Will there be any problem removing those—what did you call them, Korl?"

"Vector processor arrays," the Drazen storyteller said. "I'll order some Zarents to—I mean—I'll put together a party of hardware geeks and take care of it myself. I'll just head down there now."

"I can supervise," the old Verlock offered and rose ponderously to his feet.

"Yes, very nice doing business with you," Ronald said, quickly shaking hands with the four youngsters. "If you're ever in the neighborhood, feel free to drop in."

"Aren't you forgetting the anime special about Wanderer storytellers Flower Studios agreed to make?" Samuel asked innocently. "Surely you don't plan to leave before recording interviews for your characters. Isn't that scheduled for—"

"Another time," Ronald said over his shoulder as he shuffled after the Verlock, the only Wanderer slow enough to still be in the lobby. "Hey, wait for me!"

Nobody said anything else until the doors closed behind the last of the storytellers, and then Vivian burst out laughing.

"Would somebody please explain to me what just happened?" Julie asked.

"Me too," Bill chipped in. "Did we win or lose?"

"We won," Flower trumpeted through the overhead speakers. "Nobody has ever gotten rid of a Wanderer infestation so cheaply."

"But how about all of the work you did on the Miklat?" Julie asked.

"I'll get reimbursed for that by the Stryx, and we really did it for the Zarents," Flower said. "Did you hear Samuel beat them down to fifty thousand creds? Priceless."

"It's still a lot of money."

"Not when it's counterfeit. I bought in all the five-cred coins that the Wanderers passed off on our vendors and it came to just over fifty thousand. The Stryx will reimburse me for that as well."

"Won't the Wanderers just pass it off on somebody else now?" Julie asked.

"Caveat emptor," the Dollnick AI said. "It's a dangerous galaxy, after all."

"It's a shame they're taking one of the LARPing studios," Bill said. "I was really starting to get into role-playing."

"Running two of them was getting to be a distraction, and my Stryx mentor wants her dragon back. I'll have to look into upgrading some of my own systems if I go beyond one studio again."

"Samuel? Are you alright?" Vivian asked, shaking her husband's shoulder.

"Sorry," he said, jerking as if he'd suddenly come awake. "I'm just a bit stunned, I guess. After all those weeks of setting them up through negotiations, I was beginning to worry that they'd call my bluff."

"What bluff? The Cayl emperor's granddaughter really is due tomorrow, which reminds me, I told Flower we'd vacate our reservoir deck chateau for her. I don't think she'd be comfortable living on one of the regular residential decks, especially with all of those warriors following her everywhere."

"Our mentor's last message only mentioned a pair of hounds," Samuel said with a sly grin. "I was sort of exaggerating about the two columns of Cayl warriors. Is anybody hungry?"

"You made it all up?" Bill asked.

"Exaggerated. The Vergallian ambassador I worked for wrote a treatise on the subject of exaggeration that's become a standard reference in their diplomatic service."

"It's just past noon," Julie said. "If it's alright with Flower, we could help you move, and then we could all eat a late lunch out to celebrate. Bill?"

"I thought I was going to be here all day so I'm open," Bill said happily. "How much stuff do you guys have? Should I get a floater cart?"

"It's just the luggage we brought for our honeymoon, and some things we picked up at the bazaar that will fit in a couple of boxes," Vivian said. "The four of us could probably take everything in a single trip. The funny thing is that I was just getting comfortable with those giant

Dollnick fish swimming up to the deck and begging for food."

"You told me that you missed having neighbors, and the only time we ever saw people on the reservoir deck they were either sculling, or jogging on the catwalks," Samuel said. "Anyway, I'm just happy that Flower finally agreed to put us in a normal cabin and charge monthly rent. If our mentor approves of keeping the Human Empire headquarters on board, we can talk about remodeling or getting a bigger space later if it becomes necessary."

"This is a public service announcement for all Wanderers on board," the captain's voice sounded throughout the ship. "The Miklat will be departing at oh-eight hundred on Universal Human Time tomorrow, so you have less than twenty hours to vacate. Flower will be running her large shuttles in a continual ferry service until that time on a first-come, first-serve basis. Please restrict your gleaning to the usual towels, soaps, and sundries, or your baggage may be subject to search and seizure. The furniture in your cabins will remain on board."

"I guess we really did it," Samuel said, standing up and stretching to crack his spine. "Let's get this move out of the way and then I could go for pizza and beer."

"I'm so proud of you," Vivian said as they exited the Human Empire's headquarters. "Your first diplomatic coup and you didn't even have to threaten the use of military force, much."

"If we're going to need boxes, we can stop by Flower's delivery service and pick some up," Bill said. "I used to work there."

"We're all set," Samuel told him. "I bought a Grenouthian trader's pack at the bazaar. It's huge, and the compartments can all be separated into individual backpacks." He entered the lift tube and waited for the others to board the capsule before requesting, "Reservoir deck."

"You're lucky," Julie said. "Flower doesn't wait for me to tell her where I want to go anymore. She just takes me there."

"And what if she guesses wrong?" Vivian asked.

"She's never wrong, at least, she would never admit to it. Does the same thing happen on Stryx stations once they get to know you?"

"No, they like leaving us the illusion that we have some control over our lives. I guess subtlety isn't Flower's strong suit."

"Being right is my strong suit," the Dollnick AI broke into the conversation. "I would be derelict in my duty if I stood by and watched my inhabitants make a mess of their lives. And selecting the lift tube destinations for Julie and Bill is a beta test of a paid service I'm thinking of rolling out. I chose them as the test subjects because I know them so well."

"You might have told us that," Bill said.

"I wanted to get your natural reactions to the service. If you had known what I was doing you might have put on an act to please me."

"I don't want to discourage you, Flower, but I'm not sure there would be much of a market for omniscient lift tube service," Vivian said. "Most people would see it as an invasion of privacy."

"Really?" Flower asked. The capsule came to a halt on the reservoir deck but the doors remained closed. "How so?"

"Well, in order to know where people want to go, you'd kind of have to be watching them all the time."

"Humans are creatures of habit. The vast majority of your movements from deck to deck are commuting to work, school, or your required team sports and other scheduled ship's activities. I estimate that less than three percent of lift tube trips would require any thought on my part to determine the desired destination. But if you don't think it's a service people would be willing to pay for..."

"We don't," all four of the passengers chorused.

"Very well, then I won't offer it," Flower said, and the lift tube doors opened.

It took the McAllisters less than fifteen minutes to pack the things they'd brought from Union Station on their honeymoon and the household items they'd picked up while living on Flower. Vivian and Julie called dibs on the rolling baggage, leaving Samuel and Bill to divide the remainder into two backpacks.

"Where's your new place?" Julie asked.

"Flower said it's on a regular residential corridor and she'll talk us through getting there," Vivian said. She glanced over the edge of the catwalk at the reservoir and gave a wave. "Goodbye, giant Dollnick man-eating fish."

"Are you going to miss them?"

"No, but you have to admit that they're beautiful."

When the lift tube capsule arrived, they moved inside and the men unburdened themselves of the packs. Almost thirty seconds passed before they figured out that Flower was waiting for somebody to give the destination.

"Uh, our new place?" Samuel requested.

"Could you be more specific?" the Dollnick AI responded.

"All right, we get your point," Vivian said. "I guess even on Union Station people normally tell the lift tubes who or what they're going to visit rather than giving an actual deck or corridor number for the destination."

The capsule began to move, and Flower asked, "Did hearing Samuel say 'our new place' make you realize what you're missing?"

"Are you talking to me?" Julie asked.

"Bill too," Flower said. "As long as we're playing musical chairs with cabins, why not move in together and get on with your lives?"

Vivian put a hand over her face and choked with silent laughter, and Julie turned red from either embarrassment or anger, but Bill said, "You won't hear any objections from me. It's not like we haven't been talking about this for the last few months, Julie."

"And we would probably have gotten to it by now if Flower wasn't keeping us so busy," Julie said, scowling at the ceiling of the lift tube capsule.

"I may have heard somewhere that absence makes the heart grow fonder," the Dollnick AI said. "And for somebody who was worried about the cost of weddings, saving the monthly rent on a cabin will go a long way."

"Come on, Julie," Bill said, taking her hand in both of his. "If we started not doing things just because Flower was pushing us we never would have gotten engaged."

"I suppose you're right," Julie said as the capsule doors opened. "Okay, I'll clean out a few drawers. Bill doesn't have any more stuff than you guys and he's been living here almost as long as me," she added to Vivian.

"Isn't this your corridor?" Samuel asked as he followed the others out of the capsule. "I think I recognize the Dollnick nomenclature."

"It's just down on the left," Flower informed them through the closest speaker grille. "I'll open the door when you get there."

"Did you find them a place near us?" Julie asked.

"Yes. I thought they'd be more comfortable doing morning calisthenics in front of friends."

"Hey, that's my cabin," Bill said when a door slid open. "It's empty!"

"I had the maintenance bots move your things to Julie's cabin, swap in a larger bed, and repaint," Flower said.

"Repaint? But I only agreed to move in with Julie a minute ago."

"I assumed you would accept my suggestion and set my bots to work after you both left this morning to give the paint time to dry."

"I don't know why I even try," Julie said in exasperation. She waved open her own door and could barely recognize the cabin she'd been living in for almost two years. "Did the room just get bigger?"

"I found a better place for your next-door neighbor and connected the two cabins to make room for a home office and a nursery," Flower said. "I won't raise the rent since I benefit from your working at home. I think the nursery speaks for itself."

From the author

The next release will be a sequel to **Freelance on the Galactic Tunnel Network**. If you've read the four EarthCent Universe books starting with **Independent Living** without reading the original EarthCent Ambassador series, I recommend starting with the three book bundle, **Union Station 1, 2, 3.** You can sign up for e-mail notification of my new releases on the **IfItBreaks.com**.

About the Author

E. M. Foner lives in Northampton, MA with an imaginary German Shepherd who's been trained to bite central bankers. The author welcomes reader comments at e_foner@yahoo.com. He's also online at: facebook/E.M.Foner/

Also by the author:

Independent Living

Assisted Living

Date Night on Union Station

Alien Night on Union Station

High Priest on Union Station

Spy Night on Union Station

Carnival on Union Station

Wanderers on Union Station

Vacation on Union Station

Guest Night on Union Station

Word Night on Union Station

Party Night on Union Station

Review Night on Union Station

Family Night on Union Station

Book Night on Union Station

LARP Night on Union Station

Career Night on Union Station

Last Night on Union Station

Soup Night on Union Station

Meghan's Dragon

Turing Test

Human Test

Magic Test

Made in the USA
Monee, IL
23 February 2022

91686748R00144